LIMELIGHT

A Penny Green Mystery Book 1

EMILY ORGAN

LIMELIGHT

Emily Organ

ALSO BY EMILY ORGAN

Penny Green Series:
Limelight
The Rookery
The Maid's Secret
The Inventor
Curse of the Poppy
The Bermondsey Poisoner

Runaway Girl Series:
Runaway Girl
Forgotten Child
Sins of the Father

PROLOGUE

LONDON, 1883

The gunshot broke the silence of the still night. Its echo floated through the lanes and streets of Highgate as birds cawed with alarm, woken unexpectedly from their roost.

PC John Preston 32Y was walking past the sleepy, middle-class terraces of Bisham Gardens for the second time that evening when he was startled by the noise. Just as he realised what he had heard, a second shot rang out.

Had he also heard a scream?

It seemed the shots had come from the west side of Highgate Cemetery.

The officer sprinted to the gas lamp at the end of the street and on towards the cemetery gates.

The tall iron gates had been locked for the night. PC Preston shone the beam of his bullseye lantern over them in an attempt to ascertain how high they were and whether he would be able to climb them.

A third shot urged him to hurry.

What was happening in there?

He placed his lantern on the ground, removed his gloves and gripped the cold iron bars firmly with both hands. He tried to clamber up the gate, cursing as his boots slipped against the metal.

Three more shots followed and the officer froze as he heard them.

Someone was in trouble and he couldn't get over the gate.

He wrenched off his overcoat and stepped back before taking a run at the gates. After some considerable effort, he finally clambered over and was able to retrieve his lantern from between the bars.

The night was moonless and now silent as PC Preston followed the path through the cemetery, holding his lantern out in front of him. The other hand was wrapped tightly around his revolver.

"Police!" he called out. "Show yourself!"

There was no response.

Headstones and monuments loomed before him, pale in the lantern light. The officer jumped at the stare of a cat's bright mirror eyes. It watched him for a moment before scurrying away.

His heartbeat pounded heavily in his ears and chest. He didn't care for graveyards and had only been in this place once before. One of his uncles had been a gravedigger and it was said that he had died at the shock of seeing a mysterious shadow while hard at work one morning. This wasn't something PC Preston had dwelt on much until this moment.

The lights of London twinkled welcomingly in the distance.

If only he were there rather than alone in this dark graveyard on a cold hillside.

Despite his high collar, the back of his neck felt like ice.

If someone wanted to attack him, surely they would approach from behind, he conjectured.

He spun round, sweeping the beam of his lantern over the graves and tombs. He caught sight of a stone angel, kneeling in prayer.

But there was no living being in sight.

Who, then, had screamed?

"Hello?" he called out anxiously.

Still he heard nothing.

PC Preston continued along the pathway, uncertain of where he was heading. He felt as though he were lost in the city of the dead.

He felt confident that the shooting spree was over.

But what of the victim?

His lantern illuminated two towering stone monoliths. He made his way towards them and saw that they flanked a decorative archway, which resembled an Egyptian temple.

His mouth felt dry as he noticed an extremely faint light shining beyond the archway. Stepping forward, he peered into the darkness and his light fell on a stone avenue lined with doorways to the tombs. He would have to walk along the avenue to find out where the light was coming from.

"Hello?" he called again. His voice echoed loudly in the enclosed space.

There was no reply.

He filled his chest with air and breathed out slowly to calm his nerves as he walked beneath the archway and stepped into the avenue of silent doorways.

The flickering light grew stronger as he crept towards it.

I guessed the man in the bowler hat was a detective as soon as he approached me. I had just left the reading room at the British Museum and was hurrying down the steps to catch an omnibus that would transport me home.

The chill of the stone seeped through the worn soles of my boots and the street beyond the railings was lost in an October fog that was the colour of tea. I wanted to get back to my lodgings before the weather worsened and my feet grew colder still.

"Miss Green?"

Along with his hat, the man wore a dark overcoat and had a young, square, clean-shaven face, thick, dark eyebrows and bright blue eyes. He had an awkward but insistent manner, which suggested that he didn't wish to accost me but that his business required him to do so.

"I am Inspector James Blakely from CID at Scotland Yard." He raised his hat. "I need to speak to you about an unfortunate incident."

"Am I in trouble?"

"No, no. Of course not, Miss Green. It is in your capacity as a news reporter that I call upon you for help."

"I am no longer a news reporter. The commissioner of Scotland Yard saw to that."

He cleared his throat. "So I understand, Miss Green. I do apologise."

"I appreciate your apology, Inspector. If only it had the power to change what has happened."

"Perhaps I could speak to the commissioner about it."

"Perhaps you could. Would he listen to you, do you think?" I couldn't imagine Commissioner Dickson paying much attention to a man I assumed to be the most junior detective at the Yard.

"I can try."

"It's growing dark," I said, glancing at the thickening gloom around about us. "I should be happy to help Scotland Yard once I am reinstated at the *Morning Express*. Good evening, Inspector."

I continued on in the direction of the gate.

"Miss Green!" He caught up with me and matched my stride. "I really would appreciate your assistance."

"I am in no position to help you, Inspector Blakely."

"I wouldn't say that, Miss Green."

We walked through the gate into the busy street. The gas lamps were being lit as we reached a section of raised paving that served as a pedestrian crossing.

"Miss Green, you are one of the few people who can help with this most unusual case." The inspector was forced to raise his voice above the sound of clopping hooves and the rumble of carriage wheels.

"Can you not see that I am trying to cross the street?"

A hansom cab emerged from the grimy brown fog. I

waited for it to pass before skipping out onto the crossing, avoiding the flattened patches of horse manure as best I could.

"Miss Green!"

We reached the pavement by the Museum Tavern.

"Are you still following me, Inspector?"

"Miss Green, it is most urgent that I speak with you. It is regarding the actress, Lizzie Dixie. She has been murdered."

I came to an instant standstill. My ears felt as though they had been boxed.

I stared at the young inspector and turned his words over in my mind. "Lizzie Dixie? But it's impossible. She drowned. Years ago." I paused to think. "Five years ago, in fact."

"So we thought."

"But she did! On the *Princess Alice*."

"Yes, Miss Green. Now you must understand why I need to speak with you."

He took my arm and hurried me through the swing doors of the tavern before I could present any argument.

"We can talk in here."

The air in the pub was heavy with pipe smoke. Carved glass mirrors reflected the flickering gas lights and my spectacles quickly steamed up as Inspector Blakely led the way through the throng of drinkers to a table partitioned either side by a wooden screen.

"Can I offer you a drink, Miss Green?"

"No thank you, Inspector. I was on my way home. I can't stay long, I have work to do."

I sat down on the bench, removed my gloves and wiped my spectacles with them. Then I arranged my handbag and umbrella by my side while I thought about Lizzie Dixie.

How could she possibly have been murdered?

Six hundred people had drowned in 1878 when the SS

Princess Alice sank in the Thames at Woolwich. Lizzie's body had been recovered and buried in Kensal Green Cemetery.

I thought of Lizzie's performances and the conversations we had shared in her dressing room. I had written a number of articles on her, and that, I assumed, was why the inspector wanted to talk to me.

Could Lizzie really have survived and been living somewhere in secret these past five years? Was another woman lying in her grave?

Considering the possibility made me crave something restorative.

"Actually, Inspector, I've changed my mind," I called over to him at the bar. "I'll have an East India sherry, thank you."

When Inspector Blakely returned with our drinks, he removed his hat and overcoat and took the seat opposite me, placing a glass of thick brown stout in front of him. He wore a grey woollen jacket with a matching waistcoat and a dark blue tie.

I found his manner calm and easy. He seemed less confrontational than many of his colleagues. I took a sip of sherry, which felt pleasingly warm in my throat.

"I cannot understand what you're telling me about Lizzie Dixie." I said. "There has to be some sort of mistake."

"A mistake was made five years ago. It seems the wrong woman was identified as Lizzie Dixie after the sinking of the *Princess Alice*."

"How has this happened? How do you know that it was Lizzie who was murdered?"

"She was wearing a locket with a picture of her daughter inside it. And her husband identified her. There are many details in this case which I can go into, should you agree to help me."

I took another sip of sherry and examined my ink-stained fingers.

"You have been writing today?" he asked, glancing at the ugly blue blotches.

"I have."

I tucked my fingers into my palm to stop him looking at them.

"Do you often work in the reading room?"

"Yes, it's a warm place to work and I find all the reference books I need in there. The electric lighting is more reliable now than it was previously. How did you know I would be there today?"

"I'm a detective." He shrugged his shoulders as though he were stating the obvious. "What are you working on at the moment?"

"An article about Germaine de Staël. I read a long essay of hers today, which was important but sadly rather boring."

"Who is she?"

"She *was* a writer. A French lady of letters."

"Like yourself, then? Apart from being French, of course. And boring." He took a gulp of stout.

"I would love to be a lady of letters. It sounds like the perfect job to me." I thought of Madame de Staël writing in her opulent Swiss château and compared her with a vision of myself at the writing desk in my draughty garret room.

"Well I should like to read the article when it is published."

"I doubt you would, Inspector."

"Why not? I like to read. I'm currently reading Thackeray's *The History of Pendennis*."

"Is it to your taste?"

"I am quite enjoying it, though not as much as I did *Vanity Fair*. I can lend it to you once I am finished with it, if you would like."

"That would be kind of you, thank you. My article is hardly of Thackeray's standard, but you should be able to read it in the *Ladies' Scholarly Repository* magazine. I believe it is due to be published in January."

"I shall look out for it."

He raised his glass and smiled, and I felt the frost between us begin to thaw.

"I should rather be working on news stories as I used to."

"If you assist me I will ensure that you have exclusive news on this case before anyone else. The Yard does not have a reputation for sharing information with the press, as I'm sure you are aware."

"Had I still been a staff member on the *Morning Express* your offer might have been tempting. But how do you think an exclusive could be of any use to me now? I'm a penny-a-liner, writing anything for anyone who will pay me. My days in the news room are over."

I drained my sherry and instantly felt I should like another. I also wished to remove my hat and jacket, but I didn't want to be overly familiar with my new companion.

"You are young for a Scotland Yard, detective."

Inspector Blakely blushed in response to my rather personal comment. "The Yard's CID is growing rapidly and they are recruiting anyone they believe shows promise. Police work is in my blood, I'm afraid. My father was a chief super-intendent and my grandfather was a constable."

"It must be hard to imagine doing anything different, in that case. If I were to assist you, what exactly would you expect from me?"

"You knew Lizzie Dixie shortly before she went missing, I believe."

"Who has told you that?"

"Chief Inspector Cullen. I understand you worked with him at the time of the Doughty Street murders."

"Yes, that is correct." I felt a bitter taste in my mouth.

"Lizzie had a complicated life," he continued. "She had many acquaintances, but few people she would have called friends. I should like to find out exactly who she knew and who she engaged with socially. I need to understand what her state of mind was before she was supposed to have drowned. And I need to understand why she pretended to be dead. Do you think you can help me with these lines of inquiry? Because somewhere within this puzzle lies the identity of her killer. Her killer must have been someone close to her. One of the few people who knew she was still alive."

"So you believe the murder was planned?"

"Absolutely."

"What happened?"

"Last night, PC Preston from Highgate Y Division was walking his usual night-time patrol along Bisham Gardens when he was startled by a series of gunshots. He quickly determined that the noise was emanating from the west side of Highgate Cemetery.

"He climbed over the gates at the top of Swain's Lane and spent some time searching the cemetery with his lantern for signs of a disturbance. He eventually found the body of a woman in the Lebanon Circle, and, as the day dawned and there was more light by which to examine her, it became evident that she had been shot."

"And did he recognise her as Lizzie Dixie?"

"At first, no. After discovering she was deceased, he summoned Dr Hugh Lechmore, a physician local to High-gate, who examined her body at the location. He ascertained that she had been shot four times."

I shivered. "That's terrible. Poor Lizzie."

"She was taken to the mortuary chapel at the cemetery this morning, where Mr Cohen, a surgeon of Highgate, conducted a post-mortem examination. He discovered a bullet wound to her upper left leg and three bullet wounds to her chest. By this time, Inspector Willis of Highgate CID was present and the woman's resemblance to the late actress was realised. Before proceeding any further, Inspector Willis consulted the Yard about the confusing case. Highgate CID had come across nothing of this kind before, so the Yard has been brought in to investigate. Y Division is carrying out an extensive search of Highgate Cemetery and the surrounding area to recover the murder weapon and any other clues.

"Mr Joseph Taylor, Lizzie's husband, identified his wife's body this afternoon. I have never seen a man so shaken up. He thought she had died five years ago! Can you imagine how he must have felt seeing her laid out in the mortuary this very afternoon?"

"No, I don't think I can."

"An inquest will be opened tomorrow in Highgate. I am not at liberty to discuss further details of this case with you, Miss Green, unless we have an agreement that we will assist one another. Would you like another sherry?"

"No thank you. I will have to travel home before the fog worsens." I put on my gloves. "We all thought Lizzie was dead, but her murderer knew that she was still alive. There cannot have been many people who might have known that, could there?"

"Indeed not. It narrows down our list of suspects to a small number, but the challenge we face is finding out who those people might be. Do you and I have an arrangement?"

"An arrangement?"

"That you tell me everything you know about Lizzie Dixie and I grant you exclusive access to the particulars of the case?"

"I can tell you what you need to know, Inspector. I should like to help, as I too would like to find out who did this to Lizzie. But as I explained, exclusive news is of no use to me. I can see no benefit of an *arrangement*, as you put it. The other papers will no doubt be reporting on the story?"

"The Yard will remain tight-lipped on the matter."

"As it so often does."

"However, there is no denying that some of the morning editions will carry the story tomorrow. They will contain only what their reporters can glean from hanging around Highgate. I should be happy to share far more with you if you were to help me."

He watched me expectantly.

I knew there was a strong possibility of presenting my exclusive insights to an editor on Fleet Street and negotiating payment over it. But I sought more than that. I wanted to resume my journalistic work on a permanent basis. I was in desperate need of a regular salary.

"I will have to give it some thought. If I were reinstated as a reporter on the *Morning Express* my decision would be an easy one."

"I heard about the disagreement with Inspector Cullen over the Doughty Street murders."

"It was more than a disagreement. I believed that the wrong man had been hanged and wrote an article to that effect."

"I remember reading it."

"And did you agree?"

"Time revealed that the wrong man was, indeed, hanged."

"Jenkins was no angel, but he didn't deserve to die for something he hadn't done. Cullen doesn't like anyone questioning his judgement, does he? Within a day of the article being published he had spoken to Commissioner Dickson, who happens to be a cousin of the paper's editor. I had no chance of survival then."

The inspector polished off the remainder of his stout and dabbed his mouth with his handkerchief. I noticed that his collar was perfectly white and starched and I imagined a laundress delivering him a pile of freshly pressed shirts each week. He wore no wedding ring, so I surmised that he lived with his parents. If not, he probably had lodgings somewhere, as I did, only in a smarter location. I pictured him residing in a respectable room in a white-stuccoed townhouse overlooking a neat green square.

I picked up my handbag and umbrella.

"Perhaps I could speak to the governor about remuneration," said Inspector Blakely.

"You would pay me to help you?"

He nodded.

"No thank you."

I didn't want the inspector to think that I could be easily bought. I liked to think I had better principles than that, even though I badly needed the money.

I got to my feet feeling a little unsteady. The shock of Lizzie's murder had affected me quite deeply. "Thank you for the drink, Inspector."

"The pleasure was mine." He also stood. "I don't particularly wish to say this to you, Miss Green, but as the case progresses there is a possibility that you will be subpoenaed to attend court and give evidence."

He attempted a weak smile and I said nothing.

"I think it would be far easier if you were to cooperate at this early stage."

"I appreciate the warning, Inspector Blakely. If I were a salaried news reporter the arrangement you suggest would be most appealing. But sadly, I am not."

CHAPTER 2

The fog was so thick by the time I reached Milton Street that I was forced to rely on the noise of the trains pulling in and out of Moorgate Station to guide me the last few yards.

I wondered whether Inspector Blakely had thought me bad-tempered and unreasonable. I wanted to be helpful, but I had felt it necessary to be firm about my position. If Scotland Yard was able to take my job from me, it also had the power to reinstate me.

My lodgings were at the top of Mrs Garnett's house, close to the railway bridge in Milton Street. I met my landlady on the staircase, her steel-grey curls sprung out from beneath her bonnet and were pale against her dark brown skin. A widow of about fifty, she had come to London from British West Africa as a child. She always wore a fresh white apron.

"I have almost finished my article, Mrs Garnett."

She scowled at me, her large, dark eyes unblinking.

"I anticipate that I will receive payment for it within the week and I will then pay two weeks' rent. That will leave only one week outstanding."

"It will be two weeks' rent outstanding by then."

"No, just one week I think."

"You're forgetting this week. By the time you have paid me for the two weeks, this week will be gone and then there will be another two weeks to pay."

"I think you could be right."

"Of course I'm right." She sucked in her lips disapprovingly.

"Thank you for being so understanding, Mrs Garnett."

"Let's see how long I'm prepared to tolerate your arrears before you thank me. You look rather pale. Have you had a shock?"

"A little, yes."

"How dreadful. What happened?"

"Someone I know has died, but I hadn't seen her for many years. The news has come as a bit of a surprise."

"I am sorry to hear that, Miss Green. Your sister called for you this afternoon. She tried to bring her bicycle into the hallway again! She says she cannot leave it in the street in case it is stolen."

"She is probably right."

"But she cannot bring it into the house! I don't want it scraping the walls. The wallpaper went up only two years ago."

"I will speak to her about that, Mrs Garnett."

"Tell her not to bring her bicycle into my house. I cannot understand why people want to ride on bicycles. If people must travel on wheels, why don't they take a cab or an omnibus? People who ride bicycles cannot decide whether they belong on the road or the pavement, and it's dangerous for themselves and all other travellers. And as for *women* riding bicycles...." She sucked in her lips again. "It simply isn't *decent*. They have to wear breeches under their skirts to preserve their modesty. Everything about it is utterly ridiculous."

"I have never ridden a bicycle myself, but many people seem to enjoy it."

"At the expense of others and their own clothes. You should have seen the mud splashes on your sister's clothing."

Mrs Garnett tutted and continued down the stairs.

Tiger had pressed herself up against the window by the time I reached my room. I pulled up the sash and she jumped onto my writing desk with a miaow. I stroked her striped coat, which felt damp and cold.

Tiger had found me six years previously. I had looked up from my writing desk one chilly afternoon to find her staring in at me through the window. I had been alarmed to see a cat three storeys from the ground, but I soon learnt that Tiger was an experienced roof cat. She had a broad expanse of gables and smoky chimney stacks to explore. On a good day, she would even catch a pigeon or two out there.

The fog had masked my view of the city, so I pulled the green velveteen curtain across the window to keep some warmth within the room. With Tiger fussing around my skirts, I lit the paraffin lamp and the stove, boiled up some coffee and sat at my desk with a slice of bread and butter.

I knew I needed to finish my article on Germaine de Staël, but I couldn't stop thinking about Lizzie Dixie. I removed a thick bundle of newspaper cuttings from the bottom drawer of my desk and began to leaf through them. These were all the stories I had written for the *Morning Express*, and among them was the obituary I had written for her.

We regret to record the death of actress Lizzie Dixie (Mrs Joseph Taylor), who was drowned in the sinking of the Princess Alice on Tuesday 3rd September aged thirty-six. She will be best remembered for her famous performance of Ophelia in Hamlet at The Lyceum Theatre in 1875.

Born in Ireland in 1842, Lizzie Dixie was the daughter of Michael Dixie, a schoolteacher in Dublin. As a young actress, she took the part of Darina in The Caliph of Baghdad at the Adelphi Theatre, under Mr Sebastian Colehill's management. After touring the provinces, she returned to the London stage as Titania in A Midsummer Night's Dream at the Olympic Theatre, and then as Ariadne in The Marriage of Bacchus at St James' Theatre. She opened at the Theatre Royal in Drury Lane in Lady Audley's Secret, in which she gave a dazzling performance as Alicia.

She married the celebrated showman Joseph Taylor in 1873, a union which delighted the public and placed the adored couple firmly at the heart of fashionable society. Mr and Mrs Taylor made a popular sight riding around London in their landau, pulled by a pair of zebras.

In 1876, Lizzie appeared at The Lyceum as Lucy in Nobody's Child, which was not a success. Another tour of the provinces followed and she opened the Royal Princess's Theatre in Glasgow with a well-received performance as Mrs Seedeep in Observation and Flirtation. Her last performance on the London stage came in July of this year, when she appeared as Cleopatra in The Course of the Nile, which was cut short due to illness.

I knew I had written what Lizzie would have wanted me to. There were many details I had deliberately neglected, such as the birth of her illegitimate daughter and her real name, which had been Hannah Mahoney. Furthermore, her father had never been a schoolteacher; he had, in fact, been imprisoned in Dublin's Kilmainham Gaol.

I rested the pile of cuttings on my desk and gazed at the drab curtain in front of me. How could Lizzie have died again? It didn't make sense to me. Someone, somewhere, knew the truth behind this.

Lizzie was already well-known when I first met her in 1875. By this time, she was more famous for her marriage to Joseph Taylor than for her performances. But later that year she received critical acclaim for her role as Ophelia and the public's interest in her soared.

I met Lizzie at a reception to celebrate the reopening of the Forum Theatre. I had removed my spectacles for the occasion, as my sister had informed me that the frames were ugly and unflattering. The result was that all of the faces were blurred and I had no chance of recognising anyone unless they came up to me and introduced themselves.

Lizzie first appeared as a column of shimmering white, her pale face topped with dark curls. I had been unable to see clearly enough to recognise her, but I sensed she was important on account of her beautiful dress. As she came into focus I could see that her dress was low-cut at the bosom, pulled in tightly at the waist and covered with shiny beads. She wore strings of pearls around her neck and a small hat covered with white flowers was perched on top of her hair. Her face was heart-shaped, with dark kohl accentuating her eyes and deep red stain on her lips. Faint lines around her eyes and mouth suggested she was my senior, possibly by five years, but I couldn't be certain.

"Miss Penelope Green, I believe?" Her voice had a slight Irish lilt.

"Yes," I replied. "How do you know my name?"

"Your colleague pointed you out to me."

She gestured behind her and I recognised the tall, blurred

form of Edgar Fish rocking on the balls of his feet while conversing with another guest and pouring a drink down his throat.

"It is a pleasure to meet you, Mrs Taylor."

I sipped my champagne nervously, as I had written a rather unflattering review of her most recent performance. I prayed desperately that she hadn't read it.

"I was interested to read your review of *The Marriage of Bacchus*."

I felt a heavy sensation in my chest.

"You didn't think a great deal of it, did you?"

"I admit that burlesque plays are not to my taste."

"Perhaps you take them too seriously. Burlesque, after all, is meant to be a little bit of fun. It is mere parody."

Her green eyes sparkled sharply and I took a sip of champagne as I prepared to politely stand by my words.

"I thought the play bordered on slapstick. It could have been produced with a little more wit."

"And Lizzie Dixie's performance of Ariadne reminded you of a clockwork doll?"

"That was a terribly harsh thing to say. I am sorry."

"It is somewhat easier to write such words than say them in person, isn't it, Miss Green?"

"It is easier, yes, and I apologise. I make a point of accepting responsibility for everything I write."

Lizzie nodded and we each sipped our drinks. I desperately hoped someone else would join the conversation and put an end to this awkward situation.

"You were absolutely right, though," said Lizzie. "*The Marriage of Bacchus* was a perfect stinker. It only ran for five weeks. You may be a harsh critic, Miss Green, but you are a fair one."

I placed the cuttings back in the drawer and examined one of the boots I had discarded beneath my desk. The sole of the right boot had a hole in it and there was little chance of getting it repaired before I received payment for my article about Madame de Staël. I found a piece of blotting paper on my desk and folded the thick sheet twice. I placed it inside my boot so it would cover the hole and then pushed my foot in. It was uncomfortable, but I hoped it would at least keep my stocking dry.

Why had Lizzie pretended to be dead?

Questions repeated themselves in my mind as I readied myself for bed. I turned off the lamp, clambered under the counterpane and pulled it up under my chin.

As I lay there with my eyes open wide in the dark, I wondered what information Inspector Blakely had gathered up to this point. Tiger had curled up on my chest, her loud purr filling the silence.

I realised there was nothing to stop me carrying out some investigations of my own on this case. I wanted to find out what had happened to Lizzie. She had once been a friend to me and had made a point of helping me. Now it was my turn to help her, and it was possible that I already knew more about the particulars of her life than Inspector Blakely and his detective friends at Scotland Yard.

CHAPTER 3

I arrived at the British Museum as it was opening the following morning so that I could visit the newspaper room before it became busy.

I quickly saw that all the papers had run the story of Lizzie Dixie's murder. I perused the headlines: 'The Tragic Case of Lizzie Dixie', 'The Perplexing Mystery of the Actress Who Died Twice' and 'Lizzie Dixie Dies Again'.

The Illustrated Londoner carried a picture of a woman in a graveyard collapsing onto the ground with her arms flung wide and a look of horror on her face. At the extreme right of the picture was the hand of her unknown assassin firing a gun. 'Shot Dead in the Cemetery!' shouted the headline.

I read through the stories and was relieved to discover that they included only the most basic information on the case. I could see that an opportunity remained for me to gain exclusive insight if I chose to help Inspector Blakely.

My colleagues in Fleet Street seemed as bewildered as I was about Lizzie's death. Reading the news stories, I ascertained that there was no common theory and, as yet, no plausible answers. The stories described Lizzie Dixie as 'much-loved', 'accomplished' and 'a fine beauty'.

There was much speculation as to why she had chosen to hide after her supposed drowning. Perhaps the actress had 'fallen into debt' or 'suffered a weakness of the brain', according to one. There was general disbelief with regard to the brutality of the murder.

One newspaper implied that her murderer might have been a disgruntled fan, angry to discover she had pretended to be dead. I felt a shiver run through me as I read the line: 'If it is not Lizzie Dixie buried in Kensal Green Cemetery, then who is it?'

The newspaper reading room began to fill up with people, bringing with them scents of coffee, tobacco smoke and damp wool. I leafed through a copy of the *Morning Express* and heard a familiar voice behind me.

"Still reading us then, Miss Green?"

I turned to see my former colleague, Edgar Fish, standing behind me. He was a tall, broad man with heavy features and small, glinting eyes. A thin mousey-brown moustache ran across his top lip and I could smell stale alcohol on his breath. As usual, he had a pencil tucked behind one ear.

"I like to read all the newspapers, Mr Fish." I felt annoyed that he had discovered me there.

"You're maintaining the habits of a good journalist, then."

"Of course."

I folded the newspaper, picked up my handbag and stood up. I tried to make myself as tall as possible, though in truth I only reached his shoulder. I looked him firmly in the eye. "I *am* still a good journalist."

"So I hear." He gave me a patronising smile. "There are plentiful ladies' journals in need of writers, so I am sure it will be easy for you to find work. The grand ladies of Britain always require advice on which colour hat to wear and how to discipline their maids."

"I must go, I have a deadline."

"As do I. The Lizzie Dixie story requires my expertise."

He rubbed his hands together, as if relishing the idea of the work which lay ahead. I felt a snap of anger in my chest.

Lizzie's story should have been mine to write.

"I'm not usually up at this hour," he continued, "but this one's a Gordian Knot and there is a great deal of work to do. You knew Lizzie well, I recall. I should be asking you for comment. Who the deuce do you think did it?"

I shrugged. "I have no idea, but it is terribly sad. Good luck with the story, Mr Fish." I made my way towards the main reading room before he could anger me any further.

I worked in the reading room for most of the morning, desperate to get my article finished, but I struggled to concentrate. Propped open on the desk in front of me was a collection of Madame de Staël's essays and my pen was poised to take down notes. But the words on the pages began to dance before my eyes, and sometime later my sheet of paper bore several blots of ink and little else.

I sat back in my chair and gazed up at the thousands of books that encircled me. The shelves were stacked in three tiers, the highest two accessible via two galleries with brass railings that ran around the perimeter of the circular room. Arched windows sat above the top gallery, and presiding over them was the great dome of the reading room.

High up in the centre of the dome was a round glass window, through which bright sunlight shone, illuminating the blue, white and gold plasterwork above my head. This was the very best light by which to work, yet I was unable to focus my mind at all as thoughts of Lizzie took precedence.

"I care little for parties," Lizzie had said during our first meeting at the theatre reception. "I would rather be at home practising my lines."

"Which part are you playing next?"

"Ophelia in *Hamlet*."

"One of my favourite plays!"

"Then you must come and see it."

"I would love to. I'm reading *Othello* at the moment."

"You read Shakespeare for your own entertainment?" Lizzie's painted eyebrows knotted slightly.

"It's something my father used to do. I remember him reading the plays to me when I was young. When he is away I like to read them, as they remind me of him."

"Where is he?"

"In South America."

"What is he doing all the way over there?" Lizzie's eyes lit up with interest.

"He is collecting plants for Kew Gardens and the British Museum. He has done so for many years. His expedition is due to end within the next month and then he will return home."

"How fascinating. What is his name?"

"Frederick Brinsley Green."

"I should like to meet him and hear of his travels when he returns. I would love to travel myself. Your father must have many interesting stories to tell."

"Yes, and he is writing them down with the hope of putting them all into a book some day."

"There you are!"

The booming voice startled me. I hadn't noticed Joseph Taylor walking up towards us. He was a large man with ginger whiskers and a thick moustache, which had been waxed into upturned curls at either end. He wore a black silk top hat, a deep red tailcoat, and red-and-green chequered trousers with a matching waistcoat. He appeared drunk as he grabbed Lizzie by the waist and kissed her cheek.

Her mouth smiled, but I noticed that her eyes did not.

"Joseph, meet Miss Penny Green. She is the reporter who wrote the review for the *Morning Express*."

"Did she now?" His eyes turned on me accusingly and a sneer formed beneath his large moustache.

"There is no need to be cross, darling. I like honesty in a person. I cannot listen all the time to people telling me how wonderful I am, can I? Sebastian!"

She waved over to a tall, thin man with dark whiskers. He was by her side in one swift stride.

"Yes, Lizzie?" He wore a top hat, a dark frock coat, a cravat and a waistcoat. He had a long, angular face and his whiskers were arranged in the mutton chop style. A white carnation adorned his buttonhole.

"Please ensure that Miss Green receives a ticket for the opening night of *Hamlet*."

Sebastian nodded in reply.

"Are you sure?" asked Mr Taylor. "This ink slinger wrote a shabby review last time. She doesn't deserve to see any more of your plays!"

"Is that so?" asked Sebastian, eying me suspiciously.

"Miss Green will love *Hamlet*, I know it," said Lizzie.

"Have you met Mr Harrington yet?" Mr Taylor asked his wife.

"No, I haven't."

"He is standing just over there."

"I must go, Miss Green. It was delightful meeting you." Lizzie smiled and then she was gone.

Lizzie had been right. I had indeed loved her performance in *Hamlet*. It was cheering to witness her growing skill as an actress and the reviews were complimentary across the board. The role of Ophelia had confirmed her as one of the most talented actresses of the age.

Later that same month my father's expedition returned to Britain without him. He had vanished with his guide while collecting orchids in Amazonia. The search parties had given up all hope of finding them alive.

I remember little of my day-to-day life at that time. I know that I tried to comfort my mother and sister, but it felt as though we were each locked in our own prisons of grief. Thick walls seemed to separate me from the life taking place around me. Tiger had remained seated on my lap whenever possible, purring as if she were trying to push the grief away.

One day a parcel had arrived for me at the *Morning Express* offices. I opened it to find a three-volume collection of *The Complete Works of Shakespeare* bound in red and gilt. Inscribed on the front flyleaf of the first volume was the following message:

I am so very sorry to hear the sad news about your father. Kindest regards, Lizzie Dixie

The volumes Lizzie had given me were now well-thumbed, and the gilt had lost some of its shine. I gazed up at the light-filled dome of the reading room and prayed that Inspector Blakely would not team up with Edgar Fish to work on Lizzie's case. Neither man had known her as I had, and I felt an irrational need to be included in the investigation.

Once again, I considered Inspector Blakely's offer, but I knew the arrangement would be of little benefit to me. The work would not cover my rent or pay for a new pair of boots. I needed decent paid work, and that was why I had to finish my article on Madame de Staël, so that I could search for my next commission.

Even so, I decided it would do no harm to visit an acquaintance of Lizzie's that day. I wanted to speak to Sebastian Colehill, the proprietor of the Theatre Royal in Drury Lane. He had worked with Lizzie throughout her career and I had met him a number of times. I felt sure he could help me find out what had happened to her.

CHAPTER 4

The auditorium at the Theatre Royal was dimly lit by gas jets in round, glass shades. I sat in a red velvet seat in the stalls and waited for Sebastian Colehill.

Above me hung an enormous chandelier, which I imagined blazing with light as the audience took their seats for the performance. I could almost hear the chatter and hum of their voices and smell their perfume. Enormous scarlet and gold curtains hung in folds across the stage and, as my eyes became accustomed to the gloom, I could make out the detail of the gilded trellis and foliage moulding on each balcony.

I had watched Lizzie perform here on the opening night of *Lady Audley's Secret* and it was hard to believe that the empty seats around me had been filled with the most fashionable people in London society that night. The empty theatre appeared somewhat bereft. I felt lonely sitting here, and yet the seats and walls around me seemed to harbour every moment of laughter and sadness expressed on the stage through the years.

I felt lonely, but I didn't feel alone.

I shivered and thought of the Grey Man, who was reported to roam the corridors and auditorium, and could even be found sitting in one of the theatre seats on occasion, according to rumour. He was thought to be the ghost of the actor Charles Macklin, who had murdered a fellow actor backstage. Lizzie had told me that the presence of Joey Grimaldi was also felt here. Actors claimed to have been nudged in the back or kicked by an unseen presence, and Lizzie said she once felt as though she had been pushed out of the way by invisible hands before a section of scenery fell and almost hit her.

I had no belief in ghosts, but the back of my neck prickled as these stories came to mind. As much as I liked to dismiss tales of the supernatural, the sensation that I wasn't alone made me fearful that the figure of the Grey Man might suddenly appear out of the gloom around me. As I shivered, I felt the wedge of blotting paper under my toes in the damaged right boot.

The slam of a door to the left of the stage jolted me a few inches out of my seat. Out into the auditorium strode a tall, lean man wearing a top hat and black frock coat. As he walked towards the row where I was seated, I could see that his dark whiskers were flecked with grey. He still wore a white carnation in his buttonhole. Originally an actor, Sebastian had moved into theatre management at a young age. He had spotted the unknown Lizzie Dixie when she was just nineteen years old and performing in an amateur play. I guessed that he was somewhere around his mid-forties these days. He was as thin as I had remembered him to be, with lanky limbs and a long, pale face. He walked along the row of seats to join me.

"Good morning, Miss Green. This is a surprise." He sat down, leaving a couple of empty seats between us. "Are you still a journalist?"

"Yes, I am."

He looked at me warily, so I smiled slightly. I hoped he wouldn't assume I was here to chase a story or there was a risk he might become angry.

Sebastian removed his hat and smoothed his hair. He smelt pleasantly of violet water. "It must be a few years since we last met?"

"It was when Lizzie was still alive."

He paused before replying. "Yes, I think it was."

"The first time, that is. You have heard?"

"I have." He ran his right hand through his hair. "Just a few hours ago, in fact. I saw it in *The Times*. Unfathomable." He rubbed his face with his hand. "I honestly don't know what to think. What to say. I can't quite believe it. In fact, I don't believe it at all. I take it this is the reason you have come to see me?" He fixed me with his pale blue eyes, which had dark rings beneath them.

"Yes. I found out yesterday."

"Yesterday? Before the news was in the papers?"

"I was visited by a detective from Scotland Yard."

"Are you here doing his work for him, then? Are you going to print what I say in the newspapers?" He glared at me as if he couldn't trust what I might do.

"No, not at all. I won't be writing anything about this. Not yet. The detective asked me to help him."

"How?"

"He wants to know who her friends and acquaintances were. Somehow her murderer knew that she was still alive."

"It is odd. Most odd."

Sebastian rested back in his seat and stared at the curtains hanging across the stage, dangling his hat absent-mindedly between his pointed knees. As I watched him, I recalled an incident when I had seen him in Lizzie's dressing room several years earlier. Annie, her daughter, had been with us. She was about twelve years old at the time. She had been playing with the costumes and was trying on a red silk hat with a lace veil when Sebastian walked in with an enormous bunch of lilies.

"Another bouquet for you, Lizzie," he said. "The audience adored your performance this evening."

"Thank you. Aren't they beautiful?"

Lizzie wore a cream silk dressing gown and had just removed her stage make-up. Her face looked young and girlish for her years. She leant forward to smell the flowers. "I love the scent of lilies. Don't you, Penny?"

"I do, although I rarely have cut flowers in my lodgings. The lack of light kills off most things rather quickly."

"Including yourself?" Lizzie laughed. "I've invited Penny here to help me with Ophelia," she explained to Sebastian. "She is an expert on Shakespeare."

"No, I'm not!" I added quickly. "I read his plays, but I am not an expert by any stretch of the imagination."

Sebastian smiled. "Any help Lizzie can obtain is more than welcome, I am sure. You will be a wonderful Ophelia, Lizzie."

"You say that about every part I play. Sometimes it works and sometimes it doesn't. I wish you would be a little more honest with me, Sebastian."

"It's what I believe!"

"And how do you think this current run is going?" she probed.

"Extremely well."

"There you go again. And I don't agree with you. I think it is quite arduous."

"It is meant to be hard work. If you're not finding it diffi-cult, it means you're not trying hard enough."

"Even so, I don't believe this play is going as well as *A Midsummer Night's Dream*."

"Each play is different, as is each performance. Sometimes everything runs perfectly with seemingly little effort, and at other times it feels so terribly difficult that it's tempting to give up."

"That's how I feel at this moment," said Lizzie sadly, gazing at her reflection in the mirror.

"Come now." Sebastian stood behind her and placed his hands on her shoulders. "It will feel better again soon. It's important to remember that acting isn't all beer and skittles."

"It most certainly is not." She removed his hands from her shoulders and got up out of her chair.

"Oh Annie, look at you!" A wide grin spread across Lizzie's face. "You look beautiful in that hat!"

Annie laughed and lifted up the veil so she could see her mother properly. She looked very like her with her dark, wavy hair and pretty, heart-shaped face.

"When I decide I have had enough of this acting lark, you must employ Annie in my place, Sebastian!"

"We must begin the acting lessons very soon, in that case!"

Lizzie walked over to her daughter, lifted the hat and kissed her on the forehead. "I am proud of you, darling. I was only joking about you taking my place. If you ever think about becoming an actress you must think it over very hard, as it is not an easy profession. Promise me you won't rush into it as I did."

"I promise, Mother."

"The detective wants to find out who Lizzie was acquainted with shortly before the sinking of the *Princess Alice*."

Sebastian stopped staring at the curtain and turned to look at me. "Well, he needs to ask her husband, doesn't he? Hasn't he spoken to Taylor?"

"He has, but I can't imagine he has spoken to him in great detail yet. Mr Taylor identified her only yesterday."

"Shot. In Highgate Cemetery." Sebastian shook his head in disbelief. "Who would do such a thing? And why?"

"And why did she pretend to have drowned five years ago?" I added.

"Why indeed?" He continued to shake his head. "It's a pretty kettle of fish, that's for sure." He checked his watch. "I must dash, I have a lunch appointment. I can imagine this has caused a sensational stir in the newspaper offices. You must have a lot of reporting to do for the *Morning Express*."

"I no longer work for the *Morning Express*."

"You don't? I assumed you were visiting me as part of your journalistic inquiries."

"No, I'm not working on the story. I just wanted to speak to someone else who knew her."

"Indeed."

There was a moment of silence and I noticed his face soften.

"I wonder how Annie is," I ventured.

"Devastated, I should think. She has Taylor to look after her. I do hope they are some comfort to one another."

Annie had lived with her stepfather ever since he had married her mother. He had trained her as a performer and she was a talented trick rider in his shows. I estimated that she would be about twenty years old by now.

Sebastian put on his hat and gave me an earnest look. "Please will you come and have dinner with my wife and me? You and I both thought a lot of Lizzie, and to speak to someone else who cared for her seems..." He pulled out a handkerchief and wiped his brow. "I don't know. It just seems appropriate. Is that the right word? I am sure you agree."

"Indeed, yes. That would be lovely. Thank you."

His offer took me by surprise. *Perhaps he trusted me after all?*

"Good. Then please excuse me, Miss Green. I will send a

note to you with a date and time. You are still at Milton Street?" He tucked his handkerchief away again.

"I am."

"Good, good." He stood up and raised his hat. "Until then."

CHAPTER 5

With a fresh piece of blotting paper covering the hole in the sole of my boot, I travelled on the underground railway from Temple to Westminster Bridge station early that evening. I could only afford a third-class ticket for the train, so it was fortunate that my journey was short in the malodorous, overcrowded carriage. It was so filled with tobacco smoke that I wanted to open a window for ventilation, but I knew that doing so would only let in the smoke and soot from the engine.

I had decided to go to Astley's Amphitheatre, where Lizzie's former husband, Joseph Taylor, had a show. Posters for his production of *Sinbad the Sailor* seemed to be pasted on every spare inch of wall across London. I had never been to one of his shows and, having only ever found him cantankerous in the past, I wasn't sure what to expect.

I hoped that Mr Taylor and Lizzie's daughter, Annie, would remember me as a friend of Lizzie's. I wanted to offer them my condolences and was hopeful that they might be able to tell me something which would help me understand what had happened to Lizzie.

It still didn't seem real.

Mr Taylor wouldn't think twice about being rude and dismissive, so I hoped he would be genial towards me. I reasoned that if I watched the show before speaking to him I would have a topic with which to open our conversation.

It was dark as I emerged from Westminster Bridge station with a taste of sulphur in my mouth from the train journey. The gas lamps on Westminster Bridge lit my way over to Lambeth and I heard the puff of a steamer passing on the river beneath my feet. Lights glimmered out on the water and a couple walked arm-in-arm ahead of me. From behind, I heard the excited chatter of children.

Sinbad the Sailor began at seven o'clock and the performance was attracting a steady stream of theatregoers.

I bought a sixpence ticket from a stern woman with a heavily lined face at the box office and asked if I could speak to Mr Taylor after the show. She shook her head and looked past me in a bid to sell a ticket to the next person in the queue.

"I would like to speak to him for just a few minutes," I pleaded. In desperation, I rummaged around in my handbag in an attempt to find one of my old *Morning Express* calling cards. I located one with a bent corner among a bundle of papers and pushed it across the counter of the ticket booth.

The woman picked it up and examined it closely.

"Wait by the stage door at the end," she said after a protracted pause.

"You will tell Mr Taylor that I wish to speak to him?"

She nodded in reply and asked the man waiting behind me how many tickets he wished to purchase.

My seat was in the upper gallery, a position that afforded me a clear view of the arena. There were ramps either side of the stage leading down into a large circular ring. I recalled watching a performance at the same venue many years earlier with my father and sister.

The lights dimmed and a great fanfare of trumpets and drums ensued. A single spotlight shone onto the stage and into it stepped Mr Taylor, prompting a deafening roar of appreciation from the audience. He was clearly a popular showman.

He stood there with a grin on his face, his arms outstretched. He wore a purple tunic and breeches that glittered with bead trimmings. On his head was a purple velvet hat with three ostrich feathers in it and his hessian boots were decorated with tassels. I guessed he was about fifty years of age. His face was redder and chubbier than before, but his moustache was still bushy and ginger in colour.

"Ladies and gentlemen!"

His voice rang out clearly across the arena and I was impressed at his exuberance during what I knew must be a difficult time for him. In fact, he seemed a completely different man from the one I knew.

"Prepare yourselves for the *greatest spectacle ever witnessed* at Astley's Amphitheatre! This evening you will witness the largest number of Arab horses ever seen under one roof! Two hundred of 'em!"

He paused to allow the audience to cheer.

"We also have twenty elephants!"

Another cheer.

"Ten camels!"

More audience appreciation.

"And five lions!"

The crowd applauded once again.

"Accompanying them, we have two hundred boys and

girls, one hundred ladies and two hundred men! And among them are *fifty wild savages from the Dark Continent!*"

Whoops and gasps could be heard in equal measure by way of response to this statement.

"Yes, ladies and gentlemen. Until recently, they were unable to speak in any ordinary language and, despite my attempts to civilise them, they still eat raw flesh!"

More gasps followed.

"But please don't worry, ladies and gentlemen. I shall ensure that none of them escape into the audience tonight."

A woman behind me laughed nervously.

"And now, without further ado, I present to you Mr Joseph Taylor's performance of *Sinbad the Sailor!*"

Another great cheer rang out and up came the lights. The drums thundered and a river of horses with riders dressed in flowing blue silk and chiffon galloped from the wings onto the stage and then flowed down into the arena.

As the horses and riders galloped back and forth I could see that their movement was intended to be like the waves of the sea, and before long a great, glittering, golden barge on wheels was pulled into the arena.

Sinbad stood on top of it, waving his cutlass above his head. He wore a red turban, decorated with jewels, and a loose white shirt with baggy purple trousers. What followed was an interpretation of the Sinbad story with all of his voyages combined into one. It wasn't the faithful retelling I remembered my father recounting to me, but I found myself enjoying it all the same.

Sinbad was shipwrecked on an island, where he discovered a giant egg decorated with jewels. From this egg hatched a large bird, which was actually a beautiful Arab bay horse with impressively large wings supported on poles held by several children.

Sinbad flew on the bird's back to another island inhabited

by the savages, and there he was invited to marry the chief's daughter, who I felt sure was played by Annie. She was dark-haired and dressed in pink chiffon pantaloons with a chiffon blouse that was decorated with glittering sequins.

She and Sinbad rode off together on a pair of horses and, as I watched her stand on the back of the galloping horse and perform an array of vaults and somersaults onto its back and off again, I became certain the girl was Annie. Her skin had been darkened to give her the appearance of a savage, but the shape of her face and her eyes seemed familiar. She must have only recently heard of her mother's death, yet the girl was able to perform flawlessly. It was nothing short of remarkable.

The crowd showed their adoration for Annie and Sinbad as they accomplished their horseback tricks, and I felt sure Lizzie would have been proud of her daughter.

Had she known Annie was capable of such remarkable feats? Had she ever come here incognito and watched her daughter perform?

I reflected on my conversation with Sebastian earlier that day. He had seemed understandably upset about Lizzie's death. They had worked closely together throughout her career. It seemed he could offer no explanation for her disappearance or her murder.

Inspector Blakely would need to interview Sebastian, as he had known Lizzie well before she had supposedly drowned. But I couldn't see what useful information, if any, Sebastian would have for the inspector. He seemed as shocked and bewildered as I was.

I felt a sense of anger that Lizzie had chosen to hide her survival from us all. *Why would she do such a thing?* She must have known that a funeral had been held for her, and to allow her family and friends to grieve for her when she was still alive seemed like a vindictive deception.

Perhaps she hadn't intended to upset anyone, and perhaps something had happened which had left her with no choice but to hide. But I couldn't for the life of me think what that might have been.

CHAPTER 6

The savages turned on Sinbad, and Annie was carried away on the back of a white painted elephant and locked in a cage surrounded by lions. The audience grew quiet as the lions prowled menacingly around the arena. I felt relieved to be sitting in the upper gallery.

Sinbad wrestled the lions to the ground in a well-rehearsed routine and I was impressed by the skill of the performer as well as the way the lions did as they were instructed. There was an enormous cheer when Sinbad rescued Annie from her cage. When Mr Taylor entered the arena and invited the largest lion to stand on its hind legs, resting its paws on his shoulders, the crowd erupted and everyone stood to their feet to applaud. As I watched Annie curtsy in the centre of the arena, I recalled her as a young girl and felt a lump in my throat. I joined in with the applause, clapping until the palms of my hands hurt.

Sinbad the Sailor left me impressed with Mr Taylor's skill as a showman. Lizzie had often enthused about his work and I regretted not having seen one of his shows earlier.

◈

I left the amphitheatre with the rest of the crowd and walked down the side of the building into a lonely, dark alley where a dim, flickering light marked the location of the stage door. I knocked at the door but there was no answer, so I stood and waited.

Tiny droplets of rain sparkled in the lamplight and a gust of wind blew them onto my face. I wiped the dampness from my cheeks with my gloved hand and wondered whether Mr Taylor had already returned home for the evening. Hugging my handbag to my chest, I peered into the darkness around me, aware that this would be the perfect place for a robber to attack me and steal my bag.

Surely there must be a better place to meet with Mr Taylor. Preferably somewhere that offered light and warmth.

Just then the stage door opened and a shaft of light illuminated the alleyway. A dark face appeared, much lower down then I was expecting. It belonged to one of the savage children from the show. I wondered how many people in the audience had believed Mr Taylor's claim that the savages were truly wild. The girl looking out at me had most likely been born in London and was nothing more than an ordinary performer in the show, just like everyone else. Her dark eyes stared out at me and I was about to speak when the door was slammed shut again.

"There's a lady what's waitin' for yer, Mr Taylor!" came the girl's voice from the other side of the door.

This time I rapped sharply on the door, which opened by a scowling Mr Taylor. His ginger hair was sweaty and tousled from being pressed down under his hat. He had a cigar in his mouth, a drink in one hand, and I could see that his velvet costume was worn at the edges and too tight around his midriff.

"Miss Green. I received your calling card. Do come in."

"Good evening, Mr Taylor. I must congratulate you on the most magnificent performance of *Sinbad the Sailor*. I enjoyed it very much. As did the rest of the audience, judging by their applause." I grinned, hoping my flattery would wipe the frown from his face.

It didn't.

I stepped through the door and into a small hallway, from which a wooden staircase led to an upper storey. Mr Taylor's bulk blocked my progress any further. This, it seemed, was as far as I was to be permitted into the building. I heard scampering on the wooden steps as the girl who had previously opened the door ran off up the stairs.

An odour of animal dung lingered in the air.

"Miss Green. You work for the *Morning Express*."

"Yes." I smiled to cover up the lie. "I last saw you with Lizzie five years ago."

The mention of her name deepened his frown and furrowed his brow.

"Do you remember? She was performing as Cleopatra at the time and I met you backstage one evening."

"You're the daughter of the plant hunter, aren't you? The one that went missing."

"That's right."

"And Lizzie gathered together a substantial amount of money to fund a rescue expedition for him."

"Yes."

"Little good came of that, did it?"

"Sadly, it was unsuccessful, but I shall never forget Lizzie's generosity." I felt a lump in my throat as I spoke.

"May I ask why you are here?"

"I came to offer my condolences to you and Annie. I have just discovered what happened to Lizzie."

I saw a flicker in his green eyes, but the frown remained fixed on his face.

"I am shocked. And saddened. I cannot understand how this could have happened to her."

"And you think I do?"

"Not at all; you must be distraught. To continue with your incredible performance this evening is true testament to your character, Mr Taylor."

Once again, I hoped flattery would soften him, but I was wrong for a second time.

"I am a professional showman, Miss Green. I have been doing this job since I could walk. Twenty years ago, I watched my mother die and two hours later I was on the stage. The audience had no inkling at all that my world had just ended. The inquest into Lizzie's death was opened today, but the show must go on."

"Absolutely." I nodded sagely.

"Are you planning to interview me for your newspaper?"

"No, the reason for my visit is more personal than that. I considered Lizzie a friend and, having discovered this terrible news, I felt the need to visit the people who were most important to her."

His face reddened. "By law, my marriage to Lizzie ended when she was discovered drowned on the *Princess Alice*. I have since found out that we were still married for another five years. My wife deceived me. She wanted me to believe that she was dead!"

His lips twisted in anger and I was relieved to hear footsteps on the staircase. I hoped the presence of another person might help to subdue his temper.

I looked up the stairs and saw Annie descending towards us, dressed in a dark overcoat. I felt a smile pull at the corners of my mouth as I remembered her as a girl. Wiped clean of its stage make-up, her face was pretty and girlish, just as her mother's had been. But Annie looked pale and sombre. She glanced over but didn't appear to recognise me.

Mr Taylor pulled the stage door open behind me and peered out into the street.

"Is our carriage here, Joseph?" she asked.

He nodded in reply, closed the door and drained his glass.

"Annie?" I wondered if the girl would remember me. "I'm Penny Green. I knew your mother. I saw you many times in her dressing room. I remember that you liked to dress up in your mother's costumes."

The girl eyed me warily and then turned to Mr Taylor, as if requesting his permission to speak to me.

"And what an incredible performance," I continued. "You are an extremely skilled horsewoman."

I wanted to add that her mother would have been proud of her, but I realised the comment might have caused upset. I wanted to ask her and Mr Taylor if they had known that Lizzie had survived her supposed drowning, but the guarded expressions on their faces told me not to take the risk. I felt disappointed that the showman was determined to be so hostile.

"Annie is tired," said Mr Taylor, "and she has no interest in talking to hacks. And neither do I. I can see no reason for you to come here, Miss Green, other than to pry. I won't mince the matter: in short, I find your presence here to be an imposition."

Any hope I had harboured of finding out more about Lizzie's death was gone. *If Mr Taylor and Annie were not prepared to talk to me, what could I possibly do next?*

"I do apologise, Mr Taylor, if I have upset you. It was never my intention, I can assure you. I came here only as a friend of Lizzie's."

He opened the door and glared at me.

"Goodnight, Miss Green."

CHAPTER 7

I stayed at home the following morning to finish my article on Madame de Staël. I struggled to muster any enthusiasm for it at all after the rebuff from Mr Taylor. My conversations with him and Sebastian kept running through my mind.

How did they really feel about Lizzie's death? Had they any idea who could have harmed her?

There were so many questions I wished to ask them, but I wanted to avoid causing them any upset. I had already antagonised Mr Taylor and had no desire to make matters worse.

There was a little coal left in the scuttle, but I decided to see how much of the day I could get through without lighting a fire in the stove. Once it was lit I would treat myself to a cup of coffee. Until then, I wore a woollen dress over my nightdress, a pair of thick socks, which had once belonged to my father, and an old overcoat of my sister's, which was too long and broad in the shoulders. I wore a pair of fingerless gloves and a woollen bonnet, hoping my unusual ensemble would keep me warm for the morning, at least.

Once my article was finished I would receive payment of

seven guineas. This would enable me to pay Mrs Garnett for two weeks' rent with two pounds and seven shillings left over. I desperately needed to find more work. My salary at the *Morning Express* had been two hundred and fifty pounds a year, which had not been a great fortune, but had allowed me to pay my way. The constant worry about income frequently disturbed my sleep and left me feeling tired and dismal.

Perhaps I had been foolish to turn down Inspector Blakely's offer of payment for helping him. My pride had stepped in and I had spoken without taking the time to properly consider his offer.

I sat at my desk by the window and wrote. The sky was leaden, but there was just enough daylight by which to see clearly. The nib of my pen scratched as I wrote and the ink flowed onto the page and over my fingers. Tiger was lying out on the rooftop, peering in at me occasionally.

Eventually, my article was finished. I put my pen down, lit the fire in the stove and stitched the pages of my manuscript together as I waited for the kettle to boil. That afternoon I planned to dress myself and take the manuscript to the editorial office of the *Ladies' Scholarly Repository* in Bloomsbury.

The sound of an argument drifted up the stairwell to my door. I recognised Mrs Garnett's voice and then the second voice. It was my sister Eliza. I had no choice but to go downstairs and find out what the problem was.

I left my room and made my way down the narrow, wooden staircase and then proceeded down the wider, carpeted staircase. Mrs Garnett and Eliza were facing each other in the hallway. The front door stood open, and half-in, half-out of the door was Eliza's bicycle. It was a wide contraption with a large wheel on one side and two smaller wheels on the other. At the centre was a small, uncomfortable looking seat and two pedals. The bicycle was steered by two handles either side of the seat. Eliza had suggested in the past that I should have a ride on it, but I had never been tempted.

"I can assure you, Mrs Garnett, that my bicycle can be placed in your hallway and still leave ample room for those coming and going through the front door."

"It will scrape my wallpaper! Do you know how much this wallpaper cost?"

"And if I leave my bicycle outside it will be stolen. Do you know how much my bicycle cost?"

The two women glared at each other angrily, and Mrs Garnett had her hands on her hips. Eliza wore a smart, plaid skirt and jacket, and beneath her skirt she wore a pair of breeches and boots. She had borrowed a pair of her husband's trousers to preserve her modesty.

"Ellie!"

My sister turned and saw me on the stairs.

"Penelope! Whatever are you wearing?"

"I could ask you the same." I glanced at the trousers, which were just visible beneath the hem of her skirt.

"The pair of you," Mrs Garnett tutted and shook her head, "are one button short. It must run in your family."

"Mrs Garnett," I said. "Would you object to Eliza leaving her bicycle by the privy? I am sure it will cause no harm there."

Mrs Garnett shrugged. "I suppose so. As long as it doesn't block the privy door."

"It could still be stolen!" retorted Eliza.

"It is unlikely. The privy is well hidden behind the house."

"She can leave it there for one hour," conceded Mrs Garnett.

After steering the bicycle down the narrow passageway by the side of the house and into the courtyard, we went up to my room and had a cup of coffee.

With her height and loud voice, Eliza always seemed to make my lodgings feel smaller. She removed her hat and jacket, hanging them up on the hooks behind my door.

"It's cold in here. Those coals have only just been lit, haven't they? I take it you're wearing that strange concoction of clothes to keep warm."

She sat on the chair by my writing desk while I settled on my bed. Tiger miaowed at the window to be let in. When Eliza pulled up the sash, she crept in and then dashed beneath my bed.

Somehow Eliza caught sight of my button-up boots under the desk and picked up the one with the hole in. "Goodness gracious, Penelope, you're poorer than a church mouse, aren't you? Are you finding any work at all?"

She reminded me of our mother as her eyes bored into me enquiringly. Eliza and I were similar in appearance: we were both blonde-haired and brown-eyed, but she had always been the larger, stronger and louder one, even though she was two years my junior. Her features were sharper than mine, her nose was longer, and she had often told me she wished for a softer face like mine.

"I never understand why I am the married sister and Penelope is not," was something she frequently said. She claimed I was prettier than her, which I disputed.

"I have some work."

"And how does it pay?"

"Not quite enough."

"Then let me give you something." She picked up her handbag and opened it.

"No, Ellie, please. It's not necessary."

But my protest was weak and Eliza piled some coins onto my desk.

"That's all I have for now. I will bring more when I visit later this week."

"No, please don't. That is more than enough. I shall collect payment for my latest article this afternoon. I will be able to pay you back this evening."

"You may have the loan for longer than that. You need it. Buy yourself a new pair of boots. You look thin, as well. You must come and eat a proper meal with us. Do you have any hope of salaried work on the horizon?"

"I could apply to newspapers, I suppose, but it might be difficult to persuade them to take me on after I lost my job at one of the most prestigious publications."

"That editor, William Sherman, has much to answer for." Eliza tutted and took a sip from her tin cup. I had broken all my china and was unable to afford replacements. "You know what Mother thinks, don't you?"

"That if I had a husband I shouldn't be in this mess."

"That is what exactly what she thinks, and she has no idea how poor you are. You're in a fine pickle. You need to ask her for some money. She won't expect you to repay it."

"I know, but in return she will expect to set me up with the village curate."

Many years previously, my mother had decided that Reverend Briggs would make me an excellent husband.

"He is still a bachelor, you know."

"And there is a very good reason for that. I can manage quite comfortably when I have a salary."

"But a salary can't give you happiness and children, can it?"

"I am happy without children." I could feel my jaw tightening. These conversations with my sister always included a comment about my age, followed by a despairing look.

"Penelope, you are almost thirty-five..."

"I know," I interrupted.

"Cousin Agatha has just announced her engagement to a commander in the Royal Navy. Did you hear? I always knew Agatha would find a husband quickly. She has a pretty nose and a well-turned ankle. She is the last of our cousins to marry. To think that all twenty-seven of us are spoken for!" Eliza glanced at me awkwardly. "Except for..."

"Have you heard the news about Lizzie Dixie?"

"Yes!" Eliza's eyes opened wide with fascination. "Terribly surprising, isn't it? You knew her, didn't you? What happened?"

I told her what I had learned so far, I knew I could talk to Eliza freely, without fear of her spreading any gossip. Although she often laughed at me for being a working woman and shunning family life, she had always taken a keen interest in what I did and I sensed that she sometimes dreamed of having a job like mine.

Eliza was clever and a good writer and could have had a paid job, but instead she devoted her time to her family and her cause: the West London Women's Society. Her husband, George Billington-Grieg, was a lawyer and took pleasure in maintaining a large household of children and servants. He would not hear of Eliza working for money; to do so would have implied that he was unable to earn a sufficient wage to support his family.

"It is a true mystery," said Eliza.

"And to think that Mr Taylor didn't know that his own wife was still alive. It is no wonder he was so grumpy with me when I spoke to him."

"You spoke to him? Was that wise?"

"I wanted to pass on my condolences."

"You didn't visit him out of sheer nosiness?"

"No!" I replied, affronted.

But there was some truth in her question. My sister knew me well.

"I wish I could speak to Lizzie's daughter, Annie," I continued. "I wonder if she knew that her mother was still alive. Lizzie may have been able to hide from her husband, but surely not her own daughter? She must have made contact with her in one way or another."

"It is hard to imagine that she wouldn't have, isn't it?"

"I need to talk to Annie, but I have no idea how to do so."

"Why do you need to speak to her? You're not working on the story, are you?"

"No, I am just curious."

"Let Scotland Yard solve it."

"But don't you wonder how it all came about? Why she pretended she had drowned and was found murdered five years later?"

"Of course I wonder. I think all of us like to consider ourselves detectives when one of these cases presents itself. It is rather easy to develop an obsession with a murder, isn't it? Mother still has that ornament of the Red Barn on the mantelpiece in her dining room; the barn where William Corder murdered Maria Marten. I remember her telling me that story time and time again, and it used to chill me to the bone. That and the Ratcliffe Highway murders." Eliza shuddered. "Not to mention Constance Kent."

"My interest is not an obsession with murder," I replied. "I knew Lizzie. I worry about what her life must have been like over the past five years for it to have ended this way. And why did she decide to hide? Had her life become so very difficult? I remember the poor reviews she received for her last ever performance as Cleopatra in *The Course of the Nile* and I wonder if she struggled to cope with the criticism."

"I suppose we shall never know now, shall we?"

"I should like to find out."

"I shall always remember Lizzie Dixie for her role in raising funds for the expedition to find Father. She put a substantial amount of her own money into it. And that reminds me! I have heard from the curator at the British Museum about Father's paintings and the orchid specimens. They are going to be moved to the new Natural History building at Albertopolis in the coming weeks."

"I must ensure that I see them again before they are moved."

"And I am sure they will make an interesting display in the new natural history department. Some of his paintings would never have been found if the second expedition hadn't returned to Amazonia. Lizzie Dixie was a kind lady, even though she had a bit of reputation for loose morals. Did you mention the name Sebastian Colehill earlier?"

"Yes."

"I have only just realised that I met his wife, Mary Cole-hill, last week. She told me her husband was the proprietor of the Theatre Royal in Drury Lane. She has recently joined the West London Women's Society and seems a most pleasant lady."

We were interrupted by a knock at the door and then Mrs Garnett called my name.

"My bicycle can't have been outside the privy for an hour already, can it?" asked Eliza.

I got up and answered the door.

"A messenger boy just called with this," said my landlady, handing me a neat, white envelope with my name and address scrawled across it in black ink. I guessed it must be Sebastian Colehill's dinner invitation. Thanking Mrs Garnett, I closed the door.

"I hope you don't mind me opening this now," I said to Eliza, ripping open the envelope. "It is not often that I receive letters."

I unfolded the piece of paper and saw that it wasn't from Sebastian at all. Printed lettering at the top said: *Morning Express, est. 1837.*

I scanned the sloping writing quickly. "It's from William Sherman at the *Morning Express,*" I said. "He has requested to see me at three o'clock tomorrow afternoon at his office."

"Is that good news or bad news?"

I felt a flicker of excitement in my chest.

Perhaps Inspector Blakely had managed to have me reinstated in my job.

"I feel certain it is good."

CHAPTER 8

My new boots chafed my heels as I hailed the horse-drawn omnibus at Finsbury Circus. The downstairs seats were full, so a kind man offered me his place and went up to the roof while I sat down and felt relieved to rest my feet. I had hurriedly bought the boots that morning and my feet much preferred my old, worn pair.

The windows were so begrimed that I was unable to see much outside; instead, I read an advertisement for Jeyes Fluid before a newspaper headline caught my eye. 'Murdered Actress Shot Four Times. Killer Still on the Loose', declared the leader on *The Daily Mail* being read by the person sitting opposite me. I shivered and leant forward in my seat in an attempt to read the story, but the print was too small.

I found it hard to believe that Lizzie had suffered such a brutal end. I had been so accustomed to the belief that she had drowned that this subsequent news of her death was difficult to accept. My heart ached for Annie and I wondered how she was truly feeling. Her demeanour had seemed so cold and sombre when I had seen her after the show.

"Annie should have a proper, loving family home," Lizzie had told me during a fundraising reception for the expedition to find my father. "Joseph does his best with her, but she is not his daughter and she has reached the age at which she is resentful of him telling her what to do. I have told her she must listen to him because he is her stepfather, but she is headstrong and refuses to accept him for who he is. I married him because he is extremely successful and I feel sure that he can help me feel better about myself. He loves me and I have a deep affection for him. I sometimes wonder if that is as much love as I am capable of giving. Most of my heart is reserved for Annie. I worry about her."

I gave up trying to read the story on the paper in front of me. I hoped Mr Taylor was looking after Annie, but I couldn't imagine him having much tenderness for her in his heart.

Perhaps I would soon have an opportunity to find out what had really happened to Lizzie. I felt sure that Mr Sherman was to offer me my job again.

Why else should he ask me to meet with him?

Inspector Blakely had almost certainly spoken to Commissioner Dickson, who must have had a word with his cousin. It only seemed fair, given that my article about the Doughty Street case had been correct all along.

I hugged the handbag on my lap and felt encouraged that my fortunes were changing. I thought about the work I could do on Lizzie's story and how I could help Inspector Blakely uncover what had happened to her. The desperate need for a salary and my curiosity about the last few years of Lizzie's life made me want to work on this story more than anything else. I pictured myself in Mr Sherman's office being welcomed back as a paid member of staff. I was looking forward to seeing my former colleagues again, and perhaps Mr Sherman would invite the compositors and printers up to greet me. Maybe even the messenger boys.

The omnibus slowed to a halt and I guessed we had reached the slow-moving traffic at Bank. I got up, paid the conductor my fare and hopped off into the busy street. The sky was darkening and the flagpoles of the Bank of England were already disappearing into a foggy mist, which had a greenish tinge to it. Specks of soot floated on the air as if the fog had prevented the chimney smoke from rising upwards. Trying not to limp from the soreness of my heels, I walked a short distance up Cheapside and hailed another omnibus, which would take me along Ludgate Hill and through to Fleet Street.

Once again, it was difficult to see out of the window, but I was able to register a brief patch of darkness as we passed beneath Ludgate Viaduct. I got off the omnibus at the top of Fleet Street and was greeted by the familiar sight of the spire of St Bride's, the very top of which was lost in the descending fog. A train whistled as it passed over the viaduct behind me and pulled into the station.

My heart lifted as I walked along the crowded pavements of Fleet Street. This place had felt like my second home for more than ten years. During that time, increasing numbers of newspapers and periodicals had established themselves here, and there were now so many telegraph wires criss-crossing overhead that they could have served as a web for a giant spider.

Large lettering across the building fronts spelled out the names of the respective newspapers. I passed the *Daily News*, *The Daily Telegraph*, the *Morning Advertiser*, the *Standard* and the *News of the World*. The coffee houses and public houses along this stretch were always filled with hacks, who retired here to relax after meeting their deadlines and to share news and gossip. Mingling with the writers on the street were printers in their ink-stained clothing, bookbinders in their aprons and, occasionally, a wealthy-looking proprietor with a silk top hat and fashionably striped trousers. Messenger boys weaved through the crowd, running with pages of copy to meet deadlines.

There were more women now in Fleet Street than when I had first begun working here. A number worked as secretaries and there was a growing acceptance of lady reporters in the news rooms, so long as we took our work as seriously as the men did. My view was that we took it more seriously: spending more time working and less time drinking in Fleet Street's taverns than our male counterparts.

Many lady journalists worked on the fashion and society journals, few worked as news reporters for a daily newspaper. I had never been put off by the thought that I was an unusual case and had learnt to shrug off disparaging comments from my male colleagues.

I had always been drawn to the centre of the nation's news reporting, and from the moment I decided to become a journalist I had wanted to work on Fleet Street. My father had encouraged me in my profession, but I think he assumed I would be happy working in a quiet, provincial town in Derbyshire. He had been surprised when I told him I wanted to live and work in London. He had not been keen on the idea of his daughter being alone in the city, but he hadn't realised up to that point that I had inherited his sense of adventure.

Mr Sherman's office was on the first floor of the *Morning*

Express building. I was greeted by the roar of the printing presses in the basement as I stepped into the main entrance and climbed the narrow, wooden staircase. At the top of the stairs, one door led towards the editor's office and another towards the news room.

I knocked nervously at the door that led into the reception area of Mr Sherman's office and waited for an answer. It swung open and a compositor bustled out with a bundle of proofs in his hand, scrawled all over with Mr Sherman's corrections. If I hadn't skipped promptly out of the way, he would have bumped into me. He thundered down the stairs and I caught the door just before it closed again. I stepped into the reception area and saw Miss Welton standing there.

"Miss Green, he is ready for you now."

I had expected a warmer welcome from the editor's secretary, but I surmised that Mr Sherman was in an agitated mood, which had, in turn, dulled Miss Welton's demeanour. She was older than me by a number of years and wore a dark, woollen dress, which was buttoned up to the neck. Her grey hair was pinned neatly on top of her head and a pair of pince-nez was clipped to the end of her nose.

"Thank you, Miss Welton, it is a pleasure to see you again."

She smiled thinly in reply and gestured for me to walk through to Mr Sherman's personal office, to which the door stood open.

The editor sat at his desk, scribbling furiously onto a proof. His shirt sleeves were rolled up and he wore a blue serge waistcoat. His black hair was oiled and parted to one side, and a pipe stuck out from beneath his thick black moustache. Another compositor stood next to him, biting his lip.

"Ah, Miss Green," said Mr Sherman without looking up. "Please take a seat."

I moved a pile of papers from the only available chair and

sat down. The editor's office had greasy, yellowing walls and smelled of pipe smoke. The far corners of the room were grimy and gloomy, and piles of books and papers were stacked on the desk and all over the floor. A gas lamp hung down from a long chain over the editor's desk and a fire burned brightly in the small grate. Mr Sherman had worked in this room, at the helm of the *Morning Express*, for almost ten years.

The editor paused to examine his edits and then thrust the proof in the direction of the compositor.

"You have half an hour to get these changes made. And shut the door behind you. Don't leave it hanging open as the previous oaf did!"

The man left and Mr Sherman sat back in his chair. He took the pipe out of his mouth and regarded me closely. His eyes were pale blue and his brow was permanently creased. His bushy eyebrows almost met at the top of his nose.

"Miss Green," he began solemnly. The glum tone of his voice did nothing to suggest that he was about to offer me a job. One of the speaking tubes next to his desk whistled.

"Excuse me one moment." He leant over and spoke brusquely into the mouthpiece. "Yes?"

The person at the other end told him there was no space for the article about the Fenian dynamite conspirators arrested in Nova Scotia.

"There has to be!" he barked. "It may be a long distance away from us, but after the bombs earlier this year I tell you that the Irish Republican Brotherhood is a threat we need to be reporting on! Cut it down to two hundred words and make sure it goes in!"

There was more conversation while Mr Sherman leafed through the papers on his desk and tossed a small card in my direction. It landed on a piece of paper covered in his familiar inky scribble.

As he traded sharp words through the tube, I leaned forward and picked up the card. It had my name on it. I realised, with a shudder of dread, that it was the card I had left for Mr Taylor. The same corner was bent as it had been on the one I had left with the front-of-house woman at Astley's Amphitheatre. My heart began to pound.

Mr Sherman hadn't called me in to offer me my job back.

I was here for a telling-off.

CHAPTER 9

I clutched my handbag tightly on my lap, bit my lip, and waited to hear what Mr Sherman had to say.

Having finished with the speaking tube, he sat back in his chair and puffed on his pipe before removing it to speak.

"I can see by the expression on your face, Miss Green, that you have realised who visited me yesterday."

"Mr Taylor."

"That is correct. He was angered by your questioning of him the previous evening. Can I ask why you pretended to still be employed by this newspaper when you spoke to him?"

"I didn't pretend as such, Mr Sherman. I had to leave a card for him at the front of house and I only had my cards with the *Morning Express* written on them."

"You didn't think to cross out the name of the newspaper to clarify your employment situation?"

"I didn't, no. Although I do think a crossing out would have looked rather untidy."

"Instead, you preferred to mislead the gentleman?"

"I visited him as a friend of his former wife. I did not

introduce myself as a news reporter. I apologise. I didn't think the name of the newspaper on the card would have any bearing on the situation."

"What rot," he replied sharply. "You are a clever woman, Miss Green. I would conjecture that you are cleverer than some of the male staff here. You knew that the reputation of the *Morning Express* would guarantee you an interview with the great showman, and sure enough it did. It is only a shame that your conduct during the meeting served to upset him."

I felt a cold perspiration spread under my arms. I tried to take a deep breath, but my chest was too constricted by my corset.

"With all due respect, Mr Sherman, he was already upset at the discovery of his wife's death. I think there was little I could have said to improve his mood."

Mr Sherman pointed the shank of his pipe at me accusingly. "You were tactless to visit him and deceitful to pretend that you were still a member of my staff. I thought you were better than this, Miss Green, but it seems I was wrong. Do you think I enjoy spending my afternoons trying to calm an irate showman who is holding me responsible for the behaviour of a woman who no longer works for my newspaper? Do I look like someone who has the time to do such a thing? Can you understand how embarrassing it was to have to explain to him that you no longer work here?"

Having arrived at the office expecting good news, I now felt rather overwhelmed by disappointment. I felt the need to escape outside for a change of air.

"I apologise unreservedly for my conduct, Mr Sherman. It was never my intention to cause upset or to bring the reputation of this newspaper into disrepute."

I stood and hooked my handbag over my arm. "I shall gather up all my remaining cards, place them in an envelope and post them to you at the first opportunity, so that there is no danger of this ever happening again."

Mr Sherman took another puff from his pipe and spoke in a calmer tone. "I am sure there is no need, Miss Green. Please don't spend your money on the postage. You have learnt your lesson now, I take it?"

"I most certainly have. I won't trouble you any further, Mr Sherman. I know the evening deadline will be upon you shortly. Good afternoon." I gave him a slight bow, walked over to the door and opened it.

"Did I say I was finished, Miss Green?"

I paused with my hand on the doorknob, nervous about what I was to hear next.

"Come back here and shut that accursed door."

I did as I was told and turned to face him, but I didn't sit this time. I watched him as he retrieved a fresh pipe and a tin of tobacco from his desk drawer.

"I had another visitor yesterday who I haven't told you about yet." He opened the tin and began to fill the pipe with flakes of tobacco. "It was my cousin, and he wasn't making a social call. You know who I am talking about, do you not? Commissioner Dickson of Scotland Yard."

My heart skipped slightly.

"It seems you have made quite an impression on that young detective of his."

I felt my cheeks redden. I presumed he was referring to Inspector Blakely, but he made it seem as though I had intentionally endeavoured to impress him.

"A detective spoke to me briefly about Lizzie Dixie a few days ago," I said.

"So I understand." Mr Sherman tucked the pipe into his mouth, then shuffled the papers and books on his desk in an effort to locate a box of matches.

"This detective is working on the Lizzie Dixie case and

needs all the help he can get. He is only a young chap, as I understand it, but he happens to be the son of a chief superintendent, which strengthens his position. And it seems he has won golden opinions, despite his youth. I think Chief Inspector Cullen would serve better on the case, but what does my opinion matter? Ah! There they are."

The editor took up the box of matches and lit his pipe. "Commissioner Dickson feels that he was perhaps rather overzealous in ordering your dismissal earlier this year. He acknowledges that some aspects of the Doughty Street case were questionable."

I sighed with relief and smiled.

This was the news I had been waiting for.

"I am happy that the commissioner has finally seen sense," I replied.

Mr Sherman scowled. "He has *always* seen sense, but a man is entitled to rethink his decisions."

"Of course. Thank you, Mr Sherman."

"Commissioner Dickson feels that having you reinstated here would serve as an apology for past mistakes and would also provide his detective with a useful source of information in relation to the Lizzie Dixie case. There is a great deal of public interest in it, as you can imagine."

"Yes, I can imagine. Thank you, Mr Sherman. And do please thank Commissioner Dickson on my behalf when you see him next."

Mr Sherman dismissed this last comment with a wave and searched through the papers on his desk again. "I need a piece done on the Corrupt and Illegal Practices Prevention Act, which has just been passed in parliament."

I nodded in reply.

"Can you have that done for me by tomorrow afternoon? Just a summary; four hundred words will do it."

After the scolding, I found it hard to believe what I was

hearing. "You want me to write an article? Does this mean I have a job here again?"

"Why else would I ask you for a summary of the new act?"

"Thank you, Mr Sherman!" I felt a grin spread across my face. "I am extremely grateful that you have reconsidered my position, especially in light of the unfortunate incident with Mr Taylor. I can promise that no such incident will ever happen again."

"I am sure it won't." He held up a piece of paper and began reading it, which I took as a sign to leave.

"And once I have written my piece on the new act, I will get to grips with the Lizzie Dixie story."

"There is no need; Edgar Fish has it. There will be plenty for you to work on, don't worry. Just help the detective out when he asks you and pass on all the exclusive news to Edgar Fish. That's what I agreed with Commissioner Dickson. We help him and, in exchange, we have the exclusives."

CHAPTER 10

Although I had not been given the Lizzie Dixie story to work on, I was permitted to meet with Inspector Blakely a few days later. A hansom cab took me to Kensal Green Cemetery one morning, shortly before dawn. Once I had paid the driver, I found my way through the grey gloom towards the tall iron gates which were already standing ajar. I pushed one of them open and could just make out a ribbon of pathway snaking ahead of me. I chided myself for not bringing a lantern.

I could see the pale forms of tombs and monuments as I turned right and made my way over to Lizzie's grave. I had visited her burial place a number of times over the years, and now had to accept that I had been paying my respects to a woman whose identity was unknown. Each time I had come here, Lizzie had been living somewhere in secret. I felt a mixture of anger and sadness about it. Meanwhile, another victim of the *Princess Alice* sinking had been buried in Lizzie's grave, and on this particular morning her body was to be exhumed.

Once her coffin was removed, Lizzie would be buried. I

had been told that the early morning burial ceremony was to be kept brief and far removed from the public gaze.

A blackbird started up its early morning song, its cheerfulness at odds with the sombre environment. There was a damp, earthy smell on the cold morning air and I shivered in my black satin dress and jacket, which were suitable for mourning but offered no protection against the cold.

I recoiled as the strands of a cobweb stuck to my face, hurriedly wiping them away with my gloved hands. As I walked alone in the murk, my heart began to thud more rapidly. The crunch of my boots on the gravelled path sounded deafening. I glanced around at the sleeping places of the dead all around me, worrying that someone or something was about to jump out. I tried to calm myself and remember that I had no belief in ghosts; however, the chasm between the living and the dead sometimes felt narrow.

I walked a little faster, wishing I had arranged to meet Inspector Blakely at the cemetery gates so I had someone to accompany me through the graveyard. I thought about Lizzie out walking in Highgate Cemetery late at night.

What had she been doing there? Had she arranged to meet her killer? If so, did that mean she had known him?

I reached a fork and took the path to the right, relieved that it would not be long before I reached the grave. It was both reassuring and spooky to see lights flickering in the midst of the tombs. As I walked closer to the lights, I could hear the sound of shovels digging into the earth, along with the snort of a horse and the jingle of a bridle. On the path ahead of me, I could just make out the shape of a carriage and two horses. Presumably it was there to take the coffin away.

I arrived at the graveside and saw a small group of dark figures standing close to it, watching as two men dug in the lamplight. It didn't seem right; dead people weren't supposed to be dug up. I wished I hadn't decided to come here on such a dismal morning.

"Here it is," said one of the gravediggers. I heard the light tap of a shovel against wood as confirmation. A shiver ran down my back and I stood a short distance away from the group, not wishing to get too close to the open grave.

Someone in a bowler hat had noticed my arrival and walked over to me.

"Good morning, Miss Green."

I had only met Inspector Blakely once, but his vaguely familiar voice felt reassuring to me on a morning such as this. He held a bullseye lantern, which cast some light onto his face, and I could see a faint line of stubble on his chin, as if getting up at this early hour had not given him sufficient time to shave.

"Good morning, Inspector Blakely." I felt relieved to have someone friendly to talk to. "And thank you for helping me get my job back."

"My pleasure." I could just about see his smile in the gloom. "Although Commissioner Dickson did not take a great deal of convincing. I think he knew he had behaved a little harshly towards you. And I am not sure you should be thanking me on a grim morning such as this." He glanced at the open grave and grimaced.

"How is the investigation going?"

"Slowly," he replied quietly. "We have identified a few people of interest, but there are no firm suspects yet. It will be interesting to see who turns up this morning to see Lizzie interred. Funerals are invaluable for murder investigations as they allow us to find out who was close to the victim. The murderer himself may even turn up; it's not unheard of."

"Is that right?" I glanced around us warily.

"I might need you to help me identify a few faces."

I heard some quiet muttering from one of the men standing close by and saw that he was a vicar wearing black robes, a soft black hat and a stark white collar. I realised he was praying and wondered if I should bow my head and listen.

The gravediggers were leaning into the grave, trying to haul up the coffin under the guidance of a man who I guessed was an undertaker. On the ground next to him lay the lid of the tomb, upon which lay a sleeping angel carved in stone.

"Are you here undercover?" I whispered to the inspector.

"No, Mr Taylor is expected here and he will recognise me. I plan to stand back and watch, and I hope that my presence will not be considered intrusive."

The coffin was finally hauled out of the ground and the undertaker dusted it free of dirt with his handkerchief. The vicar's prayers grew louder and I recognised the words of the Lord's Prayer. The coffin was slowly carried over to the waiting carriage as we all stood in silence with our heads bowed. I wondered whether we would ever find out who the dead woman was.

We remained silent as the coffin was placed inside the carriage, and listened to the sound of hooves and the grind of wheels on gravel as the coffin was taken away.

CHAPTER 11

I glanced over at the dark pit, which was soon to be Lizzie's grave. The sleeping angel lay beside it. The sky was a lighter grey now and it would not be long until sunrise.

Inspector Blakely extinguished his lantern. "I was unable to find a coffee stall on Harrow Road," he said. "I struggle to do anything without my morning cup of coffee. I usually rely on the breakfast stall on Northumberland Avenue, where I get a slice of bread and butter with coffee for tuppence. And if there's time I breakfast at Russell's in Whitehall Place. Have you tried it? They do the most marvellous mutton chops, eggs and toast in there."

"Usually I like the thought of mutton chops for break-fast," I replied, "but this morning my appetite feels rather subdued."

"Mr Fish," said the inspector.

I turned to see Edgar's tall frame appear at my side. He nodded to us both.

"Rather early, isn't it?" He wore a top hat and dark overcoat, and he lit his clay pipe before peering over at the empty grave. "I see they've taken her out."

"Yes, the coffin has been exhumed," said the inspector.

"Did they take a look inside it or will they do that later? We need to know who the dead woman is."

"She will be examined by the police doctor in the mortuary," replied Inspector Blakely.

Edgar drew a sharp intake of breath. "Five years she's been down there. It's not going to be pretty."

I felt nauseous at the thought, and at Edgar's lack of tact.

"You'll let me know as soon as they find out who she is, won't you, Blakely? The public want to know the identity of the mystery woman."

"It is possible that we may never find out."

"We have to, one way or another. If the doctor can give me a physical description, we shall make a public appeal. Better still, we could get an illustration of her drawn up and someone might recognise her."

"That sounds like an interesting idea," replied the inspector.

I looked around us and noticed that a few mourners had arrived. One was a smartly dressed older gentleman, who looked familiar. He had thick, grey whiskers and wore a black overcoat and top hat. He held a shiny wooden cane by his side and the thought occurred to me that it could be a cane shotgun: a secret weapon designed for wealthy gentlemen who did not wish to carry anything conspicuous. It was probably my fancy getting the better of me, but I could picture a man such as him walking through Highgate Cemetery one evening and firing shots at a person before walking calmly away and rousing little suspicion.

He glanced at me, so I looked away in the direction of a

younger man, who also seemed familiar. He was dressed in black with a well-waxed blond moustache. He had a receding chin.

How had these men known Lizzie?

"Sir Edmund Erskine, Member of Parliament for Dorset," muttered Inspector Blakely.

"Of course," I replied, looking at the older man. "I remember him now. He was at the opening ceremony for the Royal College of Music earlier this year. I saw him accompanying the Prince of Wales. The other man is also an MP, I am sure of it. Mr Dowdeswell, I think."

"Member of Parliament for Lambeth," Edgar added.

The presence of the two politicians confirmed an uncomfortable aspect of Lizzie's life. She had been the paid companion of wealthy men. I suppose she could have been described as a courtesan.

"It's rather brave of them to turn up," said Edgar.

"I think it rather respectful of them," I said.

The pair of gravediggers rested on their shovels and took a pinch of snuff while a tall, thin figure strolled slowly towards the graveside.

"That gentleman there is Sebastian Colehill," I said quietly to the inspector. "He is the proprietor of the Theatre Royal in Drury Lane and knew Lizzie for most of her career."

"Marvellous." He retrieved a notebook and pencil from the inside pocket of his overcoat and wrote the information down.

"I shall introduce you to him," I said.

I walked over to Sebastian, unsure as to whether he would welcome a conversation with a detective at this moment. To my annoyance, Edgar Fish followed close behind us.

"Good morning, Mr Colehill."

"Miss Green!" Sebastian's pale face broke out into a smile.

"How are you?" He wore a long, dark overcoat and carried an ivory-topped cane in a leather-gloved hand.

"I am well under the circumstances, thank you."

"The same. This isn't going to be easy, is it?" He dabbed at his brow with a dark silk handkerchief.

"Mr Colehill, I would like to introduce you to Inspector Blakely. He is leading the investigation into Lizzie's death. As you can imagine, the case is an extremely difficult one, so I am sure he would welcome an opportunity to speak to you about Lizzie at some point. Not right now, of course."

I glanced at the inspector, hoping he would not start asking questions at this moment.

"Inspector, delighted to meet you."

Sebastian held out his hand and Inspector Blakely shook it.

"Likewise, Mr Colehill. In fact, my mother and I watched *The Miser of Shoreditch* at the Theatre Royal just last month. We enjoyed it immensely."

"Did you now? Well, that is wonderful to hear. I am very pleased with the show; it has broadly received good reviews, apart from one or two, but then there are always some you cannot please."

"I heard it was a rather fashionable opening night."

"Yes, it was. The Prince and Princess of Wales were in attendance, which was a great honour. I really could not have wished for anything more. I feel truly blessed to have this job, I really do."

I admired the way Inspector Blakely had instantly put Sebastian at ease.

"You were an actor yourself once?"

"I was, and so was my wife. That was how we met. But treading the boards was never to be my destiny. I discovered that my talent lay on the management side. Succeeding as an actor or actress requires more than training; the foundation is laid in something less tangible than that. It is an innate ability possessed only by a select few. You know the people I mean: those who walk onto the stage wearing the very skin of their character. Every gesture, glance and word spoken is that of their character. It is as if the actor disappears into himself for the duration of the performance. I greatly admire that ability."

"Lizzie was like that," I said.

"She was." He dabbed at his brow again. "She certainly was."

"So you knew Lizzie well?" Edgar piped up from behind me.

Sebastian seemed startled by the question. "My apologies, Mr Colehill, I should introduce myself. Mr Edgar Fish from the *Morning Express*." He extended his hand over my shoulder for Sebastian to shake. "Have you any idea who might have shot Lizzie, Mr Colehill?"

Sebastian stammered at the direct question. "Well, no, I haven't the first idea. I do not understand it at all. Are you conducting an interview for your newspaper, Mr Fish?"

"I was just curious, Mr Colehill."

Sebastian gave him a guarded look and pocketed his handkerchief. The sound of horse hooves and carriage wheels drew near, and I felt relieved that our conversation was at an end.

A bright streak of orange in the east bathed the surrounding tombs in a warm glow and the black coats of the horses shone in the early morning light as they pulled the hearse towards us. It was a polished, black, ornamental carriage with carved acanthus scrollwork and ornate finials on its roof. Lizzie's coffin lay behind extravagantly draped black satin curtains.

The hearse drew to a halt and the four men who had been walking behind it parted the curtains and carefully removed the coffin. They lifted it up onto their shoulders and I was struck by how light they found it. Lizzie had only been a slight woman. I struggled to believe she was in the coffin which was being carried towards the grave. In my mind, Lizzie had been dead and buried for five years.

How could she possibly be inside the coffin I saw before me?

Immediately behind the coffin walked Joseph Taylor in a black top hat and overcoat. He stared straight ahead without acknowledging any of the mourners. Beside him walked Annie in a long, black coat with a black hat and a black veil across her face. She carried three white lilies and I could just about see her face through the veil, but I didn't want to stare too much.

I wiped a tear from my cheek and glanced around at the small group of mourners, wondering what they each knew about the last few years of Lizzie's life and about her death. Everyone bowed their heads while the vicar said his prayers.

Was there any truth in what Inspector Blakely had said about funerals? Could one of the people present be the murderer?

I tried to still my mind and listen to the vicar's words. "In the midst of life we are in death: of whom may we seek for succour, but of thee, O Lord, who for our sins art justly displeased?"

Was the murderer listening to these words at this moment?

Lizzie's coffin was slowly lowered into the ground. "Thou knowest, Lord, the secrets of our hearts; shut not thy merciful ears to our prayer; but spare us, Lord most holy, O God most mighty, O holy and merciful Saviour..."

My heart felt heavy and I prayed that Lizzie's soul could finally rest in peace.

But I feared that peace would be a long time coming.

CHAPTER 12

"It is only half past seven," said Edgar as we walked through the cemetery with Inspector Blakely. "It feels as though it should be time for lunch."

"I think we need to find somewhere to eat a good breakfast," said the inspector.

"That's a first-rate idea!" replied Edgar.

"I had heard rumours that Lizzie had a daughter," said Inspector Blakely, "and it was useful to finally clap eyes on her."

"Did you not meet Annie when you spoke to Mr Taylor?" I asked.

"No, he didn't mention her. Rather strange, considering she is his daughter."

"She isn't."

"Oh, that explains it then."

"I'm afraid I don't know who her father is. Annie was ten when Lizzie married Mr Taylor."

"Of course. I should have realised they had not been married long enough for Annie to be his daughter."

"Wait!" I hissed.

A flash of movement next to a yew tree had caught my eye. I stared at the gap between the tree and a nearby tomb, waiting to see what, or who, was there.

But there was nothing.

"I'm sorry. I thought I saw someone."

"Who?" asked Edgar.

"I don't know. I thought there was someone there just then. Watching us."

"What did they look like?" asked Inspector Blakely.

"I don't know. I just saw a flash of something. Dark clothing, perhaps."

"A man? A woman?"

"I'm sorry, I really don't know. Please forget I mentioned it. The uncomfortable business of this morning has left me rather jumpy. I shall be glad to find a place to eat some breakfast."

"We must have a look," said the inspector, leaving the path and striding towards the tomb. "Over here, you say?"

"Please don't worry, Inspector Blakely!" I called after him. "I expect I was imagining it. I am rather tired."

But he continued walking towards the tree and the tomb, so I followed him onto the wet grass, leaving Edgar behind me on the path.

"It is nothing," I said, catching up with him.

"Ah, but it *is* something," he said looking down at the ground. "Do you see the flattened grass? Someone has been here."

I shivered and looked cautiously behind the tree, but no one appeared there. Cobwebs heavy with dew hung between the branches.

Inspector Blakely continued to look around. "It seems that whoever it was has scarpered."

I glanced across the rows of headstones and monuments. A crow landed on a nearby stone cross, but I saw nothing until another movement caught my eye.

"There!" I pointed to a dark figure in the distance that appeared to be running away from us.

"After him!" called the inspector.

He ran ahead and I followed, trying not to stumble over the graves. Inspector Blakely streaked off ahead of me as the heels of my boots sank into the soft wet grass. The hem of my dress was wet with dew and my corset prevented me from taking in the breaths required for such heavy exertion. I stopped and decided to leave the running to the inspector. I could see neither him nor the dark figure, so I turned and made my way back to the path.

Edgar was waiting there, smoking his pipe. "Did you find him?" he asked.

"Inspector Blakely has chased after him. I don't know why the man is running away, or why he should have been standing there watching us."

Edgar gave me a puzzled look and glanced towards the gates of the cemetery. "Oh, hello."

I followed his gaze and saw a group of darkly dressed men walking towards us.

Edgar cackled. "They fell for it!"

"Fell for what?"

"I spread the word that Lizzie Dixie's funeral was at eight o'clock." His small eyes glinted with glee. "Now here's a group of hacks who have missed out!"

I watched the journalists from our rival newspapers as they drew nearer and felt pleased that they had missed the small service at Lizzie's graveside. A few onlookers seemed to be following them and I estimated that between twenty and thirty people had arrived here, hoping to see something.

"Too late!" shouted Edgar. "You missed it. She's in the ground!"

A slack-jawed man, chewing on a piece of tobacco, strode at the front of the group and scowled at Edgar. I recognised him as Tom Clifford from *The Holborn Gazette*.

"What do you mean we missed it?"

"The funeral's finished, old chap!" Edgar laughed.

"You told us eight o'clock."

"I gave you incorrect information. My mistake."

Tom Clifford spat onto the ground and uttered a profanity.

I stepped away from the group and was pleased to see Inspector Blakely walking quickly down the path towards us. I walked up to him.

"You didn't catch him?"

"Sadly, no." He was breathless from running.

"Did you get a better look at him?"

"Not really." He took off his hat and wiped the beads of perspiration from his brow with his sleeve. "A fairly slight fellow. Dressed in black and he wore a cap. He was blooming fast!"

"Who was it, I wonder? And why did he run away? I cannot understand it."

"It is anyone's guess. Perhaps it was someone who has had his collar tugged by my hand in the past. He was watching us, you say?"

"That was my impression, but perhaps I was mistaken."

"Even if you were, there is no doubt that he was behaving suspiciously. Why run away like that? I can only assume he was interested in the funeral proceedings, and I would like to find out who he is as a matter of urgency." He took his notebook from his pocket and made a note in it.

"Who are all these people?" he added when he had finished writing.

EMILY ORGAN

"They have come for Lizzie's funeral. Edgar gave them the wrong time."

"I see."

Inspector Blakely replaced his hat and we passed the small crowd. Edgar was at the centre of it, laughing and joking with everyone.

"Is there anyone in that group who I need to talk to?"

"I don't think so; they're mostly hacks."

"Let's leave them for the time being, then. Has your appetite recovered yet, Miss Green? I think we should find somewhere to take breakfast and talk about the case."

◈

Inspector Blakely tucked into a plate of mutton chops in the restaurant of the Buchanan Hotel close to Notting Hill and Ladbroke Grove station. It was a small, comfortable place with crimson flock wallpaper and white tablecloths. I nibbled at my toast and marmalade, sipped at my coffee and thought about the contrast between Lizzie's first funeral and the second.

Hundreds of mourners had attended her funeral at St Paul's Church in Covent Garden five years previously, but very few had known her personally. The handful of mourners at her graveside that morning had saddened me as I realised that only a few people had ever really mattered to her.

Inspector Blakely placed his knife and fork side by side on his empty plate and wiped his mouth with his serviette. His suit, waistcoat and tie were black, and I noticed a simple gold pin on his tie. I wondered if it was a gift from someone as he opened his notebook, which lay beside his plate. His dark eyebrows knotted together in thought as he read through his notes and chewed on the end of his pencil.

"My list of interesting persons remains quite small," he

said, looking over at me. "Is there something wrong with your toast, Miss Green?"

"No." I glanced down at the half-eaten slice on my plate. "I struggle to eat much at times like this."

"Do you mind if I eat it?"

"Not at all. Are you sure you want to? It looks a bit sorry for itself with me having eaten some of it."

I passed the plate to him and he ate the toast while flicking through his notebook.

"I would like to speak to Lizzie's daughter, Annie," he said. "Do you know much about her?"

I told him about my visit to Astley's Amphitheatre earlier in the week and how Annie had seemed reluctant to speak to me.

"I wonder if she is quite influenced by Joseph Taylor's presence," said the inspector. "It sounds as though she might have said more to you if he hadn't been there. If I could somehow speak to her alone that would be preferable. Although I suppose I would need a chaperone. You could act as chaperone, couldn't you?"

"If she and Mr Taylor are happy with that, I could."

"I can't imagine Mr Taylor being happy with anything." He wrote something in his notebook.

"Me neither. He has always struck me as a cantankerous man."

"He will have to lighten his mood as I still have a good many questions for him. I also need to speak to Mr Colehill. He seems more amenable."

"I am sure he will be as helpful as he can. He was very fond of Lizzie."

"They worked together?"

"Yes, for many years. Mr Colehill first discovered Lizzie when she was nineteen years old."

"So she owed her livelihood to him?"

"I suppose she did. She performed under many other managers, of course, and her success was attributed to her own ability rather than anything Sebastian specifically did."

"But if it hadn't been for him, she might not have become an actress in the first place?"

"Possibly. Maybe she would have done so, but we will never know. Sebastian was a big help to her, and he was supportive throughout her career."

"And then we have the other suspects."

"Are Annie, Mr Taylor and Mr Colehill suspects?"

Inspector Blakely put down his pencil and grimaced. "Not just yet. One of them has to be, if not all of them. I like to describe them as people of interest. They knew Lizzie and I feel fairly certain she was murdered by someone she knew; by someone who knew she was still alive. That could make our list of suspects rather narrow, couldn't it?" He picked up his pencil again. "The other names I need to note down are Sir Edmund Erskine and Mr Hugh Dowdeswell. I assume Lizzie knew them through her work. Her *other* work," he added, raising an eyebrow.

"That sounds sensible to me," I said. "There are probably other men too."

"There may well be, and I need to track them all down. Can you think of anyone else I may have missed?"

"Lizzie had a large family, but I don't think any of them live in England. If her mother is still alive she is probably in Dublin and I know a few of Lizzie's brothers emigrated to America. I thought Lizzie had come to London with her older sister, but I don't ever recall meeting her and I don't know her name."

The inspector made a note of this. "Lizzie's father?" he asked.

"I seem to remember her saying that he had died. She told

me he was a ne'er-do-well and was in Kilmainham Gaol. The family was poor and she helped her mother make matches and sew clothes. She became a housemaid when she was fourteen."

"And Lizzie, or Hannah as she was called at that time, moved to London with her sister to work in service. Am I right?"

"Yes, they did well and found work with the wealthy Burrell family in Belgravia."

"And I've already ascertained that her brothers went to America. I have heard rumours that they are friendly with the Fenian leader, Mr O'Donovan Rossa, out there."

"I have also heard that said."

"And Lizzie sympathised with the Irish cause?"

"Yes, she did. I can't say she would have agreed with the Fenian dynamite campaign, but she supported home rule. She said the Great Famine should never be allowed to happen again and that as long as the British were in charge she worried that it would."

"Sir Edmund and Mr Dowdeswell are both liberals, and therefore more sympathetic to the Irish cause than some. Even so, Lizzie's relationship with them creates a complicated situation, especially with her brothers supporting the Fenians in America."

"You think she could have been murdered for her political connections?"

"Anything is possible at this stage, Miss Green. I am trying to determine how far my investigations must extend."

I felt reassured that Inspector Blakely intended to be thorough in his investigation. The more we talked about the case the more complicated I realised it was. "It seems that although there are only a few people of interest, there are many possibilities to consider," I said.

"Exactly. And I am not entirely sure where to start. I will be happier when I can get hold of that young man who ran away from us at the cemetery, I think he could be someone of importance to us."

CHAPTER 13

The following day I met with Inspector Blakely at another cemetery. This time the location was Highgate; the scene of Lizzie's murder. I knew this was to be another difficult day, but I decided that visiting the place where Lizzie had died might help me accept what had happened to her. Perhaps it would give me some ideas about who had committed the murder. Perhaps part of me also wanted to visit out of morbid curiosity.

I travelled by horse-drawn tram up to Highgate and then walked through the frosty residential streets and through the east side of Highgate Cemetery until I reached Swain's Lane. Inspector Blakely was waiting for me by the gate at the west side. He wore a tweed overcoat and a bowler hat.

"Good morning, Miss Green. It is a beautiful morning, isn't it?" He smiled and looked up at the blue sky. "I don't suppose it will be long before the fog returns, so we must make the most of it."

"And that is by visiting the scene of a murder?"

He smiled awkwardly. "Yes, there are many more pleasant things we could be doing on a morning such as this. But a profession such as mine does not accommodate those, as a rule."

"There must be some occasions when your job is rewarding, Inspector Blakely?"

"If I can reunite a lost child with its parent, perhaps. Or find a cat who has wandered astray."

"And remove a murderer from the streets?"

"Yes, that is extremely rewarding, and it is why I am here." He pointed up the steep lane. "Let me take you up to the gates PC Preston climbed over the night he heard the shots and the screams. We have no hope of knowing which way Lizzie entered the cemetery, but we can at least retrace the steps we know the constable took. He is due to speak at the inquest later today to tell them what I am about to tell you."

We walked up the lane alongside the wall of the cemetery towards a set of iron gates. I had worn my warmest woollen skirt, a lined woollen jacket and a thickly lined bonnet, which was tied beneath my chin and covered my ears. It was an old, rather unfashionable bonnet, but I craved warmth rather than style.

"I've alerted B Division to be on the lookout for the man who ran away from us in Kensal Green Cemetery," said Inspector Blakely. "And I've asked Y Division to be on the lookout too in case he turns up somewhere here in Highgate. Do you think we could put an appeal for information about him in your newspaper?"

"Of course. I will ask Mr Fish to write something. Hopefully we can put it in tomorrow's edition."

As we reached the gates, the inspector opened them and we stood at the top of a path from which we could see the cemetery descending down the hillside before us. To our right I saw an enormous cedar of Lebanon, which must have been a few hundred years old.

"Peace has almost been restored to this place," said Inspector Blakely. "There has been a great deal of interest from sightseers, as you can imagine. Y Division has had to deploy a few bobbies here over the past week to ensure that the sanctity of the cemetery is respected. We even had some day trippers arrive from Essex."

He pointed along the path ahead of us. "PC Preston went along here in the direction from which he thought the commotion had come."

The monuments and headstones glistened with frost in the morning sunshine and the path curved to our right, leading us towards the cedar. I felt a sickening turn in my stomach as I thought about the place where Lizzie had spent her last moments. I wanted to see it, but felt nervous that it would upset me.

What must this place have been like in the middle of the night?

Ahead of us lay London: a mass of rooftops, spires and smoking chimneys with a brownish grey pall hanging over them. Rising above it all was the great dome of St Paul's Cathedral, just a short walk from Fleet Street.

"PC Preston must have felt rather frightened that night," I said.

"Yes, I think he did. He could not have known whether the gunman had any more ammunition or not. There was a risk he might have been shot himself. We need to turn left here and make our way to Egyptian Avenue."

The path continued downhill and the earth was banked up to our right. My eye was drawn to two tall stone monoliths, and as we walked closer I could see that they stood either side of a large stone archway with ornately carved stone pillars either side of it. The ornamentation bore a resemblance to the architecture of ancient Egypt.

Three women stood by the archway wrapped up in shabby coats and with bonnets pulled tightly over their ears. They watched us and one whispered something to another.

As we walked towards the women, heading for the archway, one of them approached us.

"We come lookin' to see where Lizzie Dixie's got shot."

"Well you are very close to the place," replied the inspector.

I shuddered, but the women's faces lit up with excitement.

"Where was it then? Was it over 'ere?" asked one, pointing to a patch of ground.

Another woman lent over to inspect the gravel.

"Sarah says she can see blood in among them stones."

"I can't see nothin'."

"It's there if yer lookin' proper."

All three women peered down at the ground as Inspector Blakely and I passed them.

Beyond the archway was a stone avenue punctuated by a series of doors. They resembled a row of houses, and in some respects they were: these were houses for the dead, with the family name of each vault inscribed above the respective doorway. The avenue opened into a circle lined with more vaults, and above us the large cedar branched out over our heads.

There was something other-worldly about this place.

"Lizzie had a lamp with her," said Inspector Blakely. "PC Preston saw the glow from the archway we have just walked through, and it led him to this place."

I followed the inspector around the circle of vaults.

After a few steps, he stopped abruptly. "This is the Lebanon Circle. And this is the spot where PC Preston found

Lizzie Dixie. She was lying here with the lamp next to her, which had somehow remained lit."

He pointed to a patch of gravelled ground in front of one of the vaults. I felt compelled to read the inscription: The Family Sepulchre of Leonard Waugh.

"Are you sure?" I found myself saying.

I knew he was speaking the truth, but it seemed hard to believe. "But she was shot. There must have been a lot of..." I couldn't bring myself to finish the sentence.

"Everything was thoroughly doused afterwards."

I nodded in reply and stared at the patch of gravel once again.

"And she was just lying here? Was she already dead when PC Preston found her?"

"Sadly, yes. Even if he had found her sooner I am not certain that much could have been done to save her. She had been struck by four bullets, one at close range. She had one wound to her left leg and three wounds in her back. The wounds in her back suggest she was trying to run away. We found bullet fragments lodged in the ground beneath her body, which suggests that one of the shots was fired into her back as she lay on the ground."

The violence of her death was unbearable. It felt as though the ground was lurching beneath me and I slumped against the wall of the sepulchre for support. I could feel beads of perspiration breaking out across my forehead and my face felt cold.

"Are you all right, Miss Green?"

"Not really."

"My apologies, I should not have brought you here. I should have known better than to discuss this matter with you in detail. I know most ladies would cover their ears at hearing such things, but as you are a reporter I thought you would be..."

"I am fine, thank you, Inspector Blakely." I tried to stand upright again. "I find this upsetting because I knew Lizzie and I cannot bear to think that she suffered so."

"I understand; it is terrible. The only consolation I can offer is that the end was undoubtedly swift and she may not have known much about it. The shots PC Preston heard were fired in fairly quick succession."

"Tell me what he heard exactly."

"One shot, a pause and then a second. There was another pause before the third came and the final three shots were fired close together. I think the first shot was probably the one which hit the front of her left thigh. It suggests that she was facing her assailant when it was fired and that there had perhaps been an interaction before the shot came.

"Once she was hit, she tried to get away by running up Egyptian Avenue and into this section, the Lebanon Circle. The assailant must have followed her and two shots were fired, which we know missed their target because we found them lodged in the stone wall in the avenue. The fourth shot would have hit her in the back, causing her to fall here, and the last two would have been fired to ensure that the job was finished."

"I don't want to dwell on it." I leaned against the wall again.

"It was quick. Six shots fired and no casings found, which suggests a revolver. We have retrieved some bullet fragments and we think that the murderer first confronted Lizzie in front of the archway to the avenue."

I walked back to the avenue and looked down it in the direction of the spot where Lizzie's killer had stood in front of the archway.

"It must have been exceedingly dark here that night," I said. "Lizzie met her killer just in front of the archway. A shot was fired and she was hit in the leg. Then she turned and ran up the avenue and into this circle. The murderer fired three more shots and one of them felled her. And then the last two shots..."

I couldn't continue my sentence. Instead, I walked slowly down the avenue to where Lizzie's killer had stood. I imagined the deafening gunshots and the bright flash from the barrel of the revolver. I imagined the screams and Lizzie falling.

"I have seen enough now, Inspector."

CHAPTER 14

We took a walk, passing Highgate Ponds and up Parliament Hill. A wind had picked up from the west and the cool air was refreshing. The sun shone, birds swooped in the wind and a small boy was flying a red kite. We stood beside a small spinney of trees and gazed across London.

"Whoever killed Lizzie must have known her, mustn't he?" I said. "She must have arranged to meet him at Highgate Cemetery in the middle of the night. Why else would she go to such a place at such a time?"

"We cannot find a cab driver who took Lizzie there. I am wondering whether it was within walking distance of her accommodation."

"Her daughter must know something. I can't believe Lizzie would not have made contact with her for the past five years."

"She is on my list to speak to, as you know. I'll have to get past Joseph Taylor first, though, and he is not an easy man. There was nothing in Highgate Cemetery that made you think of anything Lizzie had mentioned to you? There was no one she knew buried there?"

"No, I don't recall her mentioning it at all. If we knew where she had been living when she was missing we would be able to locate her personal belongings. She may have had letters and diaries containing vital clues."

"Y Division is carrying out enquiries at all the homes close to Highgate Cemetery, so hopefully that line of enquiry will lead somewhere. We may be able to find out whether she was living in the area or find more witnesses to what happened that evening. We still haven't found a murder weapon or any other clue to the identity of Lizzie's murderer."

"Why did she pretend that she had drowned?"

"It's quite a quandary. When did you last see Lizzie?"

"On the first night of her play, *The Course of the Nile*. I went to visit her in her dressing room after the performance. It must have been August 1878, just a month before the *Princess Alice* sank."

Inspector Blakely removed his notebook from his inside coat pocket, leafed through it and read aloud from his notes: "The *SS Princess Alice* sank on the third of September 1878. Lizzie was known to have been travelling on the steamer after an excursion to Rosherville Gardens in Gravesend. She was travelling with a male companion, Mr Robert Holmes, who we believe paid Lizzie to accompany him that day.

"On her return journey, the *Princess Alice* collided with a cargo ship, the *Bywell Castle*, close to North Woolwich gardens at a quarter to eight in the evening. The steamer sank within five minutes and more than six hundred and fifty lives were lost."

He looked up from his notebook and shook his head. "A terrible tragedy. I remember seeing my mother in tears when she discovered the news." He looked back at the page. "Some of the passengers were able to clamber onto other vessels, but most lost their lives. Bodies were pulled out of the water for many days afterwards and two days after the tragedy a drowned woman who bore a resemblance to the actress Lizzie Dixie was found. As no one had seen or heard from Lizzie since the accident, it was assumed that this woman was indeed the actress. Her husband, the showman Joseph Taylor, identified his wife and her funeral was held the following week."

He looked up. "And you attended the funeral along with around two hundred other people."

"Yes, it was quite a commemoration. Lizzie was much loved."

"Somehow she got out of the water that day and we need to understand why she made the decision not to return to her husband and daughter. Instead, she completely disappeared."

We both looked out across London again and I couldn't stop my mind dwelling on the violence of Lizzie's death. I had reported on murders many times in the past and although I had felt great sorrow for the victims, this was the first time I had actually known one of them.

Inspector Blakely checked his watch. "I must get back to the Yard. I hope to leave a little earlier this evening and get to Battersea before sundown to help my grandfather pull up his leeks." He returned his watch to his waistcoat pocket.

"You like gardening?" I asked.

"I'm beginning to. My grandfather grows many vegetables, but is becoming too infirm to tend them. He asked me to help him last year and since then I have visited him on a regular basis. I find great solace in nurturing plants. Tomatoes." He gave me a wink. "My grandfather is particularly skilled at growing tomatoes. They are all finished now, of course, but there are still plenty of potatoes in the ground if you would care for any?"

"If they are surplus to your needs then yes, thank you."

"And leeks. I can also give you some leeks."

"That would be very kind. I have always liked the thought of having a garden one day myself. My mother likes to grow dahlias. She has quite a large garden at home in Derbyshire."

"That's where you grew up?"

"Yes, I have fond memories of our garden there. My father planned to build a glasshouse where he could grow exotic plants from the seeds which he had collected. Mother does a good job of maintaining the garden and I must ensure I am there next summer when the dahlias are flowering." I pictured the large, colourful blooms and the buzz of bees in warm sunshine. The thought was a welcome relief from the cold and the sombre cemetery.

"Yes, you must ensure that you are there next summer. I would like to try growing some dahlias next year in my grand-father's garden. They make lovely cut flowers, don't they?"

"Last summer I brought a bunch of them back to London from Derbyshire and they really brightened up my room."

"I am sure they did."

We exchanged a smile.

"Gardening must be a welcome respite from the bleakness of your work, Inspector."

"It certainly is. It's not an uncommon hobby for detec-tives. Thank you for putting the happy thought of dahlias in my mind." He smiled again. "I really must go. Now that we have done the unpleasant business of visiting the scene where Lizzie lost her life, do please think more about the last time you saw her and the conversation you had with her. Did she mention her marriage or her brothers? What was her frame of mind?"

"I will try to recall it, Inspector."

"Thank you. And thank you for all your help so far, Miss Green. I would like you to accompany me to see Mr Taylor so that I can speak to Annie with a chaperone present. Would that suit you?"

I nodded. "I am happy to help, Inspector. I will not rest until we find the person who did this to her."

CHAPTER 15

I spent the afternoon in the reading room finishing some paragraphs on the proposed withdrawal of British troops from Egypt. Before long, I felt my eyelids grow heavy. I looked up at the pale blue dome above me and tried to recall the last conversation I had ever had with Lizzie. It had been in her dressing room after the opening night of *The Course of the Nile*. I remembered that she had been in a sombre mood that evening.

It had taken her a long time to remove the elaborate hair-pieces and make-up required to play the role of Cleopatra, and once she was done she had examined herself in her dressing room mirror and frowned.

"Now I see myself again and I can no longer forget who I am. Wouldn't it be wonderful to be Cleopatra all the time?"

She wore a silky blue, kimono-style dressing gown with pink and white blossoms on it. I admired the way it shimmered in the gaslight and thought Lizzie looked beautiful without her stage make-up and with her hair brushed loose.

"You don't mean that," I said.

"Don't I?" She turned to me and placed a clay pipe

between her lips, then lit it. "I would like to spend the rest of my life being someone other than myself."

"Why?"

"Because I have done things I am not proud of to get where I am today."

"We have all done things we are not proud of."

"No, Penny. Not to the extent I'm talking about."

"What have you done that was so bad?"

Lizzie blew out a puff of smoke. "I was a maid for the Burrell family when I first arrived in London. From the moment I joined their household, I craved the lifestyle they led. The father, Charles Burrell, approached me one evening. I thought he cared for me and I was flattered by his attentions. He was a wealthy man and highly thought of, and his desiring me made me feel important. I was only thinking about myself, of course. I didn't spare a thought for his wife. I was a foolish and selfish girl back then."

"And very young. I should imagine you were frightened."

"Frightened? Why?"

"If you had turned him down you would perhaps have lost your job. Were you fearful about refusing him?"

"I was too impressed by him to turn him down. But there is some truth in what you say. I would not have been able to refuse him; he would never have let me. But that was just the start, Penny. Charles Burrell has meant nothing to me for many years now. My relationship with him was just the beginning. Once I had sinned I knew I could never be a proper wife, and I liked to be desired. Being an actress made me desirable; I could dress up and look beautiful. So that's what I did, and I made lots of money from it.

"I am a sinner and I feel the need, more than ever, to be someone else now. If only I could be in character all the time. And perhaps I am. Lizzie Dixie is the person everyone sees on stage, and then they see her socialising with the great showman, Joseph Taylor, by her side. As soon as I step out of the limelight I am just plain Hannah. And one day people will realise who I really am. They will hate me." She puffed out another billow of smoke.

"That's not true, Lizzie."

"How can you admire a flower when its bloom is fading? That's what I am now, Penny."

"You are feeling sorry for yourself. The performance has tired you out and you need to go home and get some rest."

"Perhaps I do, but in the morning I will awake and Lizzie Dixie will be older and less beautiful. She will be closer to the day when people find out who she really is. Can't you understand, Penny? My time is running out. I envy you."

"Envy *me*? Why?"

"There is no pretence about you. I wish I had learnt how to use my mind instead of my body. What a different situation I would be in now."

"You would not like to be me. I don't create and entertain in the way that you do. I am just an observer. I watch the world and I write about it."

"I am little more than someone's entertainment for an evening. You are more than that: you help to educate and inform people. You tell them what is taking place in their world. Would you like some gin?"

I nodded.

Lizzie put down her pipe and opened the door of the cupboard next to her dressing table. She took out a bottle of gin and two glasses.

"I don't like hearing you talk like this," I said as Lizzie poured my drink and handed me the glass. "You are a talented and much-loved actress. *The Course of the Nile* has sold out for the next few weeks and there will be even better things to come after this."

I raised my glass in a toast and drank back a mouthful of

gin, which burned my throat. "Does Joseph know you feel this way?"

Lizzie laughed. "All that matters to Joseph is his show."

"But he cares deeply about you."

"I suppose he does, in his own way." Lizzie drained her glass alarmingly quickly. "Do you think you will ever marry?"

"I don't know. I have never found the right man to marry."

"But you may yet."

"I may. But I am a spinster now and, if the truth be told, I am happy."

"Have you ever been in love?"

I felt my face freeze as I watched Lizzie wait for my answer.

"I was in love once." It was the first time I had admitted it to anyone. "But I am not sure that he loved me. In fact, I know that he didn't."

"Then he was the wrong man."

"He was, yes." I drained my glass and Lizzie refilled it. I never had the chance to tell her anything more.

***

I arrived at the *Morning Express* offices in time for deadline. I handed my article about the British troops withdrawing from Egypt to Miss Welton and went into the news room: a shabby place with piles of paper on every surface and a grimy window looking out onto Fleet Street. Edgar sat with his boots up on his desk, talking to a corpulent, curly-haired reporter called Frederick Potter.

"It's not the female mind which is at fault; it is the lack of schooling," said Edgar as I hung my hat and coat on the cloak stand. "Many women believe the few French phrases and needlework stitches their governesses taught them qualifies them as educated."

"And that is my point about the female mind," said Frederick. "It is unable to form a sensible view on the world. It applies a lightness to everything, which renders women incapable of understanding the important matters in life."

"I disagree slightly. I think that, with the correct education, a woman is almost as capable of working effectively as a man," Edgar replied.

"On certain tasks, maybe. But don't get me started on women and grammar. Have you ever picked up one of those fashion periodicals? They are written and edited exclusively by women, and it shows."

"Grammar is a skill that only someone with a solid education can master."

"And even the solidly educated get it wrong at times."

"Indeed," Edgar agreed.

"So what hope do women have?"

"What about Mary Ann Evans?"

"What of her?"

"Otherwise known as George Eliot. She mastered the written word."

"Garrulous and multiloquent."

"Her readers don't seem to think so," I interjected.

"That's because her readers are all women," replied Frederick. "I cannot think of a man who would choose to read a George Eliot novel unless he believed that George really was a George!"

"I've been looking for you everywhere, Miss Green," said Edgar. "Where have you been?"

"Working, Mr Fish."

"With the schoolboy inspector?"

I nodded in reply, sat down at the desk next to his and took my papers out of my bag. I looked at his long legs stretched out on the desk and his piggy eyes, and felt that I didn't want to share anything about Lizzie's case with him, even though his views on women's writing were vaguely more moderate than Frederick's.

"So what have you got for me?" He removed his feet from the desk and rubbed his hands together while trying to peer over my shoulder at my shorthand. I leafed through my papers, wondering what small details I could tell him to keep him satisfied.

"Lizzie Dixie was interred in Kensal Green Cemetery early yesterday morning."

"I know that. I was there, wasn't I?"

"Have you been attending the inquest?"

"Yes, and I can recommend it as the perfect remedy for insomnia."

"I believe PC Preston was there today explaining how he discovered Lizzie?"

"He was, and it was discussed at enormously great length."

"We need to put in a request for information about the man who was following us at the cemetery."

"Saying what?"

"Asking if anybody knows who he is. We need to describe him and explain where he was seen and at what time. Hopefully someone may know who he is."

"But we didn't even see his face!"

"No, but we have a description of the rest of him."

"A description of his back as he ran away from us. Even if we had seen his face, finding him in a population of almost five million people is a Sisyphean task."

"We need to try. Perhaps we will be lucky."

"Perhaps," he replied doubtfully. "What is Blakely's next line of investigation?"

"He is to meet with Joseph Taylor in a few days' time."

Edgar retrieved the pencil from behind his ear and wrote this piece of information down.

"You need to clarify in anything you write that Joseph Taylor is not a suspect."

"The husband? Why not? Does Blakely have *any* suspects yet?"

"No."

Edgar tutted. "The chap's taking his time, isn't he? You would think Scotland Yard would put its best detectives on a case such as this, but this young boy is all over the shop. He needs to have his ears boxed by his schoolmaster."

Edgar cackled and Frederick joined in.

"It is a complicated case." I felt the need to defend Inspector Blakely.

"So what else is happening?"

I looked at my notes. "Y Division is conducting door-to-door enquiries in the area in an attempt to find out where Lizzie Dixie may have been living for the past five years."

Edgar nodded and made another note. "And whereabouts are they looking?"

"In the vicinity of Highgate Cemetery at the present time. Inspector Blakely cannot find a cab driver who took Lizzie to the cemetery that evening, so he thinks she may have walked from her lodgings nearby."

"It is a reasonable assumption," said Edgar. "But it is hardly foolproof, is it? She may have borrowed a friend's carriage to get there, or she may have taken a tram to Highgate and walked from there. She might have travelled by train to Highgate and she could also have taken an omnibus to Hampstead and walked." He turned to Frederick and tutted as if Inspector Blakely had no idea what he was doing.

"Anything is possible at the moment. I don't envy the detective having to decide what is and isn't a priority for his investigation," I said.

"Finding out where Lizzie lived is not exactly searching for her killer, is it? The perpetrator is still wandering the streets looking for his next victim."

I thought of the man who had been watching us in the cemetery and felt a chill at the back of my neck. "Perhaps there is something in her home that might provide a clue to his identity," I said.

Edgar nodded. "It is possible, I suppose. I don't see why the killer would be leaving clues anywhere. He clearly gave this crime a good deal of thought."

"And what makes you say that?"

"It's planned, isn't it? He knew Lizzie was to be there at that hour. How many people do you know who take a walk in Highgate Cemetery at midnight? None? Exactly. The killer either lured her there or followed her. Now, if he followed her, that still doesn't explain why she was there in the first place. That is what the schoolboy inspector needs to be finding out."

Edgar closed his notebook and placed his pencil on top of it, as if he had it all worked out.

"I wonder why you are a journalist at all," I said, "seeing as you are such a good detective."

I noticed a flash of annoyance in his eyes. "Oh, I could be a detective, all right. But Mr Sherman needs me here."

"Of course." I gathered up my papers and placed them in my bag. "Do let me know when you have identified the suspect."

"It's obvious, isn't it? It's the husband, Taylor. It's always the husband."

CHAPTER 16

A week after Lizzie's second funeral, Sebastian Colehill sent a carriage to collect me for dinner. It was a smart brougham, well-polished and with a black buttoned leather interior. There was a woollen blanket on the seat for me to pull over my knees and the windows were clean, so I could see the people thronging the dark, rainy, gas-lit streets.

We made our way along Oxford Street to Knightsbridge, bumping over the uneven surface of the road and swerving to avoid the omnibuses, which stopped the moment they were hailed. Lights blazed from the many shops, public houses and restaurants.

The Colehills' home was one of the newly built terraced houses in Cadogan Square. In the light of the gas lamp, I could see that it was red brick, with ornamental details carved into golden stone around the windows and porch. I counted four storeys, but the upper floors faded into the darkness, so it was difficult to be certain. Thick curtains were pulled across the mullioned windows, and as I was led up the steps to the porch by the groom I peered down at the brightly lit servant quarters in the basement.

A maid in a white apron and cotton bonnet answered the door and showed me into an impressive tiled hallway, which was lit by an enormous chandelier. Having been relieved of my coat, hat and umbrella, I joined Sebastian and his wife in the drawing room.

"Good evening, Miss Green!" Sebastian smiled broadly and he had colour in his cheeks, presumably from the warmth of the lively fire in the large fireplace. He wore a deep burgundy frock coat and striped burgundy and blue trousers. There was a red carnation in his buttonhole and his dark hair, streaked with grey, was neatly parted.

"May I introduce my wife, Mrs Mary Colehill?"

A slender woman of about my height stepped forward and greeted me. She was handsome, with strong blue eyes and a chin which was a little too square for her to be described as pretty. Her sandy brown hair was neatly curled and pinned on top of her head and decorated with small blue flowers.

She wore a silk dress, which was turquoise with countless gold buttons down the bodice, and it fitted her so snugly that I marvelled at the tiny size of her waist. A length of gold and blue striped silk draped from each hip and looped into a large elegant bustle at her back. Her sleeves were long and tight, and trimmed with gold silk at the wrist. I wondered if my navy satin dress with the lace collar had been a suitable choice for the evening. *Perhaps I should have chosen something more colourful*, I reflected silently.

"Miss Green," she said with a smile. "How lovely it is to meet you at last. I have read some of your work. I particularly enjoyed your article on orchids in the *Domestic Botanicals Journal*."

I felt my face grow warm at the compliment. "Thank you,

Mrs Colehill. I am extremely flattered that you read it. Orchids are very close to my heart; my father had a passion for them."

"Please address me as Mary. After dinner, you must take a tour of our conservatory. Sebastian is very fond of hothouse flowers and has built up quite a collection in there." She turned to smile at her husband.

"I have indeed," he added.

"Do please sit and have a drink. Sebastian tells me you are rather partial to East India sherry."

I recalled an occasion when Lizzie had given me a bottle as a gift and we had shared some of it with Sebastian in her dressing room. "I am. Thank you, Mary."

She gestured to an occasional chair with a velvet seat. I sat down and my eye was drawn to a large oil painting in a heavy gilt frame, which depicted an ancient stone building.

"Is that a pyramid?" I asked, my article on Egypt fresh in my mind.

"The Great Ziggurat of Ur," replied Sebastian. "An ancient structure which was discovered in 1850. Since putting on *The Caliph of Baghdad* at the Adelphi, I have developed a keen interest for all things Mesopotamian. In the dining room, you will see a section of frieze which has a sphinx on it, a replica of course, and I have to admit it once served as part of the stage set for the play."

"You have a lovely home," I said.

Around the painting of the ziggurat were smaller paintings and lithographs, many of them depicting literary or historical scenes. The wallpaper was patterned green and gold, and a large bookcase containing many leather-bound volumes took up a significant section of the room. The heavy velvet drapes were dark green, with an elaborate gold pelmet running across the top of them. A small harpsichord with a tapestry cover and framed photographs atop it sat close to the window. The room also contained a polished writing desk and several glass-topped occasional tables.

One by one, I was introduced to the Colehill children; there were thirteen in total. The eldest was a girl of seventeen called Rose and the youngest was a baby boy who was carried in by the nursemaid to meet me. The Colehills clearly adored their children. Sebastian told me their names and I tried my best to remember them. Mary told me which school the boys went to and the girls' governess was even brought in to meet me.

She regaled me with information on which instruments the children played and a few of them were instructed to practise their French with me and sing a sea shanty. They were polite and well-mannered, but I was relieved that the parlour maid kept my sherry glass topped up. I didn't dislike children, but moments such as these reminded me of my lack of success in producing a family of my own.

As I sipped sherry in the well-furnished room in the large house within a fashionable district of London, I couldn't deny that I had desired this for myself. As a girl, I had always assumed this type of life would find me while I was busy writing. I had even been told that, as the prettier of the two sisters, I would have a wide choice of suitors.

I realised now the extent of the nonsense my well-meaning relatives had instilled in my mind.

Sebastian talked about the theatre as we dined, and Mary talked about her friends and acquaintances. We were joined by the seven oldest children. The younger six had already had their supper in the nursery and were being put to bed. We dined on a course of oysters followed by mushroom soup, and then a sole of John Dory followed by a course of lamb in a curry sauce. We finished off with Bakewell pudding and vanilla custard, then grapes with a goat's cheese from Kent. Each course was served with a different type of wine, and by the end of the meal my corset felt distinctly uncomfortable.

"I suppose you must have a lot to write about this terrible murder?" asked Mary.

"Lizzie Dixie? Yes, although my colleague Edgar Fish has the story. I have been helping the detective on the case, as I knew Lizzie."

"And that is how you came to know me, isn't it, Penny?" said Sebastian.

"Yes, we met backstage on numerous occasions, didn't we?"

"Terribly sad," said Sebastian in a slightly choked voice. "The whole thing is terribly sad."

I noticed his eyes were damp and decided to change the subject. "Mary, I believe you know my sister?"

She raised her eyebrows. "Who is your sister?"

"Eliza Billington-Grieg."

"Is that so?"

She seemed surprised that I could be related to someone as worthy as Mrs Billington-Grieg.

"I see the resemblance now that you mention it." She peered at my face and hair. "Eliza is tall, isn't she? An intelligent woman by all accounts."

"She is."

"She has done such good work with the West London Women's Society, which is why I requested to join. She cares very deeply about the issues in society today."

"She does indeed."

"And I think it is quite commendable that she rides a bicycle. I must ask Sebastian to buy me one."

"You wouldn't ride on it," he said.

"I would."

"But you can't ride a bicycle in normal clothes," said Sebastian. "If you rode on one wearing that dress your skirts would become hitched up and it would be quite indecent."

"Then I should wear breeches!" laughed Mary.

The children chuckled at this.

"What a ridiculous notion!" retorted Sebastian. "I am aware that some women are donning all manner of strange apparel to ride bicycles, but not my own wife. I won't allow it."

Mary laughed again.

"We have recently acquired some new parakeets, which you shall see in the conservatory Penny," said Mary. "Terribly noisome creatures. Do you have any pet animals?"

"I have a cat called Tiger."

"How lovely. She must keep you company. It cannot be easy to live alone."

"I enjoy my own company."

"Of course, you must do. Essential, I suppose, if you are going out to work instead of making time for a family."

I smiled politely and noticed Mary looking at my ink-stained fingers. I sensed her disapproval about the fact that I had a job.

CHAPTER 17

I followed Sebastian along a corridor with highly polished wainscoting. Being upright felt much more comfortable after all the food I had eaten. We paused by a doorway, which led into a small library. Sebastian looked behind us and then gestured for me to step inside. There was something secretive about his manner and I found it disconcerting.

The room was lined with books and the only light came from the fire in the small hearth. I remained standing close to the doorway while Sebastian walked over to a writing desk by the fireplace.

"Before I show you the conservatory, there is something I'd like you to look at. I'm hoping it might explain a few things." He pulled out a drawer in the writing desk and lifted out several small volumes. "Diaries," he said as he walked back to me. "They belonged to Lizzie. She left them with her belongings in the Theatre Royal dressing room."

He handed them to me. They were leather-bound and pocket sized. I felt uneasy holding them. They presumably held thoughts that Lizzie had wanted to keep to herself.

"Shouldn't we give them to her husband?"

"I think she kept them at the theatre because she didn't want Taylor to read them. You'll understand once you've read them yourself."

"I'm not sure Lizzie would have wanted me to read her diaries."

"You said the inspector wanted to know who she was acquainted with shortly before she supposedly drowned. These diaries will help to explain that."

"Could we give them to Inspector Blakely?"

"Yes, we could. If he's looking for clues about her disappearance, the diaries will give him a good grounding. It should also stop him pestering us." He smiled.

I looked at the diaries in my hand and wondered what they contained. "Having read these, do you now understand what happened to Lizzie after the *Princess Alice* sank?" I asked.

Sebastian scratched the back of his neck, as if growing impatient. "Please read them for yourself, Penny, and then let me know what you think about them. I am going away tomorrow for a few days, and when I return we can discuss them in more detail. There are five years there: from 1873 to the day before we thought she had drowned in 1878. Now let me show you the conservatory as we planned. Will the diaries fit in your handbag?"

I nodded and felt disappointed that he wasn't willing to tell me anything more. I tucked the diaries inside my bag and followed Sebastian out into the corridor again. He headed towards a doorway with a bead curtain hanging across it.

Sebastian placed his arm through the curtain and parted the beads so I could step into the conservatory. I found myself surrounded by large, broad-leaved plants in a chilly, dimly lit room. I could hear the chirruping of birds from somewhere but it was difficult to discern where they were positioned among the thick foliage. I looked up to see the iron framework of the conservatory above my head and the darkness of night beyond the panes of glass. Behind me, over the doorway, was a classically styled triangular pediment supported by two columns.

"Part of the stage set from *The Marriage of Bacchus*," said Sebastian as I regarded it. "I couldn't bear to dispose of it. It is made completely from papier mâché, yet in this light you could mistake it for the real thing, could you not? Feel it." I reached out my hand and touched the hardened paper, which had been painted to resemble stone. Sebastian walked on ahead of me. "And here is *scuticaria salesiana*," he announced. I turned to see what he was referring to.

"Beautiful," I said walking over to him and looking at the elegant orchid he held cradled in his hand. It had five green, oval-shaped petals arranged around a large, white, frilly petal marked with crimson dashes.

"I am certain your father would like to see it."

I felt surprised by his choice of words. "You refer to him as if he were still alive."

"Do you not believe that he is?"

"I don't know what to believe."

"Lizzie did her best to have him found, didn't she? It is such a shame that the expedition was unsuccessful."

"And she never knew its outcome," I replied.

The expedition to find my father had taken place in 1880 and I suddenly realised that Lizzie had still been alive then.

"On second thought, do you think she did?"

Sebastian shrugged sadly. "We shall never know. Come and see the birds."

He led me around a large banana plant towards an ornate, white-framed aviary.

"Here are my beauties," he said. "Parakeets, lorikeets, cockatiels and canaries. There is a macaw in here too, do you see him? There is also a pair of white doves."

We watched the birds hop from branch to branch of a small tree, which was planted in a pot within the aviary. Swinging perches hung from the dome of the cage.

"And you will also notice a collared dove in there. Mary found it in our garden, as the poor thing had been injured by a cat. She has been nursing it back to health again. After a busy day, I often come in here and watch the birds, and when the sun shines through the glass I fancy myself in an exotic location, such as India or Peru."

"What a lovely place to have within your home."

"See the red canary there? I call her Lizzie."

"How lovely."

I stood and watched the little bird hopping and turning her head in short, staccato movements. As I watched her, I wondered whether I should tell Sebastian that I had visited the place where Lizzie had been found on the night she was murdered. The sad heaviness of the place had remained with me.

"How is the inspector doing?" asked Sebastian. "He seems a pleasant enough chap."

"He has a complicated job to do, but he seems to be tackling it well so far."

I turned away from the bird to look at Sebastian. His face was heavily shadowed in the dim light and his cheeks appeared gaunt.

"Taylor's the likeliest suspect, of course," he said.

"You think so?"

"The marriage had soured long before the *Princess Alice* sank. You'll read about all that in the diaries."

"Do you think Lizzie falsified her death to escape her marriage?"

"It's certainly a possibility, isn't it? Taylor is a loathsome man."

"Perhaps so, but it doesn't mean that he killed her."

"It makes him more likely to have done it, though, doesn't it?"

"I don't believe he knew she was still alive."

"None of us did. Perhaps he found out and killed her in a rage."

"I am sure it is far too early to speculate, Sebastian. Scotland Yard are doing the investigating and I am certain they will find out who did this in due course. I hope they also find out why she hid herself away from us all."

"Me too." Sebastian turned to look at the birds once again and we stood there in silence, watching them chirrup and hop around their cage.

Out of the corner of my eye, I saw Sebastian's shoulders begin to shake and then he made a small chuckling noise as if he were laughing. I turned to him and was about to ask what he had found funny when I realised he wasn't laughing.

He was crying.

His cheeks were wet with tears and a watery excretion trickled out of his nose into his moustache.

"Sebastian?" I willed him to wipe his face with his handkerchief, but instead he stood there with his hands hanging limply at his sides, his shoulders shaking and his face wet and creased up.

"Who did this to her?" he asked, his eyes gazing at me imploringly. Strands of spittle stretched between his lips and I took a step back, feeling repulsed.

"Who was it?"

"I don't know, Sebastian. Do you have a clean handkerchief?"

He looked up at the glass above our heads. I followed his gaze and could see our reflection in it. A look of anguish was fixed on Sebastian's face, whereas I appeared slightly frightened.

"Why?" he called up at the ceiling. "Why did they do it?"

I became nervous that Mary Colehill or one of the children might enter the conservatory and find him in this state.

"Sebastian, please calm yourself. It is extremely distressing, but you must remain in control of your emotions. I visited Highgate Cemetery and I saw the place where–"

His face suddenly turned towards mine. "You went there? You saw where she died?"

I nodded and swallowed nervously.

"What was it like? *What did you see?*" His blue eyes were wide, wet and unblinking.

"Nothing. There is nothing there to see. It is just the cemetery. The detective took me there to get a better understanding of what happened."

"Ohhhh!"

His wail interrupted me and I began to retreat towards the banana plant.

"Thank you very much for the dinner invitation, Sebastian. It is late and I must get home. Can I ask if you would be so kind as to lend me your carriage again? I can make other arrangements if that is preferable."

Sebastian stood with his back to me. His head was lowered and I felt relieved to see him wipe his face with his handkerchief.

I waited in silence and then he spun round to face me with a grin fixed on his face as if he hadn't been crying at all.

"Absolutely, Penny. Of course. I will ask the groom to take you home. It is late. Thank you very much for your company this evening."

"Thank you for the invitation," I replied.

I tried to smile, but I felt as though I was forcing my face into a grimace.

CHAPTER 18

I managed to read some of Lizzie's 1878 diary before retiring for the night, but it was not easy to follow. Her handwriting was illegible in places and she had a habit of using abbreviations and nicknames. I wondered if her earlier diaries explained what some of the abbreviations stood for. It would take me some time to fully decipher what she had written. Her last entry on Monday 2nd September 1878 was brief:

"The Nile better than yesterday, but F still rushing his lines. When lights came on the balcony was only half full. Lunch with D - told me I have choices, but I disagreed. Tired."

Having been assured by Sebastian that the diaries would help explain what had happened to Lizzie, I felt disappointed with what I had read so far. I knew that I would have to persevere.

'Mystery Surrounds Actress's Murder' read the headline of Edgar's article the following day. 'Graveyard Killer Still at Large!' yelled the headline of *The Illustrated Londoner*, with a picture of a shadowy figure standing next to a tomb holding a gun in his hand.

There was little progress to report on Lizzie's case, but public interest remained high. The *Morning Express* offices received more than two dozen letters each day from members of the public who believed they could solve the murder. I was sure it wouldn't be long before one of the penny dreadfuls picked up the story and turned it into a sensationalist tale.

Much of my day was spent on the Egypt story, but once I had met the deadline I decided to visit Lizzie's grave before nightfall. After the fuss of the past few weeks I felt the need to pay my respects to her in a quiet and reflective manner, away from the news stories and the police investigations.

I bought a bunch of lilies, which only left me enough money to travel third-class to Praed Street, and then from Paddington Station out to Notting Hill and Ladbroke Grove.

When I reached Kensal Green Cemetery, I felt relieved to see that the sleeping stone angel had been replaced on Lizzie's tomb. I lay the lilies next to her, bowed my head and prayed that I would be able to do something to catch her killer.

As I stood at the graveside and the fog around me darkened, I thought about the last words Lizzie had said to me as we drank our gin.

"I am not sure why I chose this life. I suppose I had always liked the idea of wearing beautiful clothes and having my hair curled so fashionably. I suppose I wanted people to notice me. Perhaps I thought it would bring me happiness. But I realise now that I was only trying to escape myself. When people tell me they would love a life such as mine, I reply with the words of Shakespeare: 'All that glitters is not gold.' "

"*The Merchant of Venice*," I said to the sleeping angel. "In the play those words are written on the scroll in the golden casket." I had been unable to recall the name of the play the phrase came from when Lizzie had said those words to me; I had only remembered afterwards.

I thought of Sebastian's tears in the conservatory and shuddered. I hadn't realised how deeply he had cared for Lizzie.

Had Sebastian's tears been those of grief? Or tears of remorse from a murderer?

I had always liked Sebastian, but the incident in the conservatory had unnerved me. I couldn't understand how he had managed to compose himself so quickly after such an outburst. I reasoned that he was an emotional, highly-charged man. He worked in the theatre, so perhaps he was predisposed to bouts of melodrama.

Do please think more about the last time you saw her... What was her frame of mind?

Inspector Blakely's words ran through my head. There was no doubt that in the summer of 1878, Lizzie had been trapped in a marriage she had felt indifferent about and she had become tired of acting. The critical reviews that had followed the opening night of *The Course of the Nile* would have wounded her further. Perhaps she hadn't planned her disappearance, but the opportunity to vanish after the sinking had been too good for her to miss. Her diaries would tell me, I felt sure of that. And once I had understood them I would pass them on to Inspector Blakely.

I took the train back to Paddington station and then made my way to Praed Street, where I waited for an underground Metropolitan Railway train that would take me to Moorgate. It was ten minutes before eight, and when the train arrived it was busy. I managed to find a seat in third-class and flicked through Lizzie's 1878 diary, looking for something which could help me understand her disappearance. July of that year sounded more interesting:

"D has a plan, says he can save me. I trust D because I love him more than I have ever loved anyone."

I flicked back a few pages. *Did Lizzie explain who D was at any point?*

I didn't get a chance to find out.

The roar in my ears was hot and deafening. Somehow, my seat disappeared and I felt a sudden lurch to the left. Someone's elbow was in my chest and I was kicked by a pair of heavy boots. Everything went dark and there was a terrible crunching, shattering sound. I felt grit in my eyes and mouth, and then I realised I was lying down. Muffled groans and screams filled the air and I scrambled about, trying to get to my feet. There was a bitter stench of gunpowder.

I had no idea what had happened, but I felt relieved that I seemed to have survived it.

There were flames close by and someone was lying on the ground. I grabbed the person's coat and tried to pull him away from the fire, fortunately he began to move and someone else managed to stamp out the flames. I tripped over something and realised it was the railway track. We were in the tunnel, and up ahead I could see the lights and platform of the next station. I could also see the rest of the train, but the carriage I had been travelling in was in pieces.

The screams continued and there was also shouting. People had climbed down from the platform and were helping to drag us out of the tunnel.

"Everyone out! It's a bomb!"

With a renewed sense of panic, I managed to scramble out of the tunnel into the smoke-filled station at Edgware Road.

I climbed up onto the platform and looked back at the devastation which had been caused to the third-class carriage. The walls had either fallen in or been blown out; I couldn't tell which. I saw twisted pieces of metal, splintered panels of wood and countless shards of broken glass from windows and lamps. The fragments crunched under my boots and I was jostled on all sides by people with dusty faces, ragged clothes and blood-stained faces and limbs.

There was a burnt taste in my mouth and I saw a young boy pulling on the arm of a woman who was slumped over on the platform. I stumbled towards them to help and saw that the boy had a cut on one cheek. The woman he was holding on to began to sit up of her own accord, and I was relieved to see that she was conscious.

"Let me help you up," I offered.

My voice sounded far away and the woman was too distressed to allow me near her.

"We must get out of here," I said. "There may be another." I looked nervously at the dark mouth of the tunnel beyond the end of the train. Injured people were being dragged out, and hats, bags and umbrellas were scattered over the tracks among the pieces of train debris.

The boy rubbed at his forehead, leaving a smear of blood mixed with dirt.

I pleaded with the woman again. "We must get out of here. Let me help you."

She was young and was dressed in a dark cotton dress. Her red hair had fallen loose and there was a deep cut on one of her hands. She examined it and began to cry.

The boy was also crying.

"Come on," I said, bending down and gripping the woman by the arm. "You must get to your feet and take your son away from here. It might not be safe."

I was terrified that another bomb would detonate and felt vulnerable standing here on the platform.

The woman let me help her up. She looked at me with her dark eyes, her mouth hanging open as if she had no idea where she was.

"Let's go!" I said, guiding them towards the station's exit. I realised my spectacles were covered in a layer of grime. I tried to wipe them with a gloved hand, but succeeded only in adding more dirt to the lenses.

A large crowd had gathered on the street outside the station and several police officers were jostling people about and trying to take control of the situation.

"Tabitha!"

The woman I was with suddenly received a warm embrace from an equally dishevelled-looking woman, who I guessed was a travelling companion from whom she had become separated. Suddenly, the woman and the boy were whisked away into the crowd and I lost sight of them.

I wiped my spectacles again and realised for the first time that my handbag was missing. It was somewhere in the bombed-out carriage in the tunnel. I looked at the hordes of bedraggled people stumbling out of the station entrance and knew that I stood no chance of getting back in there to retrieve my bag or Lizzie's diaries.

Were they even still in one piece?

It was too dangerous to return.

The diaries were gone.

By nine o'clock that evening, I was sitting at my desk in the *Morning Express* news room. My hands shook as I peeled off my filthy gloves and my ears were still ringing from the explosion. Mr Sherman and the other staff gathered around me as I told them what I had seen.

"Shouldn't you be in hospital?" asked Edgar with a rare look of concern on his face.

"I am fine." Remarkably, I had only suffered minor cuts and bruises. I should have gone home and rested, but I had experienced a serious incident first hand and I was a news reporter. It was my duty to report on what had happened.

"Another bomb was thrown from a train this evening between Charing Cross and Westminster Bridge," said Mr Sherman. "Fortunately, there doesn't appear to have been as much devastation as at Praed Street and Edgware Road. We shall get a second edition out as soon as possible tomorrow morning. Miss Green, do you think you could write down as much detail as you have before then?"

"Of course, but I must fetch myself a drink first."

I could still feel grit in my mouth and taste the smoke. "I hope the little boy will be all right."

"I am sure that he will," said Edgar. "It is fortunate that St Mary's Hospital is so close to the incident."

"Potter," barked Mr Sherman. "Get yourself to St Mary's Hospital and find out the latest news on numbers killed and injured."

"I cannot get the screams out of my ears," I said.

"Those poor people," Edgar said sympathetically.

"It was the passengers in third-class who were blown up." Mr Sherman placed a glass of sherry in front of me. "Thank you," I said.

I took a warming sip and wiped the grit from my teeth with my tongue.

"I always keep a few spare bottles of sherry in my office for late nights," said Mr Sherman with a rare smile. "This attack must be the work of the Fenians," he continued. "There hasn't been a dynamite attack in London since March, so we were probably due another. Would anyone else like a sherry?"

There were nods from the colleagues standing around me.

"Good, well I shall sort the drinks. Let's get to work on the second edition."

CHAPTER 19

Perhaps it was due to the lack of sleep, but I could still feel myself shaking a little as I stood on the stepladder and retrieved a hefty, green, leather-bound volume from a shelf in the upper gallery of the reading room. I should have stayed at home to recover from the explosion, but I knew that if I took time off work Mr Sherman would give the railway bombing story to someone else.

"Here, let me help you," came a voice from nearby. I looked down in surprise.

"Inspector Blakely!"

He held up his hands to take the large book, so I passed it down to him.

"*The Short History of Ireland*," he read from the book's cover. "I dread to think how heavy the long history of Ireland must be."

I climbed down from the stepladder. "I wasn't expecting to see you here, Inspector. Do you have a reading card?"

"I'm a detective; I can get into most places without the requisite cards and tickets." His blue eyes sparkled and I thought he looked cheerier than during our previous two meetings at the cemeteries. He was wearing a navy, tweed suit under his overcoat and his usual bowler hat. "Terrible news about the explosion, and to think you were in the midst of it. How are you?"

"I am well, thank you. A few aches and I still cannot hear properly, but that is all."

"It must have been extremely distressing."

"It was odd; I wasn't really sure what was happening. I heard a terrible noise and then there was so much smoke and dust. I can't say I saw a lot really, and I didn't realise it was a bomb until I heard someone saying that it was. I am fine, thank you, Inspector."

"I am relieved to hear it, Miss Green. I visited the offices of the *Morning Express* and was told I would find you here."

"Do please call me Penny. My proper name is Penelope, but only my mother and sister call me that."

"And there is no need to address me as Inspector. James will suffice."

We both smiled, and I felt warmth in my face as I accustomed myself to the new familiarity between us.

Thankfully, James broke the silence. "There are three hundred constables guarding the underground railway today, and I hear that the Home Secretary is to introduce an Explosive Substances Act, which will give us powers to arrest anyone planning an attack such as this. The finger is pointed at the Fenians, of course."

"Yes, I'm working on the story, which is why you are carrying that enormous book about Ireland under your arm."

"It is a miracle that no one was killed."

"It is indeed. More than thirty people were treated at St Mary's Hospital, and only four remain there. I hope they make a good and swift recovery."

"Let's hope that they do."

James leant against the brass railing of the gallery and I

followed his gaze down to the people below, their heads bent over the long rows of desks, which radiated out from the circular clerks' desk at the centre of the room.

"Lizzie's brothers," I said. "They joined the Fenians, didn't they? I wonder if they had any involvement in this."

James shrugged his shoulders. "It is difficult to tell yet, isn't it?"

"But there could be a Fenian link to Lizzie's murder, I suppose?"

"It requires investigating, that's for sure. Hopefully my colleagues will identify who is behind the most recent bombing, and I will enquire as to whether any of the suspects have the name Mahoney."

"I had dinner with Sebastian Colehill two days ago and he gave me some of Lizzie's diaries. He told me they would help explain her disappearance five years ago. I began to read them but didn't get far before I lost them in the explosion."

"Oh dear, that is a shame. I must speak to Mr Colehill as a matter of urgency. He has read the diaries, you say?"

"Yes, although he did say he would be going away for a few days. I should have asked where, but you will need to make enquiries. Perhaps his wife will be able to tell you how you can contact him."

"He's gone away? That is an interesting development."

I watched James consider this and began to wonder whether Sebastian had planned his absence to avoid being questioned.

"I will look into it," he added.

"I can't believe the diaries are gone. Without them, we have little hope of finding out exactly what was happening in Lizzie's life shortly before she supposedly drowned. I feel so foolish for losing them."

"You were in a bomb explosion! You mustn't blame yourself."

"I should have kept them at home."

"Please don't worry about the diaries any more. I will speak to Mr Colehill about them as soon as possible. In the meantime, I shall be visiting Joseph and Annie Taylor tomorrow. Would you still like to accompany me? I suppose you are quite busy with this story about the bomb."

A man sitting at one of the desks below looked up at us as if we were disturbing his work, and I realised our voices probably carried across the domed space.

I lowered my voice. "I am busy, but I can find the time to accompany you. I would especially like to find out what Annie knows."

"And Taylor too. We don't have a suspect yet, but a lot of suspicion hangs on him. Do you know the house at Mile End?"

"Yes, I visited Lizzie there once."

Mr Taylor had built himself a large home behind The King Henry pub on Mile End Road. It was located on the spot where he had overwintered as a travelling showman.

"I almost forgot," said James, bending down and picking up a cloth bag which had been placed on the floor. "Potatoes and leeks."

I smiled. "Thank you, James."

"Let me carry these and the book down to your desk for you."

When I returned home that evening, there was a letter waiting for me on the hallway table. I didn't recognise the handwriting on the envelope. I picked it up, climbed the stairs to my room and opened the little window to let Tiger in. I got the fire in the stove going and put the kettle on to boil.

Then I sat down at my desk and opened the letter. I was surprised to see just a few words written on the paper, and they were written in an odd, childish hand. There was no sender's name or address.

Stay out of this. It has nothing to do with you. There will be trouble.

I held the piece of paper in my hand and stared at it for a while.

Had I read it properly? Was there some other explanation in the words that I hadn't understood? Or was this actually, as I feared, a threat?

My first thought was that it must have come from Mr Taylor as he had been so hostile towards me. If the letter was from him, he would not be pleased to see me on his doorstep with Inspector Blakely the following day.

Who else could have sent it? Was the sender referring to my work on Lizzie's case or the railway bombing story I was working on? Was it linked to the bomb?

I doubted it was Mr Taylor, as he was a man who spoke his mind. If he wished me to stay out of this, I felt sure he would ask me directly rather than going to the trouble of sending me a letter.

There will be trouble.

What did the sender mean by that?

It was a threat; only a mild one, but a threat nonetheless. I shivered. I checked the address on the envelope and everything was spelt correctly: my name and the street.

This person knew me and knew where I lived.

What struck me as odd was the way the sender had attempted to disguise his or her handwriting in the letter, and yet the envelope was written in what I assumed to be the author's usual hand: elegant, sloping writing in black ink. The letter was written in the same black ink but the writing was clumsy, as if a child had written it. This mismatch in hand-writing was clearly an oversight. The sender was trying to manipulate me but was capable of making an error.

Perhaps it was someone's idea of a joke.

The envelope bore a stamp from the General Post Office in St Martins le Grand, so that gave me no further clue, other than that the sender had posted the letter in the centre of London.

I felt hungry and tired, and my body ached.

I ate half a can of sardines with bread and butter, and drank a cup of cocoa. Then I lay awake in my bed, too wary to settle down to sleep. Instead, I listened to the raindrops rattling against the windowpane while Tiger lay next to me, licking the remains of the sardines from her paws.

CHAPTER 20

I met James outside The King Henry pub on the Mile End Road, as we had arranged. It was a crumbling weather-boarded building with a faded ale advertisement on one wall. A steady drizzle pattered onto my umbrella and an unpleasant stench wafted up from the filthy gutter at the side of the road.

My ears still felt muffled from the dynamite blast and I found myself going about my daily business with a new sense of nervousness. I felt worried that another bomb might be detonated around about me at any moment.

The Fenians were sure to strike again soon. The question was, where?

James greeted me with a warm smile, which helped me briefly forget about the bomb and the threatening letter. I had put the letter in my handbag and planned to show it to him once we had spoken to Mr Taylor and Annie.

"Are you ready?" he asked.

"I think so."

"I am not sure how best to say this," said James as we passed the pub. "But I have perhaps shared a little too much of the case with you. There are certain rules about how the Yard works with the press and I may have transgressed a few of them." He stopped and turned to me. "I can rely on your discretion, can't I?"

"Of course, James. I am here to help, not to write about the story. As you know, my colleague, Mr Fish, has the story, so you can trust me to keep everything confidential unless you instruct me otherwise."

"Thank you, Penny."

James smiled and we continued walking. "I felt certain I could trust you before I mentioned it. The Yard is extremely careful about the information it passes on to the press, for fear that an investigation could be compromised. So you and I are walking on eggshells."

"I will be careful, you have my word."

"Thank you for printing an appeal for information about the young man we saw at the cemetery. Y Division has found a witness who told them he saw a man of that description climbing over the fence of Highgate Cemetery on the night that Lizzie died."

"Really? It has to be him!"

"It sounds like this man might have been involved. There could be a reasonable explanation for him being there, but it does sound suspicious."

"Did the witness have any more information about him?"

"Sadly, no. However, I plan to speak to him myself just to be certain. Y Division is working on finding more witnesses."

We reached the rambling, dark-bricked house Mr Taylor had built for himself. Lizzie had lived here with him during their marriage and I wondered how she had ever managed to feel comfortable in this place. The building was a cluster of towers, turrets, chimneys and ornamental gables. There were many little arched windows with wrought-iron tracery and the porch was of an iron and glass construction with castings of various animals incorporated into it. A row of rusty railings ran along the front of the house, each topped with a spike.

"Inspector Blakely!" came a call behind us.

My heart sank as I turned to see Tom Clifford from *The Holborn Gazette* approach. He was chewing tobacco, as usual, and his pork pie hat was pushed back on his head, revealing a creased brow. He stopped and regarded us with his hands in his pockets. "Come to arrest Taylor, have we?"

James' face clouded. "No, I am just conducting my investigations."

"He must be the one who done it, though, don't you think?" Tom pulled out a notebook and pencil.

"Scotland Yard has nothing to say to the press at the present time."

"No? What's she doing 'ere then?" Tom pointed his pencil at me.

"Miss Green was acquainted with the deceased actress and is assisting me with the investigation."

Tom Clifford wrote this down. "And what's that mean exactly? What's she actually doin'?"

"She is doing what I have just told you. Now please excuse us."

"Bit unfair the *Morning Express* gets preferential treatment, ain't it, Inspector? What about the other papers? If you don't talk to us we'll come up with our own stories, if you know what I mean."

James walked away from Tom towards Mr Taylor's front door, and I followed.

"Is it Taylor what done it, Inspector?" continued Tom. "Is that why you're 'ere?"

A maid opened the door before we even had a chance to tug the bell pull. She showed us into a large, dingy hallway, where an enormous stuffed bear stared glassily at us with its teeth bared.

Its presence sparked a memory of Lizzie complaining to me about her husband's penchant for taxidermy and explaining how she had requested that the stuffed animals be confined to a storeroom. They had clearly reappeared over the past five years and now stared at us from various glass cases on the walls and tables.

James and I followed the maid into the drawing room, which had an unpleasant, animal-like smell. Heavy brown curtains hung at the windows, and there were many framed bill posters from circus shows on the walls. My eyes fell upon a poster showing a slim, youthful Mr Taylor dressed in a scarlet jacket and brandishing a whip, alongside several prowling lions.

The current Mr Taylor regarded us from the hearthrug, where he stood smoking a cigar. His ginger hair was neatly combed into a side parting and his mouth was hidden behind his large moustache. He wore a grey suit and the buttons on his waistcoat strained to hold it fastened.

He greeted us and asked us to sit, but he didn't offer us a drink. James almost tripped over the tiger skin rug before realising what it was.

"Oh, hello! He's a fine beast! Does he bite?" he said, examining the head of the animal, which was still attached to the skin. Its eyes were wide open and its teeth were sharp and white.

"Only if you annoy me," retorted Mr Taylor.

James and I sat down side by side on a faded red velour settee, while the showman sat in an armchair next to a stuffed otter, which had a painted plaster fish between its jaws. Hung on the wall above the otter was a shotgun. I wondered if it was the gun which had been used to kill the poor otter.

"His name's Nero," continued Mr Taylor, still looking at the tiger skin. "I only had him for three months before he kicked the bucket. Tropical animals are sensitive creatures. I bought four giraffes from Charles Jamrach last month and two of them died the day after I got 'em." He pulled out his pocket watch and looked at it. "Now, I don't have a lot of time. I have to be at the amphitheatre for midday. What can I do for you, Inspector?" He gave me a long stare as he took a puff on his cigar.

"I appreciate you taking the time to see us," said James. "I know you are a very busy man." Mr Taylor nodded. "I would like to update you on the investigation into the death of your late wife, and also to ask some further questions if I may?"

"Yes, go on."

James told Mr Taylor about the search for Lizzie's home and Mr Taylor listened patiently, nodding at intervals and puffing on his cigar. I noticed that his hands were small and his fingers were chubby. I glanced around the dowdy room and wondered where Annie was.

"And who are your suspects?" asked the showman.

"We don't have any as yet. I am still trying to build up a picture of Lizzie's life and was hoping that you could help me."

"And what is *she* doing here?" He pointed at me. "She's a hack."

"Miss Green was a friend of Lizzie's."

"So she says. I remember spending a vast amount of money on a futile expedition to find her father, that's for sure."

I bit my tongue and decided to remain quiet so not to antagonise him and ruin James' line of questioning.

"Miss Green is assisting me with my enquiries."

"So she can write all about it in the newspaper."

"We have an agreement between us that only the information the Yard is happy to make public will be printed."

"I still don't understand why she is here."

I felt distinctly uneasy. "If you think it would be easier for me to leave, I can do, Inspector," I said.

James gave me a look that urged me to remain patient. "Your presence is no problem at all Miss Green, please stay. We will not be here long, will we, Mr Taylor?"

"Absolutely not."

"I would like to ask you how Lizzie was feeling shortly before the *Princess Alice* sank."

"That was five years ago!"

"I realise that, but I am trying to understand why she would have chosen to hide somewhere for the last five years. Was she suffering from some form of distress? I understand the reviews of her performance in *The Course of the Nile* were far from top notch."

"They were damned awful, the poor girl."

"So she was unhappy?"

"Of course she was!"

"And may I ask how the relationship between you and your wife was at that time?"

"No, you may not!"

"Did she seem unhappy to you?"

"Yes, she did. I just told you that."

"So I can make the assumption that there was some strain on your marriage, given that your wife was feeling unhappy?"

"There was, yes. She was miserable."

"Was she miserable only about the reviews or was there something else that was causing her unhappiness?"

"How would I know? There's always something the matter with women, isn't there? They're rarely happy and they seem to think that it's the job of every poor, confounded fellow to somehow deduce what the cause of the upset is."

"Would you say that your wife suffered from mood swings?"

"Yes, she was like all wives! But every other wife would have come home after escaping from a sinking steamer. To have hidden away as she did baffles me beyond all measure. She should have come home, where her husband and daughter were waiting for her! To put us through that grief as she did..."

He trailed off and took an extra-long puff on his cigar. He blew the smoke out of his nose in a drawn-out exhale and I watched it swirl down into a small cloud above Nero's head.

I wished I had found the opportunity to read Lizzie's version of events in her diaries. I hadn't realised how unhappy her marriage had been until this moment.

"I will never understand how she could have done that to us. She left us. What was she thinking? She left us to mourn at her funeral and she never came back. She never returned to the family that loved her."

He stared at the fireplace and I could see that his eyes were moist.

"When did you discover that your wife had hidden from you, Mr Taylor?"

"When you arrived on my doorstep eleven days ago, Inspector!"

"And you had no inkling before then?"

"None! What are you suggesting here?" Mr Taylor leant forward in his chair and glared at James.

"I am not suggesting anything, Mr Taylor. I am simply clarifying the facts."

"Clarifying the facts seems to suggest that you're pinning this on me."

"I am not pinning anything on anyone, Mr Taylor, please be assured of that. I am a long way from finding a suspect."

"That's because you're sitting idly in my drawing room and are not out there looking for him."

"Can I ask you what you were doing on the night of the twentieth of October, Mr Taylor?"

"There! I knew it!" Mr Taylor jabbed his cigar in James' direction. "You're accusing me of murdering my wife, are you not, Inspector?"

"No, I am not. This is a standard question, which I am putting to all of Mrs Taylor's acquaintances. It is in your interests to be helpful to me, Mr Taylor."

"Is it? I was at the amphitheatre hosting a performance of *Sinbad* and then I returned here with Annie, just as I do every evening, Inspector. And if you need alibi witnesses you can find fifteen hundred of them who watched the performance!"

He clearly thought this last comment a smart one. Having delivered it, he rested back in his chair to finish his cigar.

"Thank you, Mr Taylor. I realise this is not easy for you, and I appreciate you taking the time to answer my questions. I wonder if I might speak to Annie now?"

"No, you may not."

"Is she here this morning?"

"She may or she may not be."

"Mr Taylor, I am trying to find your wife's murderer. I would appreciate your help in this matter."

"And what could Annie possibly know of any of this?"

"That's what I would like to find out. Please may I speak to her?"

"You may speak to her for one minute." Mr Taylor held up a single podgy finger to emphasise his point before turning his head over his shoulder and roaring loudly, "Annie!"

CHAPTER 21

M r Taylor stared ahead of him and said nothing as we listened to the light footsteps on the stairs and then watched the petite form of Annie Taylor walk into the room. She wore a grey and cream striped cotton dress and her dark hair was neatly plaited and pinned to her head.

James and I rose as she entered the room. She stood beside Nero's tail and stared at us, unsmiling, her hands folded in front of her.

"This is Inspector Blakely," said Mr Taylor. "You recognise him, don't you, Annie? And this woman's a scribbler and claims to have been a friend of your mother's. She accosted us the other evening at the stage door."

"Hello Annie," I said. I smiled, hoping to put the girl at ease. To my surprise, she gave a slight smile in response.

"May I request that I speak to Miss Taylor alone?" asked James. "Miss Green will act as chaperone."

"Never. Fire away with your questions, Inspector. You have one minute, remember?"

I sighed quietly. Mr Taylor seemed keen to control the situation as much as he possibly could.

"It is good to see you again, Miss Taylor," said James. "I wonder if I can ask you a few questions about your mother."

The girl nodded in reply.

"How old were you when the *Princess Alice* sank?"

"I was fifteen, Inspector."

"And you were living with your mother and stepfather, Mr Taylor, at the time?"

"Yes."

"It must have been a very distressing time when you thought your mother had lost her life in the sinking."

"It was."

"Recent events have shown that your mother was, in fact, still alive after the sinking of the steamer. It seems that she made a home somewhere and lived there in secret for five years. Did she make any attempt to contact you during those five years?"

Annie shook her head and I watched her face closely to see whether I could detect any signs of a lie. I couldn't believe that Lizzie would have kept herself hidden from her daughter. I understood why she might have wanted to get away from her husband, but surely not her own daughter.

"And you are sure that you heard nothing from her at all?"

"No, nothing." She shook her head again and looked at the tiger skin with a glum expression.

"Thank you, Miss Taylor. And can you tell me where you were on the night of the twentieth of October?"

"There you go again!" shouted Mr Taylor. "Annie couldn't possibly have murdered her own mother. What a preposterous question! She was performing in the show! She was with me for the entire evening!"

James patiently waited for Mr Taylor to stop shouting.

"Miss Taylor, can you please confirm where you were on the night of the twentieth of October?"

"I have just told you!" yelled Mr Taylor.

"For the sake of procedure, I would like to hear it from Miss Taylor."

"Damned confounded procedure!"

"I was performing in *Sinbad*, Inspector, as I do every evening at the present time."

"Thank you, Miss Taylor. And when did you hear of your mother's death?"

"The first or the second time, Inspector?"

"The second."

"It was when you came here to tell us."

"Thank you, Annie."

"You have had more than your minute," said Mr Taylor, looking at his pocket watch. "Time for you to leave, Inspector, and I don't want any of this conversation reported in the newspapers, Miss Green. If it is, there will be trouble."

There will be trouble.

My heart flipped. Mr Taylor had used the same four words written at the end of the mysterious letter I had received just the previous day.

◈

"I have no idea why Lizzie married Mr Taylor," I said as we walked along Mile End Road, looking out for an omnibus to take us back into town. The rain pattered onto our umbrellas once again and I was thankful that Tom Clifford seemed to have melted away. "He's a rather bad-tempered gentleman."

"I suppose Lizzie's death has come as a shock to him. Some of his anger is probably related to the discovery that she left him and hid herself away."

"And that is why he must have killed her."

James stopped and looked at me. "You think he did it?"

"He must have."

"His manner is too confrontational and blustering for a guilty man. I think he would be more acquiescent and eager to help if he had done it. He would have done anything he could to deflect attention away from himself. He admitted the marriage was unhappy. Do you think he would have been so honest if he had murdered his wife?"

"Perhaps he is bluffing. Acquiescence is out of character for Mr Taylor. Perhaps he thinks an element of honesty and acting in his usual manner is more likely to deflect attention." I pulled the envelope out of my handbag. "Look, he wrote me this letter."

I handed it to James and he gave me a puzzled frown. "Mr Taylor wrote you a letter? Why would he do that?"

"Open it and see. I shall hold your umbrella for you."

I sheltered James with his umbrella and watched as he opened the envelope and pulled out the letter. His frown deepened even further as he read it.

"When did you receive this?"

"Yesterday."

"And why do you say that Taylor sent it to you?"

"Because of those last four words: *There will be trouble*. Didn't you hear him say the exact same thing as we left? He told me not to print our conversation with him in the newspaper or there would be trouble. That's exactly what it says in the letter."

James pushed his lower lip out in thought. "This is a curious letter, indeed." He examined the envelope. "The author has written the note with his left hand, but addressed the envelope with his right."

"How do you know which hand was used?"

"Look at the note. You can see from the ink strokes that the author pushed the pen along the paper from the left. He went to the trouble of disguising his writing and then used what I suspect is his usual handwriting on the envelope, which is a slip-up. He probably realised what he had done after it was posted. And it was sent from St Martins le Grand, I see."

"This needs to be compared with a sample of Taylor's handwriting," I suggested.

"That would be one way to ascertain whether it is him or not. But even if it was found to be him, what would that tell us? That he is a grumpier man than we first realised?"

"Maybe we should return and confront him with it."

"Let's leave it for the moment, but please keep it somewhere safe. It might be useful to us, or it might not. You're not worried about the threat, are you? The majority of people who send these miserable missives have no intention of acting on them; they simply wish to frighten the recipient. You're not frightened, are you?"

"No," I said, trying to appear braver than I felt. "I know it's someone playing a trick of some sort. But I should like to find out who it is."

"I am sure that we will."

James handed the letter back to me and we continued on in the rain. A dishevelled woman offered us watercress and her wares looked so soggy and limp, and her clothing was so soaked through, that I bought a sorry-looking bunch from her out of pity.

"So is Taylor a suspect?" I asked.

"We need to know where he was at midnight on the twentieth. He says he was at his performance, but he would have had time afterwards to get to Highgate by midnight. We only have his word for it, so we need an alibi witness. If he had discovered that Lizzie was still alive and was hiding from him, that could have angered him. That is a possible motive for murdering her."

"A strong motive. Do you think that Annie was telling the truth?"

"It is difficult to tell. If her mother had made contact with her after her supposed drowning, it would have been difficult for Annie to keep the secret from Mr Taylor. He seems rather protective of her and I understand that she has been a performer in his show for about ten years now. Working and living with him would have left her little time to see her mother without him suspecting something."

"I wish I knew whether he and Annie were telling the truth."

"That is the challenge with detective work; you never know for sure. And now I must find Mr Colehill and ask him about Lizzie's mood shortly before the sinking of the *Princess Alice*. If he can confirm that she was unhappy, I think it is safe to assume that she chose to pretend that she had died in order to escape the cause of her unhappiness: whether it was the downturn in her career, her marriage or both. The problem we face is that Mr Colehill is currently missing."

CHAPTER 22

S ir,
   I am sending you my thoughts on the frightful death of the acclaimed actress Lizzie Dixie. I consider myself a Christian man, with two feet firmly planted on the ground. However, I can only surmise that the unfortunate woman's death was caused by a supernatural force. Occurring, as it did, in the witching hour, and among the vaults of the dead, surely points to this hypothesis.

I once considered myself an agnostic with regard to the spirit world, but a phantasmagoric incident I experienced during my time of service in the Afghan Campaign has altered my mind on the matter.

Therefore, I fear that the murderer shall never be caught, for it is likely that Scotland Yard lacks the ability to arrest a malevolent spirit. Our best hope is that the demon has returned to the pit of Hades, from whence it came.

Yours,
Captain Thomas Rees-Dundas

I placed Captain Rees-Dundas' letter on my desk in the news room and began to read the next.

"We are receiving two dozen letters a day about the case," said Edgar, with his hands in his pockets and rocking on the balls of his feet beside my chair. "The public is hungry for news and we need to give them something. What's the latest from the young inspector?"

I looked up at him, taking in his heavy jaw and small eyes. "Not much that we can print at the moment."

"Why not? Does he have a suspect yet?"

"Not yet. He has interviewed Mr Taylor and Annie Taylor, but we cannot report on that."

"It has to be Taylor. He found out she wasn't dead and murdered her in a fit of passion."

"Rare though it is, I find myself agreeing with you. But why would he do such a thing at midnight in Highgate Cemetery? What would either of them be doing there?"

"He arranged to meet her there."

"Why would she voluntarily meet him if she had been hiding from him?"

Edgar shrugged his shoulders. "Taylor would have worked something out, I am sure of it. The problem I have is that there is a great deal of gossip and rumour out there and I wish to publish some facts. Now, is the schoolboy inspector treating Mr Taylor as a suspect or not?"

"He thinks Mr Taylor has a possible motive."

"So he is a suspect?"

"Not officially."

"That means he is, however?"

"No, it doesn't."

"So what am I supposed to write about?"

"The inquest?"

Edgar groaned. "I've slept through much of it so far. We have been given the exclusive rights on this story and we cannot write about any of it. What is Blakely up to, exactly? You haven't been distracting him, have you?"

"Why should I do that?"

Edgar looked me up and down. "Not every detective has a woman on his arm during the course of his investigations."

"I am not on his arm!" I felt anger rising inside me but took a deep breath and calmed myself. "Lizzie was a friend of mine."

"Of course."

The news room door slammed and Mr Sherman strode in.

"Miss Green, where have you got to with the railway bombings story?"

I put down the pile of letters. "I am almost done. The latest from New York is that O'Donovan Rossa is claiming responsibility for the bombs, although Scotland Yard thinks it more likely that it was the independent work of the Clan na Gael Society."

"That sounds rather typical of O'Donovan Rossa's ego," said Mr Sherman. "So your article is finished?"

"Almost."

He checked his pocket watch. "I need it in one hour."

"Absolutely."

"She is refusing to give me anything on the Lizzie Dixie story," Edgar piped up.

"Is that so?" Mr Sherman eyed me questioningly from beneath his bushy eyebrows.

"There is not much we can go public with at the present time," I explained.

"There must be something. Have you seen how many letters we are receiving each day on the matter?"

"I have been reading them."

"Blakely's dragging his heels," said Edgar. "The people want a suspect. And they want him captured."

"Absolutely," said Mr Sherman, scowling at me as if I were somehow responsible.

"We cannot come up with a convenient suspect just because the public demands it," I replied. "This is a newspaper and we report on real life. If the people want sensationalist stories, they can read the penny dreadfuls."

"That doesn't help me much, does it?" said Edgar. "I've been given one of the biggest murder stories we've had in London for years and very little to report on it."

Mr Sherman scowled even more deeply.

"The bombings are another big story," I said. "Why not give Edgar the Fenian story, Mr Sherman, and I will take Lizzie's?"

"No, Lizzie's story is mine," said Edgar.

"But you are writing about it only with second-hand knowledge," I said. "You are relying on me to pass on the information."

"Is that not what we agreed?" said Mr Sherman. "You help the Yard and Edgar does the write-ups."

"He needs to get out there," I said. "He needs to meet regularly with Inspector Blakely to discuss the case and he needs to be talking to people."

"I do talk to people!"

"Talking to other hacks in Ye Olde Cheshire Cheese doesn't count." The moment I said this I regretted it, but I couldn't help feeling angered by Edgar's laziness.

"That's enough, Miss Green!" said the editor. "I will not have you casting aspersions on your colleagues. Go and get your story finished. I want it on my desk in thirty minutes' time."

"I thought I had an hour?"

"Not any longer. Get on with it. And next time you meet with Inspector Blakely, Edgar must accompany you."

"Edgar *comes with us?*" I felt my shoulders slump. The

thought of spending any more time with Edgar was horrifying. I had grown accustomed to the dynamic of working alone with James. It wouldn't be the same with Edgar hanging around. I felt certain he would ruin it all.

Edgar grinned at me and I scowled in return.

CHAPTER 23

I met Eliza at the British Museum the following morning. She was waiting for me in the portico when I arrived, wearing a smart green woollen jacket over a matching dress.

"Penelope! You look tired. Are you eating enough? There is no excuse not to now that you have a salary again."

I gave Eliza a weary smile and told her that I was well and eating as I should. She tried to reply but began coughing instead.

"I should have ridden my bicycle here," she said, thumping her chest. "The smoke and soot on the underground railway seems worse every time. But I took the train to make a statement to those dynamite bombers that they cannot disrupt our daily lives! When were you planning to tell me that you had been blown up? I had to read your report in the newspaper to find it out!"

"There was nothing to tell; I was unharmed."

"I do worry about the job you are doing."

"It was nothing to do with my job! I just happened to be on that train."

"Well I think it is all rather terrifying. I don't know where the Irish plan to plant their dynamite next. It is quite a worry. We should give them home rule and be done with it."

I gave my sister a small purse of coins and she looked at it in surprise.

"You do not need to repay me yet."

"I dislike having debts hanging over my head. I have paid my landlady everything I owe her, so it is right that I pay you now. Thank you for helping me buy a new pair of boots."

It was the last day we would see our father's botanical drawings and plant specimens before they were moved to the new natural history department of the British Museum in South Kensington.

Eliza and I climbed the staircase to the upper floor and walked through the galleries of the zoological collection to reach the botanical section. The stuffed animals in the cases lining the Mammalia Salon reminded me of the poor dead creatures in Taylor's home and I felt a shiver as I thought of the man.

"Have they caught Lizzie Dixie's murderer yet?" asked Eliza, as if she had read my thoughts.

"No, it is a complicated case."

"Who do you think did it?"

"I don't know. I am realising now that more than one person had a motive. There is her husband, but then some of her brothers are Fenians, so there could be a political motive."

Eliza paused by a case of weasels and ferrets. "Well I do hope you're being careful. You know how Mother worries. Whatever you do, don't tell her you were bombed. She would raise an army to drag you back to Derbyshire!"

We walked into the next salon. "Here we are," she said. "Look, half the room has already been emptied."

A small man with a wide moustache and kid gloves

glanced up at us as he slowly placed some pressed plant specimens into a packing case.

"The Greens?" he asked us.

"I used to be," replied Eliza. "I'm Billington-Grieg now, but Penelope is a spinster and very much still a Green. Will you be packing my father's plants and drawings today?"

"I will indeed," replied the man.

"You will be careful with them, won't you? They are all we have left."

Eliza's voice began to choke and I rested my hand reassuringly on her shoulder. We had never talked in detail about our father's disappearance. I think we had both reached the conclusion that he was no longer alive, but the thought of admitting that to one another was far too distressing. I had stopped believing that he would return, but I still held a very small measure of hope that one day he might.

"I will be careful, Mrs Billington-Grieg."

I looked at the arrangement of drawings and pressed orchids in the case.

"If it hadn't been for Lizzie we should never have seen these," I said.

Father's sketchbook had been discovered by the rescue expedition in a hut which he and his guide had used shortly before they vanished. It had contained sketches and watercolours of orchids, and three of the most complete drawings had been removed from the sketchbook and put on display in the museum. They had been roughly drawn in pencil, then washed over with watercolour before my father had added finer details in black ink. Each time I looked at these pictures I imagined him with his sketchbook on his lap, his straw Panama hat on his head and his tongue protruding slightly with concentration as he worked.

"The expedition may not have found your father, but it did find these marvellous drawings of the *Scuticaria*," said the man with the wide moustache. "You must be very proud of him."

"I am," I replied with a warm sensation in my chest.

I took my leave of Eliza once we had returned to the main entrance of the museum.

"I have to work in the reading room," I told her, mindful of a few more paragraphs I needed to write about the railway bombings.

"What about lunch? The Holborn Restaurant offers a wonderful Ladies' Shopping Menu with the choice of a hot or cold luncheon. Can I not tempt you?"

"I have a deadline."

"Of course." Eliza rolled her eyes. "Well you must come to the next meeting of the West London Women's Society. It is high time that we received some coverage in your newspaper."

"I would be delighted to. Just let me know the date of the meeting and where it is to be held."

"We take turns to host and the next meeting will be held at the Colehills' home. It is a rather marvellous place in Cadogan Square."

My stomach flipped as I thought of Sebastian's dramatic breakdown in the conservatory.

"I know it," I said.

"You have been there?" asked Eliza, deflated that I was not as impressed as she had hoped.

"I have, and Mary Colehill spoke most enthusiastically of you and the society when I dined with her and Sebastian."

"Did she indeed?" Eliza smiled broadly. "Well that is another thing you have neglected to tell me. A rather flattering thing to hear though. We are meeting on Wednesday at three o'clock and will be joined by a speaker on dress reform."

Eliza glanced towards the doors of the reading room. "You will find time for lunch, won't you? You are terribly thin and pale."

"I will see you at the meeting, Ellie." I gave her a quick kiss on the cheek and hurried away.

CHAPTER 24

That evening I made myself some cocoa and sat at my writing desk looking out of the window. It was an unusually clear night and I had extinguished my paraffin lamp so that my room was in darkness and I could see the stars in the sky. I could just make out the three twinkling stars of Orion's Belt; I remembered my father pointing them out to me. On nights such as this, I felt it would be nice to have someone by my side to look at the stars with.

Tiger sat on my desk next to the volumes of *The Works of Shakespeare* Lizzie had given to me. Lights twinkled from the trains trundling in and out of Moorgate station, and now and again a plume of steam and smoke rose up into the night sky. Here and there I saw lights in windows and I wondered what was happening in those rooms. It would have made sense to draw the curtain across the window as a cold draught was blowing in through the gaps in the frame, but I couldn't close the curtains against the stars. They twinkled and shone at me and I wondered what secrets lay up there in the night sky.

A sharp rap at the door brought me back to my senses. I

turned on my lamp and opened the door to find Mrs Garnett standing there.

"A gentleman is here to see you." Her lips were pursed tight and the whites of her eyes gleamed in the gloom. "I don't usually permit gentlemen to enter the house at this hour, but he tells me he is a detective."

"James?" I heard the panic in my voice and knew that something must be wrong.

"He tells me his name is Inspector Blakely. Perhaps he plans to arrest you!"

I ignored her and went to gather up my jacket, hat, scarf, gloves and handbag.

"Please tell the inspector I will be with him shortly."

James was waiting in the hallway wearing a dark overcoat and the familiar bowler hat. He looked up and smiled at me as I scurried down the stairs, but his expression quickly became serious again.

Mrs Garnett stood close by, watching with interest.

"I am so sorry to disturb you, Penny. Would you like to come with me to St Thomas' Hospital? I have a cab waiting outside."

"What has happened?"

"It's Annie Taylor. She has been shot."

"Shot?" My legs almost gave way beneath me and I grabbed the bannister post to steady myself.

"Who's been shot?" asked Mrs Garnett. "Your sister?"

"No, Mrs Garnett. I shall explain on my return."

"We must go," said James.

I followed him out of the house.

"How is she? Who shot her? When?" My heart pounded in my chest.

"We don't know," he replied as we stepped out onto the

dark street. "But she was shot during this evening's performance."

"At the amphitheatre?" I paused for a moment and pictured Annie standing on the back of a horse, cantering around the arena in her flowing pink chiffon and sequins. "She was performing at the time?"

"Yes."

I pictured Annie falling from the horse like a dead weight. I imagined the screams and the panic the shots would have caused.

"And no one else has been hurt?"

"Not seriously. A few people were injured in the scramble to escape the building, but it is a miracle that no one was seriously hurt or trampled."

"Poor Annie! How is she?"

"We must go and see."

I climbed into the dark interior of the cab.

"And no one knows who fired the shots?"

"No yet."

James climbed in next to me and closed the waist-high doors in front of us. "There was a lot of pandemonium, as you can imagine, and because there were so many people it will be a struggle to locate all the witnesses. But we will do our best. There are officers there from Lambeth L Division as well as the Yard. We need to find out who saw what before people drift off home and we lose our chance to speak to them. Let's go driver!"

The cab moved off.

"It must be the same person who shot Lizzie, don't you think?"

"It is certainly possible."

"Why would anyone want to harm Lizzie and her daughter? I don't understand it."

"Neither do I. We cannot be certain that the two shootings are connected."

"But they have to be, don't they? What are the chances of them not being?"

The cab trundled along and I noticed that the poor horse in front of us was walking with a slight limp. Most of the shops on Queen Victoria Street were in darkness, but lights were glimmering from the pubs and churches. My face was cold in the night air, so I pulled up my scarf to cover my mouth and nose.

"I cannot understand why we didn't turn off for Southwark Bridge a few hundred yards back," said James. "It would have been quicker to take the route south of the river. This cab is taking us the long way round."

"I feel sorry for the limping horse."

James turned to me, his face dimly illuminated by the lights from the street. "I suppose our prolonged journey gives me time to update you on another development. Y Division has discovered Lizzie's home in Highgate."

I felt my jaw hang open.

"Lizzie's home?"

"It is little more than two rented rooms at the top of a house on the high street. It is very unassuming; the sort of place you would walk past without giving it a moment's thought. In fact, I have done just that on a number of occasions."

My mouth felt dry. "What is inside it? Have you been there? Has Y Division uncovered any clues?"

"Not yet. I plan to visit tomorrow."

"Was she living with anyone else?"

"No one else has been discovered at the property yet, so

she may have been living alone. Y Division is speaking to the landlord."

"She must have disguised herself to live on a busy high street and not be recognised."

"She may well have done. But don't forget that everybody believed she was dead. So even if someone had noticed a resemblance to Lizzie Dixie, they would have given it only a passing thought. Their senses would have told them that there was no chance it was her."

"I'm pleased the Highgate police have found out where she was living. I believe that will be a big help to us."

The cab lumbered over Westminster Bridge and I saw the sprawling lights of St Thomas' Hospital glimmering across the river from the Palace of Westminster. We disembarked outside the enormous hospital on Lambeth Palace Road and walked through the main gate to the colonnaded entrance.

After making some enquiries, we located Annie's ward on the third storey.

"She cannot receive visitors at the present time," said a nurse standing guard at the door of the ward. She wore a high-collared, navy blue dress, a white hat and a long white apron.

"I am a detective and I have to catch the person who injured her," pleaded James. "I appreciate that she is badly wounded; however, it is of the utmost importance that I find out all she knows so that I can get back out there and find the person who did this. Annie knows me. She knows both of us. We spoke to her just a few days ago because we are investigating her mother's death. You do know that her mother was Lizzie Dixie?"

I could see that James had convinced the nurse. She

nodded solemnly and allowed us to pass. "Just a very short visit, please Inspector."

The ward was long, with two rows of iron bedsteads. I estimated that there were a dozen or so on either side. Each wall was lined with arched, curtained windows, and a strong, medicinal smell hung in the air. The floor was so clean that it sparkled in the light of several gas lamps hanging from the ceiling on long chains. All the patients were women, and I saw a small huddle of people standing around one of the beds halfway down the ward to our right.

"No gentlemen allowed, please sir." A nurse planted her hand firmly on James' chest and pushed him back towards the door.

"But I am a detective!" he remonstrated. "I have just been permitted to enter!"

"Not now, sir. The patient needs to rest. I have already turned away the Lambeth police."

James looked at me, his eyes urging me to continue towards Annie's bed. I left him arguing with the nurse and walked on ahead.

Joseph Taylor was easily recognisable at Annie's bedside with his fox-red hair. Two nurses stood beside him. I felt my pace slow as I thought about how little I wished to speak to him again.

He was a murderer, surely?

Or was he?

I noticed how tenderly he held Annie's hand as she rested on two plump white pillows. I didn't know Annie well, and I wasn't sure that she wanted me there, but it was a relief to see that she was comfortable enough to be sitting up in bed.

"Hello," I ventured, my voice wavering as I spoke. "What terrible news, Mr Taylor. I have just heard."

"I suppose you will be writing about this in your newspaper tomorrow!"

His eyes glared at me from beneath his red eyebrows. The two nurses stared at me too.

"Is she a news reporter?" one of them asked.

"Yes, she is, and she is constantly hanging around like a bad smell."

"Please could you leave the ward, madam?"

One of the nurses took my arm and tried to lead me away. I stood my ground, concerned that James' attempts to find out what had happened to Annie were being thwarted at every turn.

"The inspector needs to speak with Annie," I said to Mr Taylor.

"Not now he doesn't," replied the showman staring at the entrance to the ward, where James still stood remonstrating with the nurse who had detained him.

"But we need to find out what happened," I said.

"Annie was shot. That's what happened! We are darned lucky that the amphitheatre is merely spitting distance from here. She needed urgent attention, and thankfully she received it."

"Madam, can you please leave?"

I looked back at James, then at Mr Taylor, wondering what I could do to persuade the group to let us remain here.

"She can stay," said a weak voice.

I turned to see Annie looking up at me, her dark hair clouded around her pale face.

"Is she a friend?" asked the nurse.

"She was a friend of my mother's."

Mr Taylor made a derisory snorting noise.

The nurse removed her hand from my arm. "In which case, just a few moments please, madam. Miss Taylor must rest."

She and the other nurse left Annie's bedside. I walked towards Annie and saw that her shoulder was heavily bandaged.

"None of this goes into your newspaper!" fumed Mr Taylor.

"The story is already out there," I said, "and it is important for the public to know the facts about what happened at your show this evening. There were many people there, and they will all be giving friends and neighbours their accounts. It is my job to tell people what really happened instead of allowing rumour and gossip to spread. I will not write anything of my meeting here with Annie this evening, I can assure you of that."

Mr Taylor grunted in reply.

"It is your shoulder that was injured?" I asked Annie, looking at the heavy bandaging.

"It isn't too bad. The bullet just caught it, but nothing has lodged there. I have hurt myself more from falling off the horse." She tried to lift her head from her pillow. "My neck... and my back. They hurt."

"Don't move, Annie," said Mr Taylor. "Just stay as you are."

"You didn't see who did it, I suppose?"

"How could she?" hollered Mr Taylor. "She was standing on a galloping horse!"

"You were lucky not to have been more injured than you are," I said, thinking of her poor mother dying of her gunshot wounds in Highgate Cemetery.

Someone must also have wanted Annie dead. But why?

"I will be all right." Annie smiled weakly. Her eyes remained on mine, as if she wanted to say something more but couldn't.

There was a silence between us and I could hear the voices of James and the nurse at the far end of the ward.

"Would you like to speak to Inspector Blakely?" I asked Annie.

"Perhaps Joseph should first. Why don't you go and see him, Joseph, and find out what he wants?"

"I suppose he might be of some help if we're to catch the lunatic who did this to you," said Mr Taylor with a sigh. "Mind what you tell this woman; she's a member of the scribbling race."

He pointed his forefinger at Annie and then at me before walking off in James' direction.

I looked back at Annie and she stared at me expectantly.

"How are you feeling?" I asked, unsure of what else to say.

"I saw her," she whispered.

"Saw her?" I leaned in closer so that I could hear her.

Annie looked nervously past me to where Mr Taylor and James stood.

"I am sorry I lied," she continued in a whisper. "I felt so bad about it, because I know you are trying to find out what happened to my mother." She gulped as if trying to swallow back tears. "I saw her. We used to meet."

"You knew your mother was still alive?"

Annie nodded.

CHAPTER 25

"But Joseph didn't know she had survived the *Princess Alice*." Annie whispered so quietly that I could barely hear her. "He thought she was dead."

I nodded and smiled, pleased that Lizzie had not deserted her daughter.

"When did you last see her?" I asked quietly.

"Three weeks ago." Annie's eyes began to fill with tears, and I knew this was a risky subject to discuss. Mr Taylor would surely return and wonder what I had done to upset her.

"How was she?" I still struggled to comprehend that Lizzie had been alive so recently. Despite the tragedy of her death, I felt happy that she and Annie had continued their relationship.

"She was well. She seemed happy." Annie smiled through her tears.

"That's good to hear. And where did you meet?"

"Vauxhall Pleasure Gardens. We always met there and no one ever suspected."

Meeting in such a public place seemed risky to me. "Do

you know for sure that no one suspected your mother was still alive? Could someone have seen you and recognised your mother?"

Annie shook her head. "I don't think so. She disguised herself very well."

"Did she mention any trouble she was experiencing? An argument or someone she had fallen out with?"

Annie didn't reply; instead, she looked up the ward and I turned to see Mr Taylor and James approaching us.

"The Inspector would like to ask you some questions, Annie," said Mr Taylor. "I've told him to be quick and to get back out there and look for the man who committed this despicable act."

"How are you, Annie?" asked James. "Can you tell me what happened?"

"One moment I was on my horse, Moonbeam – we were cantering – and the next moment I fell. It was only when I was lying on the ground that I realised my shoulder felt as though it was on fire. Even then I didn't know I had been shot. It happened too quickly for me to put my hands out. I hurt my head and my neck."

"Did you see the gunman, Mr Taylor?"

The showman shook his head glumly. "No, the shots came from somewhere in the crowd. I have no idea where; there was complete chaos as soon as the shots rang out. Everyone wanted to get out of there."

"Why would someone do this?" I said, mystified. "Why would someone hurt Annie?" The dour expressions on the faces of James and Mr Taylor told me they shared my senti-ments. "Is the man who did this the same man who shot Lizzie?"

James looked at me. "It's a possibility."

"He wanted to kill me!" said Annie. "Just like he killed my mother!"

"Now, now, we don't know that," said Mr Taylor, gently resting a hand on her shoulder. "Please don't worry, Annie. I will protect you."

He gave her his handkerchief to dry her eyes and I felt sure then that he couldn't have murdered Lizzie. He was bad tempered, but he also seemed kind-hearted.

Unless this was a clever deception?

"Will he try to shoot me again?" asked Annie.

"Of course not," said Mr Taylor.

"You are in a safe place now," said James. "They will look after you here and you will recover quickly, I feel sure of it."

I noticed that James did not answer her question.

I felt worried for Annie. She looked so small and vulnerable lying in her hospital bed, and I felt certain that the same person was behind her shooting and that of her mother. I wanted to suggest that she was moved to a hospital out in the countryside, far away from London where the attacker couldn't find her again. But I decided not to voice my idea for fear of alarming the girl further.

"L Division are doing everything they possibly can to find the assailant," said James. "And the Yard will help them. We will not rest until he's found, you have my word."

"Poor Annie," said James as we descended the stairs on our way out of the hospital.

"She's in danger now, isn't she? That man intended to kill her. She is terrified and so would I be."

"We must be looking for the same man who shot Lizzie."

"I don't understand why he would do this. What has Annie done wrong?"

"She is Lizzie's daughter, and perhaps that is all the reason he needs."

"What if he tries again?"

"We'll have to catch him before he does."

I hadn't seen James look worried until now.

We walked out onto Lambeth Palace Road and stood by the railings under a gas lamp so that we would be visible to passing hansom cabs. I told James what Annie had whispered to me about meeting her mother.

"I had a feeling she would confide in you!" I could hear the glee in his voice. "This is extremely useful information indeed. I wonder, though, if Annie's knowledge that her mother was still alive led to her being targeted."

"It's difficult to say. If only we could find that man who was watching us in the cemetery. I think he may be the answer to all of this."

"He might well be, but experience tells me we should be wary of following only one line of enquiry. With that in mind, I would like to ask you to accompany me to dinner."

"Really?" My voice was shrill with surprise and I cleared my throat in embarrassment. "For the purposes of this investigation."

I felt my cheeks grow hot and I was pleased that James was unable to see my face clearly in the gas light. "Of course."

"Have you heard of Le Croquembouche on Great George Street in Westminster?"

"Yes, the restaurant has quite a reputation, I hear."

"I would like to dine there this Friday, but I am more likely to blend in with the clientele if I have a lady to accompany me. You would be of great assistance, of course. Le Croquembouche, as you are likely aware, is where the politicians take their mistresses, courtesans and just about anyone who isn't their own wife. It is the type of place Lizzie may have frequented. The two men at her funeral — Sir Edmund Erskine and Hugh Dowdeswell — were politicians. I need to begin investigating the courtesan work Lizzie did."

"You are hoping to see the two MPs there?"

"Yes, and I am also hoping that we may be able to speak to one or two of the women and find out what they knew about Lizzie and her relationships with these men."

"Do you think they would be willing to talk to us?"

"They have to; time is against us now. If Lizzie's murderer also attacked Annie, we need to stop him before he attacks again."

CHAPTER 26

"Here we have it," said Mr Sherman with pride, "a Remington Standard Two."

We stood around Miss Welton's desk and admired the shiny new machine with its rows of round, lettered keys. We watched as Miss Welton wound a sheet of paper around the roller at the top.

"Now then, Miss Welton, you show 'em," said Mr Sherman.

Enjoying her moment in the limelight, Miss Welton sat at the desk and adjusted her skirts before rubbing her palms together and stretching out her fingers in preparation.

"Well, are you going to type something?" asked Edgar.

Miss Welton scowled at him before holding both hands out over the keys and taking in a sharp breath. "What shall I type, Mr Sherman?"

"Anything you like, my dear."

"Right. So."

With a firm push of her forefingers, Miss Welton depressed the keys and narrow metal pegs sprang up towards the paper and then down again. We stood and watched as she searched for each letter before pushing the key down.

"Just one letter at a time?" asked Frederick Potter. "This is rather laborious."

"I have heard that in America people are using these machines very quickly," said Mr Sherman. "They call it type-writing."

"But the letters aren't even in alphabetical order," said Edgar, leaning over and inspecting the rows of keys.

"They have been arranged so that the most commonly used letters are most easily reached."

"So why is the letter *A* so far over on the left? Surely it should be in the middle?"

Miss Welton appeared a little red and flustered with the conversation going on around her as she tried to concentrate.

"That will do, Miss Welton, that will do," said Mr Sherman. "Now show 'em what you have typewritten."

Miss Welton wound up the piece of paper so we could read it:

Ryle Britania. Britannia rile the wwaves

"Excellent, Miss Welton, excellent. And thank you for the demonstration. What do you think, gentlemen?"

"I don't think much of the machine's grammar," said Edgar.

"It has potential," I said.

"Our hands are perfectly suited for writing," said Frederick. "Why use a machine?"

"For the uniformity of the script," replied Mr Sherman. "It would save me eye strain trying to decipher your handwriting, Potter, which reads as though a drunken spider with ink-soaked legs has staggered across the page."

"But if we were to use this machine, we would never make the deadline!" said Edgar.

"Perhaps when Miss Welton is a little more proficient she could typewrite our articles for us," suggested Frederick.

"That isn't a bad idea," replied Mr Sherman, although I noticed Miss Welton's mouth tighten. "Keep practising, Miss Welton, and I think we may yet revolutionise our way of working."

I walked back to my desk and Edgar followed behind me to continue a conversation we had begun earlier.

"So you have already written some paragraphs on Annie Taylor's shooting?"

"I was with her last night, and Mr Taylor and Inspector Blakely were also there, so I was able to get all the information first hand."

"But I have the Lizzie story. And I am supposed to be accompanying you when you meet the schoolboy inspector."

"Yes, but this isn't the Lizzie story; it's about the shooting last night at Astley's Amphitheatre. Annie simply happens to be Lizzie's daughter, and James just happened to be close to where I live when he heard the news. He knocked on my door as I was the nearest news reporter."

I had invented this last reason and I could tell that Edgar suspected as much.

"So what else am I supposed to write about? I can state that Lizzie's home has been found, but am not allowed to say where?"

"No, because it would attract unwanted attention and the police are busy trying to carry out their investigations at the property."

"But I can say that it is in Highgate?"

"If you must."

"If I must?" replied Edgar with a frown. "We tell the people what's happening, remember? I can say that it's in Highgate if I want to and that it is in the vicinity of the high street."

"No. Mentioning the high street is too specific."

"But it's part of the story! Everyone wants to read of how the actress falsified her own death and then lived in an unassuming abode for five years, which people walked past every day with no inkling that she was there! Even the neighbours had no idea who she was."

"You can still print that; it is a good story. Just don't mention anything to do with the high street."

"But people want to read about a location they know and can identify with. It's not far from where the trams run. People want to know these things!"

"And do you plan to control the crowds when they descend on the place and hinder the police from doing their job?"

"What rot. The problem with that schoolboy inspector is that he's too damned protective about this story. There is hardly anything to report on from one day to the next! And I have almost given up on the hope that a suspect will be named. I think I'll get myself up to Highgate and have a look at this place myself."

"I should also like to visit it."

I wondered what clues about Lizzie's life lay in the house.

"But *I'm* on the story." Edgar pushed his hands into his pockets and fixed his small eyes on me.

I knew that I would be in trouble with Mr Sherman if I didn't invite Edgar to the dinner at Le Croquembouche. James and I would be there for the purpose of the investigation, so Edgar would have to be there now that the editor had decided he must accompany us.

I glanced at Edgar and tried to form the words I needed to ask him to join us. He was the last person I wanted to be there.

"Are you free on Friday evening?" I asked, the words reluctantly spilling out.

"What? Friday?" Edgar's eyes opened wide.

"Inspector Blakely and I are dining at Le Croquembouche."

"You're having dinner? You want me there?"

"It's part of the investigation."

"Oh, I see." Edgar breathed out with relief. "Yes, I am free."

"Another argument?" asked Mr Sherman, striding towards us.

"No, we were just arranging dinner," I said.

"Were you now?" Mr Sherman raised an eyebrow and grinned. "Well, well, what a turnaround. What have you got for me on the railway bombings, Miss Green?"

"Two men are still being treated for their injuries at St Mary's Hospital, and the Chief Inspector of Explosives, Colonel Majendie, is examining the damaged carriages, which have been taken to a depot at Neasden."

"Good."

"My article is almost finished. I will give it to you before I leave to report on the West London Women's Society this afternoon."

"Now that's more like it," said Edgar. "A women's society. Women's matters. That is what you should be concentrating on."

"The West London Women's Society is keen for some coverage in the *Morning Express*," I continued, looking at Mr

Sherman and ignoring Edgar. "Perhaps we could include a few paragraphs in the Saturday features?"

Mr Sherman grunted in reply. "I don't think our readers are too concerned with women's matters. Make sure you get your article on the railway bombings handed in to me before you go anywhere."

CHAPTER 27

I arrived at the Colehills' home shortly after three o'clock. I tugged the bell pull and wondered whether Sebastian had returned from his trip away. I estimated it had been a week since he had left.

The maid led me into the drawing room, from whence the chatter of lively voices came. I stepped into the room and saw that it was filled with colourful, well-dressed ladies perched elegantly on settees and occasional chairs.

"Penelope!" Eliza rose out of her chair and came to greet me. She wore a purple woollen jacket over an oddly baggy purple skirt.

"Miss Green, welcome." I turned to see Mary Colehill at my side, greeting me with a wide smile. She wore an attractive burgundy and cream striped bustle day dress trimmed with lace. Her face was powdered and her neat hair was pinned with ribbons and bows. "You and your sister look very much alike," she added.

"Do you think so? Eliza is much taller."

"But there is a strong resemblance in your features. I have

seen a portrait of your father at your sister's home and I now see his likeness in you. Do please come and sit down."

Eliza introduced me to the group. "This is my sister, Penelope. She was exploded by the railway bomb last week! Can you believe she is still in one piece?"

There was a collective gasp, followed by enquiries after my health. Having reassured them that I was well and that my ears were almost recovered, Eliza told me everyone's name.

"You have met Mrs Lennox before, have you not? And this is Mrs Ferguson."

I nodded and smiled, desperately trying to remember who was who. My eye was drawn to the picture of the ziggurat on the wall and I thought of Sebastian once again.

Would he be angry when he found out that Lizzie's diaries had been destroyed?

"My sister is a writer on the *Morning Express*," announced Eliza, eliciting a murmur of approval. "She is to feature the West London Women's Society in that acclaimed newspaper. Isn't that wonderful? You are aware, I am sure, that it is a national paper."

I smiled weakly and hoped that Mr Sherman would finally agree to include a paragraph about the society. I feared that Eliza was hoping for a column on the front page.

Mrs Henrietta Henderson of the Rational Dress Society was introduced and she addressed us from the hearth rug. I took out my notebook and pencil in readiness to make notes and to show enthusiasm for the subject.

Mrs Henderson was in her forties and had an eagle-like appearance about her brow and nose. Her grey hair was brushed firmly back from her face and pinned into place with little decoration. Her blue jacket and skirts were of a similar design to Eliza's, and when she invited my sister to stand next to her to demonstrate their clothing I saw that their skirts were divided, so that in fact they both wore a pair of extremely baggy trousers.

"You will observe," said Mrs Henderson, waving her arms and lifting her knees energetically, "the freedom of movement which such apparel offers. The heavy, long skirts to which we are so accustomed interfere with our natural locomotion. Imagine if men were forced to wear such garments! Would they tolerate them? Of course not. A divided skirt requires no petticoat and therefore the amount of material required to be carried about the waist is lessened."

"I agree with the sentiment behind dress reform," said Mrs Lennox, who had a small feathered hat perched on her head, "but can a divided skirt ever look as elegant as a dress? I hope you will not be offended, Mrs Henderson, if I opine that your divided skirt is neither an item of fashion nor beauty?"

A discussion ensued about the aesthetics of practical clothing and I made notes and found myself agreeing with much of what Mrs Henderson said.

Afternoon tea was served during a discussion about corsetry.

"My dear friend, Mrs Nettleship, has created an evening dress which requires no corset at all," said Mrs Henderson.

Gasps of surprise mingled with the chink of china teacups.

"But surely only for a woman with a good figure?" queried Mary Colehill.

"I will never go without my corset," said Mrs Lennox. "There is much hullaballoo about the dangers of tight lacing, but most women only lace to reduce their waists by an inch or so. I cannot see anything dangerous in that."

I glanced at Mary Colehill's wasp waist and she caught my eye, so I quickly looked away.

"Tight lacing does not respect a woman's natural form," said Mrs Henderson. "However, if a woman wishes to lace, then it is her choice to do so. Dress reform merely provides women with an alternative."

"French shoes are dangerous," said Mrs Ferguson. "My niece broke her ankle after falling off a pair of high-heeled French shoes."

"Any high-heeled shoe interferes with a woman's mobility," said Eliza.

"I like shoes with high heels," said Mary Colehill, smiling apologetically. "And I lace tightly because I enjoy the support it offers and my husband admires my small waist. While I am respectful of dress reform, I cannot see it as something that I would embrace. I think women's clothes are very pretty and comfortable these days. Can you imagine having to wear hoop petticoats as our poor mothers did? It is important to remind ourselves of the progress we have made."

"I worry that dress reform will render all our clothes ugly," said Mrs Lennox.

While Eliza put up a new defence for the divided skirt, my mind began to drift to thoughts of Annie and the identity of the man who had followed us in the cemetery. If he was the same man seen at Highgate Cemetery, we needed to hear of a sighting of him at Astley's Amphitheatre on the night Annie was shot. If that could be confirmed, we would surely know who the killer was. The real difficulty would be in catching him.

My attention returned to the room when I realised the topic of conversation had changed to Lizzie.

"She was a woman of loose morals, of course," said Mrs Lennox. "It is an established fact that such women have little regard for their personal safety."

"I heard she was a courtesan," added another woman.

"Many actresses are," said Mrs Ferguson. "And I read in

The Holborn Gazette that she had secretly been in prison for the past five years. Her death was faked to cover up the shame."

It seemed Tom Clifford had resorted to making up stories, as he had threatened.

"And once you are a courtesan, you are simply inviting all men to treat you in a certain manner," said Mrs Lennox. "A violent death is not something a normal woman need worry about."

"On the contrary, Lizzie was quite normal," I said. I felt all eyes in the room on me, so I cleared my throat and continued. "Her childhood was poverty-stricken and she became an actress when Mr Colehill, Mary's husband, discovered her talent."

The women's gaze shifted to Mary, who smiled uncomfortably.

"His intentions were honourable, of course," I added with a smile in Mary's direction. "And he helped Lizzie realise her dreams. It was later in her life that she realised being a successful actress could not bring her happiness. And she made decisions which she later came to regret. Can't the same be said for all of us?"

There was silence as some drained their teacups and others found things to inspect on the cuffs of their sleeves.

"Yes, Penelope, absolutely," said Eliza loudly. "I think we can all agree that it is a tragic event, and I am sure I speak for all of us when I say that the culprit must be found immediately, for he is clearly a dangerous man."

There were noises of approval from everyone except Mrs Lennox, who gave me a hostile stare.

Eliza got to her feet to conclude the meeting. "Thank you to Mrs Henderson for her enlightening talk, and thank you to all of you for the lively discussion today. This is what I adore about the society; every woman here has her own opinion and is not afraid to offer it. Can you imagine what a difference there would be if men were present? The conversation would be dominated by their interests and we would simply have to nod politely at one another while they got on with it. When do you think the article will be published in the *Morning Express*, Penelope?"

"I will confirm a date with Mr Sherman."

"Thank you."

I had told Eliza what she wanted to hear, but I felt guilty about not being entirely truthful. I had yet to convince Mr Sherman to publish the article.

Before I left, I thanked Mary Colehill for hosting the meeting.

"Is Sebastian still away?" I asked.

"Yes, he is in Glasgow working at the Royal Princess's Theatre. I expect him home very soon."

It seemed that Sebastian had a valid reason for being absent.

"I am sure you will be pleased to have him home again when he returns. If you are planning to write to him, it may be worth mentioning that Inspector Blakely would like to speak to him on his return. He is speaking to everyone who knew Lizzie Dixie, of course."

"Of course," Mary smiled. "I suppose it is to be expected. Sebastian has been very saddened by her death."

"They knew each other for a long time."

"Yes, they did." Mary smiled. "It has been lovely to see you again, Miss Green, and I look forward to reading the article about the society."

I found myself leaving through the front door at the same time as Mrs Lennox.

"I hope you don't think I was disagreeing with you earlier," I said.

"But you were, weren't you?" she replied. She had sharp grey eyes and the feathers on her hat quivered as she spoke.

"I did not mean to cause any offence. I do find I get a little upset about Lizzie's death. I knew her quite well."

"Did you, indeed?" said Mrs Lennox. "Well so did I."

I felt stunned by the remark as I watched her march down the steps towards a waiting carriage.

CHAPTER 28

James was already waiting for me when I arrived at Le Croquembouche on the Friday evening. I had done my best to appear well-dressed, wearing the style of clothing Mrs Henderson avoided: a tight corset beneath a red silk bustle dress trimmed with gold fringing. The heeled satin shoes I wore had been in my possession for many years but had rarely been worn, and I had bought some silk flowers and bows for my hair. I had pinned them around a small velvet hat, which was fixed at a fashionably precarious angle.

James wore a smart, dark evening suit and I was amused to see that his tie was red silk, like my dress.

"Good evening, Penny. You look resplendent!" He raised his hat and grinned.

"Do you think we will pass for a wealthy man and his mistress?" I asked, but the moment I had said it I felt embarrassed.

"Absolutely," he replied. "You had better take my arm so that we look the part."

I was startled by the sound of running footsteps, and a tall figure loped out of the darkness.

"Sorry I'm late," said Edgar. He smelt of beer, as if he had just stepped out of the pub.

James gave me a quizzical glance.

"Mr Sherman has said that Edgar must accompany us because he is working on Lizzie's story," I explained.

"How good to have you with us this evening, Mr Fish," said James. "I will ask the waiters to set the table for three."

Le Croquembouche had an elaborate frontage with carved-stone ivy leaves clambering around the Doric columns that stood either side of the door. Large green and gold striped awnings hung across the curtained windows and a row of gas lamps flickered along the facade. The window boxes were crammed full of colourful chrysanthemums and clumps of trailing ivy.

A footman dressed in a red tailcoat opened the door for us, and we stepped into the warm bustle of the restaurant. It was smaller than I had imagined and most of the tables were taken. A strong scent of perfume mingled with the tobacco smoke and I cursed inwardly as my spectacles misted over.

My ears were filled with the rumble of lively conversation and laughter. A waiter took my jacket from me and we were shown to a small, intimate table at one side of the room. Through the mist on my lenses I could see a white tablecloth, a vase with a rose in it and an array of shining silver cutlery.

At James' instruction, an extra place setting was laid out for Edgar and the three of us managed to fit around the table, elbow to elbow.

As we sat down, I removed my glasses and placed them next to my soup spoon. I self-consciously rubbed at the small ridge they always left at the top of my nose.

"You look like a different person without your gig-lamps," said Edgar.

I noticed that James was staring at me in surprise.

"An improvement? Or should I put them back on?"

"No, don't put them back on. We can pretend we're with a different woman this evening, can't we, Inspector?" Edgar laughed loudly.

"Call me James," he replied quietly.

"Do you think Penny looks better without her glasses, James?"

"I wouldn't like to say so, as that might make Penny feel as though she shouldn't wear them, and obviously she must do so because she needs them."

"I do. I can scarcely see a thing without them."

"There you go, you see, so you must wear them. But not wearing them from time to time is also agreeable."

James seemed flustered with his words and I began to wish that I hadn't removed my spectacles at all.

I pretended to study the menu while glancing over it to look at my fellow diners. I could just about make out the blur of their faces. Most of the men appeared older than their female companions.

"Do you think all the men in here are politicians?" I asked.

"A fair few, I should say," said James. "Do you see a velvet curtain behind me?"

I squinted over his shoulder.

"Yes, what is behind there?"

"The private dining booths for people who do not wish to be seen. Or should I say, do not wish to be seen in the company of the people they are with."

"How do you know that? Have you ever been behind there?"

"No! But I have been told about it."

Edgar chuckled and lit his pipe. "I expect all sorts of shenanigans go on behind that curtain. I wouldn't mind having a peek." He laughed again, this time so loudly and gutturally that I noticed a lady looking over at our table. Edgar picked up his menu. "Let's choose some grub."

The waiter took our order and I wondered how I would be able to eat anything having laced my corset so tightly to fit into my dress.

"Are you expecting Sir Edmund tonight?" James asked the waiter casually, as if the politician were an old friend of his.

The waiter shrugged nonchalantly and left our table. A moment later, the oily-haired maître d'hôtel appeared. "You enquired about Sir Edmund Erskine, sir?" he asked in a heavy French accent.

"Yes, that's right. I wondered whether you were expecting him here this evening."

"And who is asking?"

"James Blakely. I am a friend of his. I bumped into him recently and he told me he would be dining at this esteemed establishment within the next week or two, so I thought I would look him up."

"Very good, sir. I will pass on your message when I next see him." The man bowed and left our table.

"Well, I thought it was worth a shot," said James.

"I like your style," said Edgar. "Ask and it shall be given. Knock and the door shall be opened. What are you going to say to him if he's here, old chap?"

"I will buy him some drinks to loosen his tongue and find out what his connection to Lizzie might be. In the meantime, let's keep an eye on who else is dining here. I think it would be useful to speak to some of the women, if possible. Lizzie must have known one or two of them. I am not sure how we can manage to speak to them, though. You might need to help me in that regard, Penny."

"I can help too," said Edgar, straightening his tie. "I've spotted a gal over there who knows my sister. I'll go and speak to her after the soup."

During our course of turtle soup, I told James that Sebastian would hopefully be returning soon.

"Good, it is rather urgent that I speak with him. It is useful that you have found out where he is, because if he doesn't return very soon we will have to get some men up there to visit him. It is a long way to travel."

"The journey takes a day from Euston Station," said Edgar.

"It is looking rather likely that I will have to book a ticket and take the train."

"What do you need to talk to him about?" asked Edgar.

"James needs to find out what Lizzie's diaries said. I lost them in the explosion."

"And a little more than that," said James. "Y Division have discovered some new information."

"What?"

"The constables questioning Lizzie's neighbours in High-gate have discovered that there was a regular visitor to the house."

"Who?"

"A gentleman who visited often and stayed overnight in some instances. He has been described as a wealthy man with his own carriage — a brougham — at his disposal. Apparently, the carriage was seen to stop further along the road so that it was not clear which house the man was visiting. This appears to have been an attempt to keep his visits secret. He also appears to have taken pains to conceal his identity by wearing a dark and sizeable Ulster overcoat; however, the constables have ascertained that this mysterious gentleman was a tall, slender man with dark whiskers. And he often wore a top hat."

CHAPTER 29

"Sebastian Colehill," I said slowly. "He has a brougham and he is tall with dark whiskers."

"We cannot confirm that he is the gentleman in question, but he certainly fits the description."

"He knew that Lizzie was still alive!"

"What a cad," said Edgar.

"We don't know for certain that he and the mysterious man are one and the same. You can see why it is rather urgent that I question him."

"But the chap is not the murderer, is he?" asked Edgar. "Surely it's Taylor?"

"If only it were that simple. Remember that we are visiting this restaurant for a reason. We are here to investigate whether the person who killed Lizzie came from the world of politics. These men sitting around about us have a voracious appetite for power and all that goes with it, and they don't mind who they trample on to get what they want." James raised an eyebrow to emphasise his point.

"So you don't think it's Colehill or Taylor?" asked Edgar.

"Instead, you think the murderer is one of these high cock-alorums sitting around us?"

"Keep your voice down," I hissed.

Edgar placed his serviette on the table next to his empty soup bowl. "I don't mean to offend, Inspector, but I think you're barking up the wrong tree. Taylor should have been arrested a week ago. I don't understand why you choose to lead a merry dance around the entire thing. Excuse me while I go and say hello to my sister's friend."

I felt pleased that Edgar had left the table for the time being, but his absence brought with it a ticklish sense of intimacy between myself and James. It occurred to me that the waiters would assume we were a couple and the thought made me uneasy. There was only a short distance between us at the table; presumably an intentional ploy to keep customers' conversations discreet. It was perfect for detective work, but I felt abashed at the physical closeness.

"It seems Sebastian lied to us," I said, after taking a large sip of wine. "When I spoke to him at the theatre about Lizzie's death he pretended he had no idea that she had still been alive!"

"We don't know for sure that he was Lizzie's visitor."

"But it has to be him, doesn't it? I think it would be unusual for another man who looked like Sebastian and had the same carriage to be visiting Lizzie."

"I agree that it is likely to have been him. And he may have lied, but perhaps he gave you Lizzie's diaries to explain the truth. I dare say her life must have become quite complicated for her to pretend that she had drowned. She may have written down her reasons and perhaps he thought it best you learnt what really happened in her own words."

"It is possible. He probably assumes that I understand

everything now. My biggest regret will always be the loss of those diaries."

"All is not lost if I can speak to the man. I only hope that he is in Glasgow as his wife says he is. If he has run away we are in trouble."

"And what of the investigation into Annie's shooting? I can't help but worry about her."

"St Thomas's Hospital is probably a good place for her to be for the time being; she will be safe there. Inspector Lloyd from the Yard is working on the shooting with L Division. They are still tracking down and interviewing all the people who were present that night. It's incredible when you think that so many people were there and yet so few seem able to help in identifying the man who fired the shots. He has managed to hide in plain sight by virtue of the sheer number of people in the place at the time."

"Perhaps Sebastian is closer than we think. Perhaps he shot Annie. If everyone is led to believe that he is in Glasgow, no one would suspect him, would they? He could have killed Lizzie and shot her daughter."

"We will find out in due course."

"Do you think so? At the moment it feels quite impossible that we will ever discover the truth."

"The truth always reveals itself in the end."

The waiter brought the next course of turbot in lobster sauce to the table.

"We talk about the investigation so much," said James, "that we seem to find little time to talk about anything else. What do you do when you're not writing?"

"Not a great deal. Writing takes up much of my time. I suppose I read a lot, both for pleasure and for work."

"Have you always been bookish?" asked James as we began to eat.

"Yes," I said proudly. "I have. Bookish with a sense of adventure, just like my father."

"Bookish *and* a sense of adventure? Do the two go hand in hand? I am intrigued!"

"Perhaps I am making it out to be more exciting than it is. I like the adventure of investigating a story. It introduces me to a whole host of people and places that I would never otherwise encounter."

"Such as Lizzie Dixie's dressing room?"

"Exactly."

"What is the most interesting place you have visited in the course of your adventures?"

"Venice."

"You have travelled to Venice?"

"Yes. I undertook my own version of the Grand Tour about ten years ago. How about you? Have you done a good deal of travelling?"

"Oh, I haven't yet left the British Isles. I once visited an aunt in Dover and she told me she could see France on a clear day from her top floor window. That is the closest foreign connection I have. I suppose I have seen a great many interesting places here in London as a result of my work."

"I can imagine."

"Some of the rookeries have to be seen to be believed."

"I have visited a few for the purpose of my news reporting."

"When you contrast the sheer misery of those infernal slums with a place such as the restaurant we are sitting in now, it strikes me that there is a great deal of inequality in our world."

"I agree. Sadly, there is."

"Cotelettes de mouton à la Provençale," announced the waiter as he presented us with our next course.

"Now that is an extremely fancy way of saying mutton chops, don't you think?" said James after the waiter had left.

I laughed. "Do you think we should tell Edgar that his food is on the table? He missed the last course."

I put on my spectacles in a bid to locate him among the diners.

"He's sitting in the corner over there," said James. "He looks rather engrossed."

I looked over to where James was pointing and saw Edgar talking animatedly to a woman with golden hair.

"Shall we fetch him or leave him?"

"I think we should leave him," said James. "He might be undertaking some investigative work."

We exchanged a glance and laughed. James loosened his tie.

"I suppose that when you are not doing police work you are tending your grandfather's vegetables?" I asked, taking off my glasses again.

"Yes, I do, although less so during the winter months. During the coldest spells of weather, I play chess with him. I am rather partial to the game, as is my sister."

"I have never played chess before."

"Never played it? Then I must teach you!"

"I should like that."

The light from the candle on our table danced in James' eyes and gave them a warm glow. I smiled and busied myself with my meal.

The mutton was followed by a sirloin of beef and York ham. As I sipped at a glass of claret. my corset began to feel distinctly uncomfortable.

"We have to speak to some of the ladies here," said James.

"It would be useful to find out whether any of them were acquainted with Lizzie."

"But how could we speak to them? They are all with their companions."

"Perhaps we should approach any woman who leaves on her own."

"That might cause her alarm. Besides, are any of these women likely to leave alone? I assumed their arrangements would be for the night."

"I am not sure," said James. "I don't know much about how these arrangements work."

"Perhaps Edgar's sister's friend knew Lizzie."

"Let's ask her to ask him."

"You mean *ask him to ask her*."

"No, the other way around."

"No, it's not. The claret has gone to your head."

"You're right, it has. I don't think I should be carrying out investigations while drinking wine. I am sure you would agree, however, that, at the current time, this investigation is turning out to be rather pleasant." He raised his glass and grinned.

I raised my glass in reply. "It certainly is."

I hoped fervently that Edgar wouldn't return to our table and ruin our conversation.

After a dessert of beignets aux pommes and Queen of Puddings, I rested my serviette on the table, feeling certain that I would be unable to eat again for at least a week.

In the blurred background behind James, I noticed that the velvet curtain had been pushed to one side as a man walked out towards us. I could not see him clearly, but I could tell that he was wearing a dinner suit. He had grey hair either side of his balding head and thick grey whiskers. As he drew nearer, he stumbled slightly and I guessed that he was inebriated. He looked familiar, but I couldn't think why.

"I can't say we are doing very well in talking to the customers here," said James. "I thought it would be a little easier than it has been."

"Mr James Blakely?" slurred the drunken man. He had reached our table and stood staring down at James, who leapt awkwardly out of his seat.

"Sir Edmund. What a surprise!"

"Blakely. Where do I know that name from? Your face is familiar."

"Detective Inspector James Blakely."

"Detective Inspector?"

"I saw you at Lizzie Dixie's funeral."

"Lizzie's funeral..." he repeated as he retrieved a cigar tin from the inside pocket of his jacket. He swayed slightly as he did so.

"Of course! Lizzie! Yes, her funeral. Damn shame." He took a cigar out of the tin and fumbled about for a painstakingly long time as he tried to return the tin to its pocket.

"Now, when was that now? Just last week, was it not? First thing in the morning. They had to dig that poor gal out of there before they put Lizzie in. Damn shame. Hang on..." Sir Edmund stood staring at James and swayed slightly as he pointed his cigar at him. "You're the police, aren't you?"

I held my breath, waiting for the mood to turn hostile.

"That is correct," said James proudly.

"Detective. Yes! So you know Cullen? He is chief inspector now, is he not?"

"That's right."

"Damn fine fellow, Cullen. Damn fine. I need a match."

He searched his pockets and turned to look at me as he swayed again. "Good evening, madam."

"Good evening, Sir Edmund," I replied.

"You with her?" The cigar was pointed at me, but he addressed James.

"Yes, that's right."

"Listen, young fellow, I'm finding it ever so tiring standing up. How about you come and join me out the back?"

"We would not wish to intrude, Sir Edmund."

"Come on." Sir Edmund gave James a hefty slap on the shoulder. "I know you're the police, but any friend of Cullen's is a friend of mine. Come along! You can bring *her* as well."

He began to stagger back towards the curtain and James grinned at me.

"This is too good an opportunity to miss," he said. "We might find out something useful."

I nodded as I picked up my spectacles and handbag. James carried our drinks and we followed in Sir Edmund's wobbly footsteps.

CHAPTER 30

Behind the curtain was a dim, wood-panelled corridor containing a row of curtained booths. I could hear muted voices, both male and female. A loud peal of feminine laughter startled me.

"Where is she?" I heard Sir Edmund say in the corridor ahead of me. "Which one's she in? My apologies, old chap, I thought she was in there. Oh, here she is. Were you hiding from me, Lola?"

Nervously, I followed Sir Edmund and James into a booth. I was concerned that Sir Edmund would realise I was a reporter and not James' companion at all.

And what would Lola make of me when she saw me? I wondered. *She would surely realise that I was not a courtesan with my spectacles firmly gripped in my hand.*

There was no time to dwell on this as I was swiftly shown to a seat in the elaborately decorated alcove. On one side was a mirrored wall and a velvet chaise longue, upon which a languid-eyed woman with beads plaited into her dark hair was reclining. She wore a low-cut, beaded bodice and long black silk gloves, which reached to her elbows. Her lips were stained a dark red, and, although she stared at me, her manner did not strike me as unfriendly.

Next to her was a man who looked about thirty. He was dressed in a dark suit and had a well-waxed blond moustache and a receding chin.

"Hugh!" said Sir Edmund. "I have found some friends!"

He slumped onto the chaise longue between Lola and the man I now recognised as the MP, Hugh Dowdeswell. James and I sat on chairs either side of a glass-topped occasional table, which was home to a lamp with a fringed shade.

Hugh puffed on a cigar and regarded us with a suspicious look. Lola had a drink in her hand and the table next to her was covered with empty glasses. Sir Edmund had finally found a match and managed to light his cigar.

"You don't mind if I smoke, do you?"

James and I shook our heads.

"Hugh's already smokin'," said Lola.

"And?"

"There's no need to ask to smoke if someone's already smokin'."

"Is that correct etiquette, Hugh?" asked Sir Edmund. "If you're smoking there's no need for me to ask if anyone minds me smoking?"

"Well, it would make sense that you needn't ask," said Hugh.

Lola picked up a clay pipe from among the empty glasses and filled the pipe with tobacco from a small tin. Sir Edmund held out a match for her.

"This is James," said Sir Edmund. "He is an inspector, but we needn't worry about that as he works with my good friend Chief Inspector Basil Cullen. And this is his companion." He looked at me. "I don't recall your name, madam."

"Beth," I replied.

From the corner of my eye I saw James give me a quick

glance, as if he wondered why I was lying. I wanted to tell him that I was terrified of being found out.

"Pretty name. My daughter is called Beth," said Sir Edmund. "And this is Lola. She often keeps me company, don't you, Lola?"

The woman nodded and smiled as she placed the pipe between her dark lips.

"And this is Hugh." Sir Edmund gave his friend a gentle punch on the shoulder. "He's a capital fellow."

Hugh smiled with one side of his mouth while Sir Edmund stumbled up from his seat, pulled the curtain to one side and shouted out: "Two bottles of champagne in here!"

Then he returned to the chaise longue and sat down heavily.

"We were saying that I last saw you at Lizzie's funeral," said James.

"Were we?" replied Sir Edmund. "That's right, I remember now." He took a long puff on his cigar. "Damn shame."

"Did you know her well?" asked James.

"Very well. She was a damn fine gal, wasn't she, Lola?"

"You knew her as well?" asked James.

Lola nodded.

"And Hugh was fond of old Lizzie, weren't you, Hugh?"

Hugh puffed on his cigar and stared at James as if he objected to the inspector's presence.

"*Beth* here," James emphasised my name as if struggling to remind himself of it, "also knew Lizzie."

"Did you now?" Sir Edmund asked me. "A fine actress, she was."

"It was quite a shock to find out that she was still alive, was it not, Sir Edmund?" asked James.

"Damn shock!" replied the politician. "I thought the gal had drowned, and that was a terrible shock in itself."

"And to think someone's gone an' murdered 'er," said Lola, her forehead furrowed.

"I cannot think why anyone would do such a thing," said Sir Edmund.

"Lizzie led a complicated life," ventured James. "She had relationships with a number of people. Do you think someone might have wanted to have her silenced? Do you think that is a risk when you are a courtesan?" He addressed this question to Lola, giving Sir Edmund a cursory glance as he did so.

Lola raised her eyebrows and the lines on her forehead deepened. "Nah, I've never been in danger meself." She sucked deeply on the pipe and puffed a billow of smoke out into the centre of the room.

"But what about Lizzie?"

"I dunno 'bout Lizzie."

"But courtesans are required to be discreet?"

"Of course."

Sir Edmund had been swaying absent-mindedly while smoking his cigar, but he suddenly looked over at James as if he had only just realised what he was talking about.

Hugh continued to watch the young inspector.

"If a courtesan was indiscreet, what do you think would happen to her?" James asked Lola.

"I dunno. She wouldn't go round talkin' in the first place, so it wouldn't 'appen." Lola scowled. "Do you think that's what's 'appened to Lizzie?"

"What happened to her?" asked Sir Edmund.

"That Lizzie might of talked and got murdered for it. That's never 'appened, as it?"

"Never."

Hugh leant forward with his elbows on his knees and stared at James. "Just what exactly are you up to here, Inspector?" His voice was low and syrupy. "My friend, Sir Edmund, said you were nothing to worry about, but you're asking questions."

"Hang on there. What's he doing?" asked Sir Edmund, raising his voice.

"Nothing," said James.

Sir Edmund screwed up his face in bewilderment.

"James is simply trying to understand the motive behind Lizzie's murder," I said. "It seems so senseless."

"I don't want any detective business in here!" slurred Sir Edmund. "I'm off-duty and so are you, young sir. Meanwhile, these lovely gals are very much *on* duty."

He leant towards Lola and slung an arm across her shoulders, then he looked questioningly at the distance between James and myself.

"Where did you find this one, then?" Sir Edmund asked James, pointing his cigar at me once again.

"She is a friend of a friend."

James coughed and I smiled benignly, hoping that Sir Edmund and Hugh would believe us.

A waiter arrived with two bottles of champagne and four glasses on a silver tray. I did not relish the thought of the bubbly liquid swilling around in my over-indulged stomach.

"Thank you, good man. Pour it out, pour it out!" said Sir Edmund. Then he turned back to James. "A friend of a friend, you say? So you are friends?"

"Of sorts," said James. "I couldn't trouble you for a cigar, could I, Sir Edmund?"

"Of course!" The politician stood up and fumbled about for his cigar tin once again.

Hugh stubbed out his cigar and took a glass of champagne from the waiter. He struck me as decidedly more sober than

Sir Edmund, and there was something about his calm demeanour which I found unnerving.

"Damn fine gal, Lizzie. Highly thought of," said Sir Edmund. "Very highly thought of, especially with the high panjandrums." He gave James a wink.

"Is that so?"

"Even the Grand Old Man took a shine to her."

James' face remained impassive and I made sure that mine matched his. The Grand Old Man Sir Edmund referred to was Gladstone, the Prime Minister. Rumours had abounded in Fleet Street for some time that he visited prostitutes, but nothing had ever been proven. I took a sip of champagne and the bubbles fizzed uncomfortably in my chest.

"When was that, then?" asked James casually as Sir Edmund handed him a cigar.

"Edmund," said Hugh. "There is no need to talk about any of this."

"It was before she was drowned," continued Sir Edmund, ignoring his friend. "Or before we thought she was drowned. I don't know when that was. Three years ago? Ten years ago? I can't remember now. I can't find my matches, old chap."

"Here." Lola handed them to him.

"You didn't hear it from me about the Grand Old Man," continued Sir Edmund. "He is loyal to Catherine, so far as the public is concerned. More than forty years they've been married."

"He has a reputation to protect," said James. "If what you say is true, he must worry about people talking."

"He doesn't," said Hugh coldly.

"Hugh should know. He is related to the Grand Old Man by marriage on his mother's side. And no one will ever talk," added Sir Edmund. "They wouldn't dare."

"Why? What would happen to them?" asked James.

Lola looked at James anxiously, realising what he was

trying to coerce Sir Edmund into admitting.

"I don't know." Sir Edmund took a gulp of champagne. "They would be silenced one way or another, I suppose."

"Nothing would happen," said Hugh, glowering. "No one would be silenced. You are asking leading questions, Inspector. And I suspect you are trying to put words into Sir Edmund's mouth."

"I wouldn't let him dare do such a thing!" said Sir Edmund. "Put words into my mouth? What a nonsense. Anyway, forget about all that business. Did you know that Lola here has partied with the Prince of Wales? It's no secret what *that* man gets up to. How I envy him!" Sir Edmund chuckled. "Although when I was last in Paris I did manage to get to Le Chabanais. Have you ever been there?"

James shook his head.

"If there is one thing Paris does well, it's brothels." Sir Edmund laughed again. "Rupert!" he cried out as a young man's head appeared from behind the curtain.

"Are you talking about Le Chabanais again, Sir Edmund?"

"I certainly am, old chap. Come in, come in."

He stood up and a young, thin, well-dressed man and a blonde woman in a purple and gold patterned dress stepped into the booth. There was barely room for all seven of us and the alcove was permeated with a sickly-sweet perfume.

"Detective Inspector James... what is it again?" asked Sir Edmund.

"Blakely."

"A detective?" asked Rupert.

"Not to worry, old fellow. He knows Cullen and he's off duty, and he's turning out to be a fairly decent sort of chap."

"Is that so?" said Hugh.

"This is his companion," continued Sir Edmund. "I can't seem to recall her name."

"Beth," said Hugh, glaring at me.

"This is Rupert Cornwallis-Deedes," announced Sir Edmund. "He mashes all the girls. His father is an old friend of mine and a bit of a masher too. And who's this thunderingly fine gal?"

"Kitty," replied the blonde girl with a grin.

"Simply divine. Now, take a seat, won't you both?" Rupert and Kitty sat on the chaise longue while Sir Edmund remained standing in the centre of the small room. "Now there's nowhere for my good self to sit! Damn it! Lola's lap will have to do."

Sir Edmund fell back drunkenly on top of Lola and, with the exception of Hugh, everyone seated on the chaise longue laughed.

I glanced at James and grimaced. He smiled uncomfortably in response.

"Now, this is cosy," said Sir Edmund. "All I need do now is rest my feet up like so."

He lifted up his legs so that his body reclined backwards and rested across the laps of Lola, Hugh, Rupert and Kitty.

"Hold on to me! I don't want to fall off!"

There was more laughter and Sir Edmund puffed on the stump of his cigar before examining the tip. "Damn thing's gone out." He threw it onto the floor. "Kitty, darling, would you care to remove my spats?"

"Of course, Sir Edmund."

"And while you're at, it you can remove my shoes too. A chap needs to be comfortable."

I gave James a frantic glance and he cleared his throat.

"Thank you for your hospitality, Sir Edmund. It is time for us to leave."

James got to his feet and I followed suit.

One of Sir Edmund's shoes was already off, revealing a red silk sock with a large hole, through which a toe was protruding.

"Must you? So soon? The evening has only just begun! You're going to miss all the fun. Could you massage my feet, please, Kitty? There's a gal." Sir Edmund give a deep sigh of pleasure as Kitty began kneading his toes. I felt my overfull stomach lurch beneath my corset and could taste the lobster sauce again.

"Thank you, Sir Edmund. Goodbye!" I said quickly as I headed for the curtain.

"Why did Lizzie ever have anything to do with that man?" I asked James as we journeyed back to Milton Street in a cab. "He is so repugnant."

"Money, I suppose. Why would anyone spend time with him? He has to pay for company as no one would offer it voluntarily."

I laughed.

"How are you feeling?" he asked.

"Better now, thank you. It was the toe massage that finished me off."

I was relieved that I hadn't been ill. The horrible lurch in my stomach had made me dash out of the restaurant, to the great concern of the waiters. In the darkness of the street, I had managed to loosen my bodice and corset, and, after a few breaths of outside air, I had begun to recover.

"It is quite a revelation that Lizzie became so well connected," said James. "Did you know about Gladstone?"

"No, she never mentioned him to me. I knew that he had watched her perform at the opening night of *Lady Audley's Secret*, but I knew of no connection other than that. We only have Sir Edmund's word for it, though."

"That is true. But this has me wondering. If she had a liaison with Gladstone and then did or said something indiscreet, perhaps that put her life in danger. Perhaps that was why she went into hiding."

I stared at the dark, misty road ahead. "I don't think you can bring the Prime Minister into this. It is completely improbable."

"If not him, then possibly someone else," said James. "There could be any number of men at Westminster who were worried about an indiscretion they had committed with Lizzie."

"But why should she be indiscreet?"

"Perhaps someone treated her unfairly. Perhaps there was something she did not agree with."

"But if she had broken her vow of secrecy, she would never have been able to work again."

"Exactly, and that might be why she chose to disappear."

The theory seemed solid enough.

"You think that perhaps she got into a situation she couldn't see a way out of?"

"Undoubtedly! Why else would she disappear? And she may also have been fearful. Perhaps Taylor found out. Gladstone is a deeply religious man and has been married for a long time," continued James. "He has several children who are doing well for themselves. You and I both know that rumours about him have been circulating for a good while, but if the public ever found out the truth that would be a different matter. It might be that Gladstone has nothing to do with it, but he may have other men who look after these things for him. Perhaps they take matters into their own hands without his knowledge. If a courtesan happened to be indiscreet and needed to be silenced, there are people out there who would deal with such a matter."

"It is a horrible thought. I wish there was no possibility of it being true."

"As do I, but we cannot ignore it."

CHAPTER 31

"I think a few paragraphs on the West London Women's Society would fit rather well on the features page of the Saturday edition."

I had decided to put the idea to Mr Sherman again as he sat at his desk scribbling on proofs. He stopped and frowned at me.

"And what exactly does the West London Women's Society do? Don't tell me, it's another group of irritable women requesting suffrage."

"Not exactly, no."

"Good. Hopefully women will soon realise that politics is not suited to the fairer sex. There is good reason for the House of Commons to exclude female parliamentary reporters. They simply don't have the heads for it."

"I cannot think of anything less interesting than being a parliamentary reporter, Mr Sherman."

"Exactly! There you go, you see! You don't have the head for it."

"Oh, I have the head for it, all right, but I would rather

work on the stories the public is actually interested in. The West London Women's Society does believe in campaigning for women's suffrage."

Mr Sherman groaned and Frederick Potter joined us.

"I call for remark that it is impossible to give women the vote unless they fight in wars," said Frederick. "How can they be expected to have a recognised opinion on war if they never fight?"

"Not all men fight," I replied. "Some are too old or infirm, yet they can still vote. Have you ever fought in a war?"

"That's not my point," replied Frederick haughtily. "Women don't fight, but they are the wives, mothers, daughters and sisters of men who do. And as women associate war with the loss of their men, they have a biased opinion upon the matter. Ergo, women are not suitable to vote. Allowing them to do so would be an act of folly."

"But women pay taxes," I said. "If they pay taxes to the government, should they not have a say on how the government spends their money?"

"That is enough!" said Mr Sherman, raising a hand to calm us. "This argument can run for eternity if it is permitted to do so. What else is this women's society working on, Miss Green?"

"Dress reform."

"Even worse!"

"My sister rides a bicycle, Mr Sherman." Frederick sniggered and walked off.

"Now don't get me started on bicycle riders!" He wagged a finger at me. "One of them steered his contraption directly into the omnibus I was travelling on last week. It was a miracle no one was hurt and it caused a cursed hullaballoo on Oxford Street, I can tell you."

"Don't you think that some of our readers might be

bicycle riders themselves and therefore interested in the practical clothing which is required for riding a bicycle?"

"A handful of them might be, but not enough to warrant a paragraph in the Saturday features."

"Some members of the West London Women's Society are now wearing divided skirts..."

"That's enough." Mr Sherman held up a hand to stop me. "We had all this a number of years ago with bloomers; those frightful, oversized undergarments from America. I thought they had been long forgotten. Please don't tell me they are the height of fashion now."

"Not bloomers, Mr Sherman. Divided skirts."

"Miss Green, may I remind you that our deadline is looming and we haven't yet finalised the edition for tomorrow morning. I am certain that our fine proprietor, Mr Conway, will not want to see features on bicycles and bloomers, or votes for women, in his newspaper."

"Shouldn't the *Morning Express* reflect changing public opinion?"

"Yes, it should, but not the opinion of a few bored housewives in the suburbs. Miss Green, I need a paragraph on the plans for the Suez Canal before the day is out. Do you think you could manage that for me?"

I nodded and left the editor's office, aware that I would not make any further progress that day. It would do nothing to stop me trying again, however. I wondered how I could phrase my words more effectively so that I didn't mention angles that instantly put him off.

I passed Miss Welton's desk and noticed that she had neatly typewritten on several pieces of paper. I picked one up.

"It seems you are mastering the art well."

"Thank you," she replied.

"I should like to learn myself. Typewriting looks so much better than handwriting, doesn't it?"

"It does; I am very pleased with it. I can show you how to do it, if you like?"

"I would be very grateful if you could. Thank you, Miss Welton."

"Oh dear, oh dear, oh dear." I turned to see Edgar swaggering towards me with his hands in his pockets. I hadn't seen him since the dinner at Le Croquembouche the previous Friday and I did not like the smug smile on his face.

I placed the piece of paper back on Miss Welton's desk.

"What is it, Mr Fish?"

"Tut, tut, tut."

I felt my right fist clench.

"What are you trying to tell me, Edgar?"

"The schoolboy inspector's off the case!" he said with a grin.

"Inspector Blakely, you mean?"

"Yes, your friend, the inspector."

"Off the case? What are you saying?" My eyes searched his irritating face for meaning.

"He's off the case. He was removed over the weekend." Edgar took his hands out of his pockets and walked back to the news room. I followed him.

"So who is assigned to it now?" My heart felt heavy in my chest.

"Cullen," he replied, sitting down in his chair and removing the pencil from behind his ear. "Finally, the case will be pulled out of the fire!"

I had disliked Chief Inspector Cullen ever since the wrongful conviction in the Doughty Street case.

"But Inspector Blakely was making good progress. I don't understand!"

"No, he was not." Edgar laughed scornfully. "He had no

suspect when Taylor should have been arrested as soon as it happened."

"Taylor may not have done it. Inspector Blakely needs evidence before he can arrest a suspect."

"He has evidence! What more does he need?"

"It is not enough."

"Anyway, Cullen will decide what to do next. I feel relieved that the investigation is in safe hands now."

I couldn't quite comprehend what I was hearing. It made no sense to have James removed from the case. I wondered how he would be feeling at this moment. After all his hard work, he probably felt quite devastated.

"I don't understand," I said. "Cullen can't just remove him for not having arrested anyone yet."

"No, but I think we both know that it is about something more than that, don't we?" Edgar leaned back and fixed me with his small, glinting eyes.

"What do you mean?" I couldn't for the life of me fathom what he was talking about.

"A certain beano with Sir Edmund Erskine?" He smiled.

I felt my stomach turn at the reminder.

"Plying an honourable gentleman with drink and attempting to force a confession about Lizzie Dixie from him?"

"That did not happen!"

"That's what Sir Edmund and Hugh Dowdeswell claimed when they made an official complaint to Scotland Yard about the schoolboy inspector's behaviour. If Blakely's father hadn't been a chief superintendent, he would have been given the old heave-ho."

"Sir Edmund and Mr Dowdeswell are lying!"

Edgar gave a derisory snort. "Sir Edmund Erskine, a man of the establishment who has been the Member of Parliament for Dorset for more than thirty years, and his esteemed colleague are both lying?"

"It wasn't the way they described it. Sir Edmund invited us to have a drink with him and we talked a little, but Sir Edmund was already half-seas-over before that happened. Hugh said very little. I think Sir Edmund is embarrassed that we witnessed his drunken behaviour and is trying to exact some form of revenge. Sir Edmund was mistaken, as is Cullen. By removing Inspector Blakely from the case, he is making a huge blunder!"

Edgar shrugged. "Go and tell him that yourself if that is your sentiment."

"I shall!"

I turned and walked away, and as I did so I heard Edgar make a comment to Frederick about women and their short tempers. I wanted to walk back and tell him in a loud voice what I thought of his rude, lazy attitude and his condescending demeanour. Instead, I took a deep breath and was ashamed to feel tears pricking my eyes. My throat felt tight as I collected up my handbag, hat, coat and umbrella and left the news room.

I strode along Fleet Street in the rain, passed the Royal Courts of Justice, St Clement Danes church and then into the narrow thoroughfare of Wych Street, with its old, timbered buildings and shop bay windows piled up with books. Although it was only mid-afternoon, the street felt dingy under the leaden November sky. I pulled the high collar of my jacket up around my neck and wished I hadn't left my scarf at home that morning.

I had planned to go to the reading room, but I felt the need to walk until every last drop of anger had left my body. I felt incensed that Sir Edmund and Hugh Dowdeswell had lied.

Had Sir Edmund woken the morning after our evening together and realised he had said too much about his relationships with courtesans and about Lizzie's connection with Gladstone? He had probably felt ashamed and acted on it.

Perhaps the answer to Lizzie's murder lay somewhere in Westminster, I conjectured. *By having James removed from the case and installing his friend Cullen in his place, Sir Edmund and Hugh Dowdeswell were simply protecting themselves and their friends. If Lizzie had been killed by someone because of her connections with politicians, and perhaps even the Prime Minister, there would be no chance of her murder being properly investigated.*

I clenched my teeth until my jaw ached. I wanted to shout; I wanted to strike someone. I glared at a man who happened to walk a little too close to me in the street and noticed him shrink away from the furious expression on my face.

No one could help Lizzie now. James was no longer allowed to work on the case. Annie lay injured in hospital, and Taylor and Colehill seemed intent on protecting themselves. Who was to find out what had happened to her?

I paused by the columned facade of the Olympic Theatre, where Lizzie had performed in *A Midsummer Night's Dream*, and felt the anger begin to drain from me. Once again, tears sprung into my eyes.

Perhaps I had no right to do anything for Lizzie. Perhaps I should have heeded the warnings in the anonymous letter writer and from Sebastian. I wasn't a detective. I wasn't even assigned to report on Lizzie's story. Perhaps she hadn't even considered me a friend?

But I thought of Lizzie in her tomb beneath the sleeping angel, and of her daughter in her hospital bed, and I felt a strong sense of injustice that these two women had been attacked. The opportunity to find the culprit was slipping away. Worse still, attempts could potentially be made to cover up what had happened.

Instead of turning right up Drury Lane and heading towards the British Museum, I turned left and walked down to The Strand. From there, I would hail an omnibus to Westminster.

CHAPTER 32

I wasn't surprised that Chief Inspector Cullen kept me waiting at Scotland Yard. I perched on a wooden chair in a drab, chilly, smoky office, which was busy with police officers working at desks and striding in and out of the room with piles of books and papers.

Perhaps Cullen was hoping that if I were left alone long enough I would make my departure, but I was determined to wait as long as it took to see him. I wasn't going to allow Lizzie's case to lapse. I leafed through some new notes I had made about the railway bombings and drafted a few rough paragraphs in my notebook.

"Miss Green."

Inspector Cullen stood over me, his thick grey moustache twitching impatiently beneath his bulbous nose. He stared down at me through his silver-rimmed spectacles and I smiled to see whether his manner would soften. It didn't.

"Inspector Cullen," I said cheerily as I got to my feet. "Thank you for seeing me at such short notice. I realise you are extremely busy."

"Indeed," he replied, marching off towards a large desk in the far corner of the room. I noticed it was in prime position beside a little stove, which was trying its hardest to provide the room with some heat.

Cullen gestured for me to sit in a chair as he seated himself behind the large desk. He laced his thick fingers together and rested his hands on his desk. His suit was made from a dark wool and his waistcoat boasted a smart line of shiny gold buttons. His face and narrow eyes gave nothing away; no doubt a skill he had developed during his many years of detective work.

"It is some time since we last met," I said. "A year perhaps?"

"I believe so."

It was unlikely that he had forgiven me for the article I had written defending the man he had ensured was hanged for the Doughty Street murders.

Cullen checked his pocket watch, signalling that I was already taking up too much of his valuable time. "How can I help you, Miss Green?"

"I am concerned that Inspector Blakely has been removed from the Lizzie Dixie case. I had been working with him on it."

"Yes, I am aware. I ensured that you could return to your job to do exactly that."

"Thank you. I am surprised that Inspector Blakely is no longer on the case as he was doing a good deal of excellent work and Lizzie was a friend of mine. I am concerned that, by removing him, the case may be jeopardised. It is most urgent that the young man who followed us in the cemetery is found and that Sebastian Colehill is questioned about his relationship with Lizzie."

"You see this next to me, Miss Green?" Cullen slapped his

large hand onto a pile of papers on his desk. "This is what we, at Scotland Yard, call a *case file*. Every note, interview and piece of evidence Inspector Blakely has collected during the course of his thorough investigations has been compiled into *one file*. We are required to create such a file for each case and it proves itself exceptionally valuable when a case passes from one officer to another, which, I can assure you, Miss Green, is a *regular occurrence*. We are very sure of our procedures here at the Metropolitan Police, so there is no cause for concern." He laced his fingers together again and stared at me. "Is there anything else?"

"Do you still require my help with this case?"

"If Inspector Blakely has done his job properly, which I am certain that he has, all of your assistance has been documented in here." He tapped the case file again. "If I have need of your help again, Miss Green, please rest assured that I shall contact you, courtesy of Mr Sherman, at the offices of the *Morning Express*."

I sat back in the chair, feeling disarmed by Cullen's patronising manner.

"Sir Edmund," I ventured. "I heard that he and Mr Dowdeswell complained to you. What they said is not true."

"How do you know what they said?" Cullen's forehead was furrowed.

"I heard they had alleged that Inspector Blakely and I gave Sir Edmund too much to drink and then tried to extract information from him, but that is not at all what happened."

"Water under the bridge, Miss Green." He waved a hand in the air dismissively. "Water under the bridge."

"I do not want James – I mean Inspector Blakely – to have been removed from Lizzie's case unjustly."

Cullen's eyes narrowed. "There is nothing unjust about how this case is being managed."

"That is reassuring."

Cullen got up from his chair and walked around the edge of his desk towards me. He lowered his voice as he perched on the edge of the desk and looked down at me.

"You are a news reporter, Miss Green, and I wasn't born yesterday. I know you are here to get something more from me."

"No, I wished only to correct any misunderstanding about what happened between Inspector Blakely and Sir Edmund."

"Inspector Blakely does not require your mothering, Miss Green; the chap is more than capable of standing up for himself. And may I take this moment to add that your working relationship is closer than that which is normally expected between an inspector and a news reporter. It is no great shame that Inspector Blakely is no longer working on the case. If you want to know the real reason why I have taken it over, I can tell you now that I think you already know it."

I assumed a puzzled expression.

"The connection with Westminster. I believe Sir Edmund may have let slip just how involved Lizzie was with the man at the top. This requires careful handling, and I don't want Inspector Blakely biting off more than he can chew. I am protecting him."

"And will you also be protecting Sir Edmund and Mr Dowdeswell?"

Cullen looked startled, as if he had been stung by a wasp. "What are you implying?" he hissed.

"If Lizzie was murdered by someone at Westminster, will it be properly investigated?"

"How *dare* you question my integrity?" A small piece of spittle shot out of his mouth.

"I wasn't questioning it, Inspector Cullen, I merely wish

to ensure that Lizzie's murder is thoroughly investigated, no matter who is guilty of it."

"Oh, it will be, I can assure you of that." Cullen rose from his temporary seat on the desk and walked back round to his chair. "Because if there was any risk that it wasn't, you will take pains to write about it in your newspaper. Am I right?"

I smiled. "Yes, Inspector Cullen. That is correct."

The rain hammered down on my umbrella as I walked across the puddle-filled courtyard of Scotland Yard. My conversation with Inspector Cullen had done nothing to reassure me that there would be a fair investigation into Lizzie's case, but I felt better having let him know that I would be keeping a close eye on its progress. I wracked my brains to ascertain whether there was anything else I could do to ensure that Lizzie's murderer and Annie's attacker would be found. I did not relish the thought of leaving it all in Cullen's hands.

"Penny?"

I looked up to see James standing in front of me. He was with a tall, long-nosed colleague. Both wore dark coats and held large umbrellas.

"James!" I smiled broadly. "I heard you had been removed from the case, so I came to see Inspector Cullen to find out what is to happen next."

"Did he tell you much?"

"Not really."

"He likes to play his cards close to his chest."

"And he and I don't have a good history," I added. "I am so sorry to hear that you have been moved after everything you have done on the case. It felt as though we were making progress, albeit it not as quickly as some would have liked."

He held my gaze and his lips moved almost imperceptibly,

as if there were something he would have said had his colleague not been standing beside him. "It is commonplace in the police force," he said with a shrug. "I have other cases to work on, and I know that Inspector Cullen will call on me if there is anything he needs help with, as I am sure he will do with you."

"Yes, he said he would."

"Good."

We looked at each other for a moment longer and I made a move to leave, not knowing what else to say.

"I will continue to take a keen interest in the case, of course," said James.

"As will I," I replied.

"I am certain that it won't be long before we work together again, Miss Green."

James raised his hat and smiled, so I said goodbye to him before continuing my walk across the wet courtyard with a heavy sensation in my chest.

"Miss Green!" Tom Clifford from *The Holborn Gazette* ran up to me. He had no umbrella and his hat looked soggy. The sight of him made me feel even more glum.

"Are you following Inspector Blakely?" I asked.

"I was until he told me he was no longer on the case. What are you up to?"

"I'm working."

"As am I, Miss Green. But what are you specifically doing here?"

"I don't have to tell you, do I?"

Tom gave an empty laugh. "No, I don't suppose you do, Miss Green. What's the latest on the case now that Blakely's off it?"

"Only Cullen knows. You'll have to ask him yourself. Did you write a story about Lizzie being in prison for five years?"

"Yes. I heard from a source that's where she was."

"Who?"

"I never give my sources away, Miss Green."

"Of course. Good day to you, Mr Clifford." I stepped past him.

"Should I speak to Cullen, then?"

"You can try."

CHAPTER 33

I t had been almost a week since Annie's shooting and I
had heard nothing more about her condition. I assumed
she was still in hospital and thought of her lying alone
in the hospital bed.

Was Mr Taylor her only visitor?

I bought her some chocolate creams and made my way to
St Thomas' Hospital in the early evening, timing my visit so
that Mr Taylor would be at Astley's Amphitheatre, which had
reopened a few days previously.

I didn't know what I would do if I bumped into Mr
Taylor. It would have been more sensible for me to stay away,
but I felt the need to look out for Annie. With little progress
in finding the person who had shot her, I worried that the
police would forget about her. I couldn't deny that I was
interested in hearing more from her about the meetings with
her mother, but only if she volunteered the information. I
couldn't visit her as a news reporter asking questions on this
occasion; I had to visit only as a friend.

I found Annie sitting up in bed with a cream woollen shawl wrapped around her shoulders. Her dark hair was well brushed and hung down at one side of her head like a curtain. There was colour in her face, her blue eyes were bright and she looked well, even if she appeared a little gaunt. It was a relief to see that she had no other visitors and I felt happier still when she smiled at me. Her shoulder was still heavily bandaged.

"Do you mind me visiting you?" I asked. "I won't stay long, but if you would rather not speak to me, I would understand."

"Why should I mind?" asked Annie. "Please sit down." She gestured towards the wooden chair at the side of the bed.

"How are you feeling?"

"Much better, thank you, though I don't think I'll be able to perform for a while. It will be some time before I get full movement and strength back in my arm. And my neck and back are still painful."

"You will manage it eventually."

"I hope so. I worry that Joseph will find another performer who will be good enough to replace me permanently."

"He wouldn't do that."

"I shouldn't be so sure."

"He cares about you."

"Do you think so?"

"Yes, I am sure of it. He is protective of you, I can tell."

"Caring and being protective are not necessarily the same thing."

I nodded. "That is true. But he loved your mother very much and therefore I am sure that he cares for you somewhere deep within his heart."

"I hope so."

"Have the police made any progress in finding out who did this to you?"

"Not that I know of. Inspector Lloyd has visited me twice and asked me all manner of questions. I don't have a great deal to tell him, though. I was unaware of exactly what happened. I think he is trying to speak to everyone in the audience, but that will take some time."

"Do you think the person who shot you could have been the same person who took your mother's life?"

"I don't know." Her lower lip wobbled slightly, so I was mindful to take greater care about the questions I asked her.

"What do you think?" she asked.

"I don't know either. It is possible, though. It's important that they catch him as soon as they can. I just wish there was more that I could do."

"The police are doing their best."

"I am sure they are."

A nurse came over and straightened the bedclothes, as if she were trying to listen in on our conversation. It occurred to me that Mr Taylor might have asked the hospital staff to keep an eye on Annie's visitors.

The nurse left again.

"I cannot understand it," said Annie. "Who would want to hurt us both?"

"That is what we need to find out. I think I'm beginning to understand why your mother pretended she had drowned on the *Princess Alice*. But surely she didn't have to hide away like that. Could she not have just retired from acting?"

"She wanted to get away from Joseph. Their marriage had been an unhappy one for a long time."

"She could have just left him. Women don't have to stay in unhappy marriages these days."

"The thought of a divorce was too much for her. Being so

well-known, she felt she would not have been able to do such a thing. The public had become so accustomed to seeing her and Joseph in their carriage pulled by zebras. Everything about their relationship was a big show."

"That is to be expected, I suppose, when you put a showman and an actress together."

"They enjoyed putting on the show, didn't they?" said Annie, her face brightening. "They were rather glamorous for a time, weren't they?"

"They were indeed! Their shows, appearances and parties filled many column inches."

Annie smiled to herself. "I felt quite proud sitting in the landau with them as we rode around town with everyone staring at the zebras. Those days were fun."

"It was rather drastic of your mother to pretend she had drowned on the *Princess Alice*. Misleading her own family like that must have taken some doing."

"Joseph was devastated, as was I." Annie's eyes became damp. "And when I received a note from her a few weeks after her supposed death, I wasn't sure what to think."

"She sent you a note? I'm surprised you managed to keep it a secret; it must have been extremely distressing."

"I don't think I had fully accepted her death by then, so reading a note from her felt as though my dreams had been answered. And when I saw her at Vauxhall Pleasure Gardens, it was incredible." Annie smiled at the memory. "I remember Mother had cut and dyed her hair an odd brown colour, and she wore some extremely drab, dark clothes, quite unlike anything I had ever seen her wear before. I remember thinking she looked very strange." Annie laughed. "But no one recognised her!"

"Did you ever visit her at her home?"

"No, I never went there. She told me she lived in north

London and that was all I knew. We met each month and we walked together, rain or shine. When it was very cold the walk was a little shorter than usual, but she always kept our meetings, and so did I. I wish we could have had a normal relationship like other mothers and daughters."

"And was she happy, do you think?"

"It is difficult to tell. She was proud of me, I know that. She told me she had disguised herself one evening and come to see me perform, and I feel very happy that she did that. She knew what I had become."

"Do you think she regretted hiding?"

"No, I think it was what she wanted. She never showed any desire to act again; I think she felt her time was over. I don't know what she did with her days, but I know that she was fond of reading the newspapers because she liked to keep up with what was going on in the world. And books. She read a lot of books. I think she was leading a very quiet life, and perhaps she was content with that."

"Annie, do you mind if I ask you a question about your father?"

"My father?" Her expression grew wary.

"Do you mind talking about him?"

"I suppose not. I don't really know him."

"But you know who he is? Did your mother tell you?"

"Yes."

Annie didn't seem to want to tell me, so I made a guess at someone I had been thinking about for a few days. "Is your father Sebastian Colehill?"

"I don't know him as well as I know Joseph." She pulled the shawl tighter around her shoulders.

"It seems he knew that your mother was still alive."

"Did he?"

"He hasn't admitted it yet. In fact, he's reportedly in

Glasgow at the moment and the police are keen to talk to him. Did you ever see him and your mother together while she was hiding?"

"No, never. Mother didn't really talk about him to me."

"Did she care for him?"

"It is difficult to tell. She kept that side of her life private. I don't know whether she loved my father or not."

"When did she first tell you about him?"

"I don't know. I have always known that my father worked in the theatre and I remember meeting him when Mother was in various performances. He never spoke to me about being my father, but she had explained that he was, so that was all I needed to know, I suppose. He has always been friendly towards me, but not too close because he is married with a family, and I'm quite sure they don't know about me."

"I am sure they don't."

I found myself harbouring a new animosity towards Lizzie and Sebastian. *Why had they had a love affair when he was married with a family?*

I thought of the delightful Colehill children practising their French with me and singing songs. I imagined the sadness they would harbour if they ever discovered their father's affair or learned that they had a half-sister.

I considered the evenings backstage with Lizzie and Sebastian in a different way now. The fleeting glances and touches had been between two lovers trying to conceal their affair. Naively, I had assumed they had enjoyed a close working relationship and nothing more.

Annie stifled a yawn and I realised our conversation had probably tired her. I reached out and gently held her hand, which was resting on top of the bedclothes. "Thank you, Annie. It means a great deal to me that you have spoken so honestly about your mother. I want to find out who did this terrible thing to her and to you, and I won't rest until I do so."

"Thank you. I think the police are doing their best."

"They may be, but I intend to keep a close eye on them, even if it is not my place to do so. Your mother deserves to rest in peace. She was kind to me and I want to return that kindness, and that also means looking out for you. Your step-father is not the most affectionate of people, is he?"

Annie smiled. "He isn't, but he's not a bad man. I tell him that if he wasn't so rude people might like him a little better. But when he takes centre stage in his shows, that's when he becomes someone else. I think it is those moments he saves himself for. I have grown quite fond of him over the years, and he's as close to a father as I'll ever have. All this business has upset him dreadfully and, unfortunately, he conducts himself rather rudely at times like this. If you ever got to know him better you would find out that he is not such a bad man, after all. He has always been fair to me considering that I am not even his daughter. And he has had to raise me as though I am. I feel indebted to him."

Perhaps I had thought rather harshly of Taylor, I conjectured.

I made a note to myself to think better thoughts of him the next time we met.

"When you are feeling better we must talk again and I will tell you my memories of your mother and what I remember of you when you were younger. I remember you had a nanny called Mrs Rathbone."

"I remember her!" Annie laughed. "She was a strict lady, but she taught me a lot."

A nurse strode over to us. "You do know that visiting time has finished?"

"Let me know when you are discharged from here, won't you?" I said to Annie.

She nodded in reply as I leant over and gave her a quick embrace. She felt so small and vulnerable in my arms.

As I walked away from Annie's bed, I prayed that she would stay safe. My biggest fear was that the person who had shot her would try to harm her again. I couldn't imagine Taylor or Colehill harming her. Like Cullen, my thoughts were turning to Westminster.

CHAPTER 34

I returned home the following evening to find *The History of Pendennis* by Thackeray waiting for me on the hallway table.

"The detective left it here for you," said Mrs Garnett, regarding me with her arms folded.

I felt disappointed to have missed James.

"Thank you. I am looking forward to reading it, although I have heard that it is not as good as *Vanity Fair*."

"It's not," said Mrs Garnett, "and I prefer Charles Dickens. I wouldn't bother with *Pendennis*."

"I shall try it all the same, thank you, Mrs Garnett."

"I wouldn't waste your time. Read *David Copperfield* instead."

"I have read it, thank you."

I picked up James' book and tucked it inside my handbag.

Later the same evening, after a meal of leek and potato soup, I sat by the stove in my lodgings and began to read *The History of Pendennis*. Tiger dozed on my lap and I had only reached the letter from Arthur Pendennis to his uncle about his engagement when my eyelids began to feel heavy. I slept briefly, but was suddenly startled by loud voices downstairs.

I removed Tiger from my lap, walked over to my door, opened it and listened. I heard Mrs Garnett's voice and a gruff male voice, followed by a stomping sound on the stairs.

"Excuse me, sir!" said Mrs Garnett.

I listened to the footsteps striding quickly up the first two flights of stairs. I assumed they would stop there and that the man would visit one of the rooms below mine. But, to my horror, I heard the footsteps continue on the wooden stairs which led up to my room.

"You have no right to march into my house in this manner!" called out Mrs Garnett.

I quickly scampered back into my room, quietly closing and locking the door. Then I sat in my chair and listened nervously.

All was briefly quiet before a loud hammering noise sounded on my door.

My skin prickled and I could feel myself trembling.

"Who is it?" I called out in the most carefree voice I could muster.

Was it the person who had sent me the threatening letter?

"Sebastian Colehill," came the reply.

My hands gripped the arms of my chair and I remained rooted to the seat.

He had returned.

"Hello, Mr Colehill."

"Open the door!"

"Mr Colehill!" came Mrs Garnett's voice. She had clearly caught up with him on the stairs.

I had not encountered Sebastian in a temper before and I felt afraid.

Surely he couldn't cause me any harm with Mrs Garnett present.

He would probably shout, but I could cope with that. Keeping my door closed was likely to enrage him further.

I walked over to my door and opened it.

"Sebastian! What a surprise! How was Glasgow?"

I grinned widely in an attempt to diffuse his mood. He glared at me. The carnation in his buttonhole was wilting and his whiskers looked unusually unkempt.

"Sebastian, what is the matter?"

"Stop standing in the doorway as if butter wouldn't melt in your mouth and ask me to come in."

I didn't like the way his tall, dark frame loomed over me or how his cold, blue eyes pierced mine. I felt my knees weaken.

"Are you all right, Miss Green?" asked Mrs Garnett. "Do you know this man? Would you like me to call for help?"

"I know him. Thank you, Mrs Garnett, for your concern. I shall leave my door open."

Mrs Garnett nodded and remained where she was, her dark eyes wide with concern. As I moved to allow Sebastian into my room, Tiger dashed under my bed.

I offered Sebastian my chair, but he stood in the centre of the room with the top of his hat almost touching the rafters. I thought of his home and how modest my lodgings must seem in comparison.

"Would you like a drink?" I asked.

"No thank you."

"How can I help?"

"Help? What a strange offer. I had a visit today from the police."

"Really?" I tried to force my face into an expression of surprise.

Sebastian glanced over at my writing desk and his eyes narrowed. He glared at my pen and paper as if they somehow posed a threat to him.

"Chief Inspector Cullen came to see me because someone has been spreading dreadful rumours that I was seen at the house in which Lizzie apparently hid!"

I felt reassured that Cullen was continuing the investigation from where James had left off, but I wasn't sure why Sebastian was accosting me about it.

"I am not aware of any rumours, Sebastian."

"No? Then what are you aware of?"

I took a breath and tried not to show him how frightened I was.

"All I heard was that Lizzie's home had been discovered in Highgate and that neighbours had said she had been visited by a man matching your description."

His eyes narrowed further.

"Many men look like you, of course, so it does not mean that you were the visitor. Inspector Cullen is simply following up on the information he received."

"That's what you call it, is it? Following up? You do realise this means I will be treated as a suspect?"

"You won't at all. I am certain the inspector will be speaking to several other men as well."

"Have you any idea how upset my wife is?"

"I can imagine it must be very distressing for her."

"I told Cullen that he should have read the diaries and then he would have a full understanding of my relationship with Lizzie without coming to my home and speaking to me as though I were a criminal. Did you not pass the diaries to the police?"

My heart thudded heavily in my chest and I slowly shook my head.

"No, they were lost."

"Lost? *How?*" He took a step closer to me.

"They were destroyed in the bomb explosion on the underground railway," I stuttered. "I had been to the cemetery to visit Lizzie and I was reading her diaries on the train, and then the explosion happened and I lost my handbag and everything in it. I'm so sorry, Sebastian, I can't tell you how much I wish I had kept those diaries safe. Every day I am filled with regret that I lost them." I felt my voice begin to crack.

Sebastian rubbed his brow and sighed. I watched him cautiously and held my breath.

Was he a violent man? Would he harm me?

"That is a shame. A great shame," he said quietly. "But it's not your fault, it was an accident. At least you were unharmed."

I began to breathe again. "Thank you for being so understanding. I realise those diaries must have meant a lot to you."

"Yes, they did. But not so much that I was unwilling to lend them to you and the police. I felt they would do the explaining for me. I knew the police would come calling as soon as I was informed of her death and the last thing I wanted was for them to visit the house."

"I am sorry."

"I don't want any of this finding its way into the *Morning Express*, is that clear?" He raised his finger to emphasise the warning.

"It won't, I can assure you of that. I tried to read the diaries before I lost them, but there was a lot in them which didn't make sense to me. Lizzie referred to someone with the initial D, do you know who that is?"

"Not without being able to read them again and sadly I can no longer do so. I remain confused about your role in all of this. I hear you have been visiting Annie."

"Yes, I am worried about her."

"Why?"

"Because someone tried to kill her! And I am frightened that they will try again."

"They would be foolish to attempt it."

"They would, but I still worry for Annie's safety."

"Leave the worrying to me. In fact, it is probably best if you stay out of this altogether. You claim you were Lizzie's friend, and you even persuaded her to pay for an expedition to find your father in South America."

"I didn't persuade her, she offered!"

"You hung around in her dressing room after her performances."

"She invited me!"

"It was no friendship. You are a hack." He gestured towards the writing desk. "You are interested only in your next story."

"That is simply not true!"

Sebastian took a step towards me and I instinctively cowered.

I had to fight back.

"Tell me why you lied to me!" I exclaimed.

"I lied to you?"

"Yes, you knew that Lizzie had not drowned on the *Princess Alice*."

"And why should I admit that to a news reporter?"

"When I visited you at your theatre, I visited as a friend of Lizzie's. I felt shocked and concerned by the news of her death and I wanted to speak to the people she knew and cared about. It was a way of coping with my grief. I didn't visit you in pursuit of a story."

"No?" I shook my head. "You call yourself a friend of Lizzie's, but you barely knew her at all," he snarled. "Do you think she ever considered you a friend?"

"She paid for the expedition to find my father."

"With Taylor's money. She did that to help bring an

eminent plant hunter home. There was no need for you to read any kindness into it. I can't trust you and the only reason you have been following that detective around like a faithful dog is to find something to write about. I invited you to my home for dinner as a friend, but I realise now how foolish I have been."

"This is a misunderstanding, Sebastian. I do not wish to write malicious stories about you or anyone else. My job is to report on what is happening, and I am desperate to find out who did this to Lizzie. And to Annie. I remember Annie as a little girl and it is terribly upsetting to think that someone could be so cruel to her. She has lost her mother and now someone has attacked her. She could have been killed! We need to stop these people and I want to help. Lizzie helped me and now I want to do something for her. I want to find out who killed her and why."

He sighed.

"You knew she was still alive," I said quietly.

Sebastian nodded.

"And Annie also knew," I continued.

His eyes searched my face, as if he was trying to decipher how much I knew about Annie.

"Did she? Well, I wouldn't know about that."

"Who do you think shot Annie?"

"I have no idea. You think I did it?"

"No, of course not. Why would you? Annie is your daughter, is she not?"

A long pause ensued.

"Yes, she is," Sebastian said finally. He took a handkerchief from his pocket and wiped his brow. "Like you, I cannot understand why anyone would wish to harm her."

"You could help by telling the police everything you know. Cullen is keen to understand what Lizzie has been doing these past five years."

"I will cooperate with them, I would be foolish not to. But my wife now knows that I have not been truthful with her, and if my children find out, or any of my colleagues or the public..."

"The police will be discreet. And so shall I."

"As long as I have your assurance on that, I will rest a little easier." He refolded his handkerchief and returned it to his jacket pocket.

"We want the same thing, Sebastian. We both want to find the person who shot Lizzie and Annie. Can we trust each other?"

"We can try."

CHAPTER 35

As I descended the stairs the following morning and walked across Mrs Garnett's hallway, an envelope on the table caught my eye. I walked over to it and realised, with my heart thudding heavily, that it was addressed to me.

My name and address were written in black ink, but the letters were scrawled awkwardly, as if someone had used their weaker hand to write.

It had to be another letter from the anonymous sender. And this time he had remembered to disguise his writing on the envelope.

I picked up the letter and examined the postmark to see that this one had also been posted at the General Post Office in St Martin's le Grand.

I used Mrs Garnett's engraved silver letter opener to slice along the top of the envelope, then I pulled out the letter and opened it to see that it was similar to the previous one.

You ignored the last warning. Keep looking behind you.

I instinctively turned and looked at the carpeted staircase behind me. Obviously, there was no one there, and I felt foolish for doing so. But the hairs on the back of my neck prickled unpleasantly.

As I had supposedly ignored the last warning, did the sender plan to carry out his threat? Was he actually going to do something to me, or had it merely been written to frighten me?

If the letter was intended to frighten me, it had worked. I had thought that Taylor had written the first letter, but I was beginning to doubt that now. It might only have been a coincidence that he had used the same phrase: *There will be trouble.*

I didn't want to believe that Sebastian Colehill had sent it to me.

Perhaps it was Cullen, I surmised.

I had upset someone but was struggling to think who it might be.

I folded the letter, placed it back in its envelope and tucked it into my handbag.

"An interesting letter for you this morning, Miss Green?" asked Mrs Garnett as she carried a mop and bucket into the hallway.

"Of sorts." I could feel myself trembling.

"And how is your sister? She hasn't brought her bicycle here recently."

"She is well, thank you, Mrs Garnett. In fact, I am meeting her for lunch today."

"Do send her my regards. Is she still wearing trousers under her dresses?"

"She is wearing divided skirts now."

Mrs Garnett stared at me and sucked in her bottom lip. "A divided skirt? What is that?"

"I can ask her to visit and give you a demonstration."

"No, there is no need." She squeezed out the mop and

began to clean the tiled floor. "No need at all. You two sisters are off your chumps."

"When will Mr Sherman publish your article on the Society?" Eliza asked while we dined in the Refreshment Room at St Pancras Station.

She was due to travel by train that afternoon to visit our newly betrothed cousin, Agatha, in St Albans and had asked me to join her for lunch.

We sat at a small, round table by the steamed-up window. Eliza was proudly wearing her divided skirt with a matching tweed jacket. I chewed on a mouthful of ham and pickled cucumber as I slowly considered how best to reply to her.

"He is taking his time," added Eliza as she shovelled a forkful of beetroot into her mouth.

"He needs a little more convincing."

"I thought you had already convinced him?"

"I have *almost* convinced him."

"Either you have or you haven't, surely?" Eliza scowled.

"Mr Sherman isn't that straightforward."

"I am sure he isn't." She sighed. "Perhaps I should give up on the *Morning Express*. I have a good friend at *The Pall Mall Gazette*. I wonder if he could help instead."

"I will be able to convince the editor," I said, offended that she would so quickly consider an alternative newspaper. "Just give me a little while longer. He is quite traditional and is always worried about what the proprietor will say. And I must be honest with you, Ellie, I have had to spend a great deal of time on the underground railway bombing story. I haven't made the society's news a priority."

"You're busy, I understand." She attacked a tough piece of

boiled beef with her knife and fork. "I read that two of the bombing suspects have been named."

"Yes, the news from Dublin is that a reward is being offered in return for information on the whereabouts of John McCafferty and William O'Riordan."

"Both criminals, I presume."

"McCafferty organised the raid on Chester Castle to seize the arms stored there. It failed because of an informant."

"How are these people allowed to roam free, wreaking havoc in such a manner?"

"If the police knew where they were, they wouldn't be." I thought of Lizzie's brothers and wondered if they had played any part in the conspiracy. I hadn't heard the surname Mahoney mentioned as yet.

"If they had been locked up the first time they wouldn't be out there now causing more trouble. Why would bombing the underground railway make anyone sympathetic to their cause? I feel terribly sorry for the famine the Irish endured, but this isn't the proper way to respond, is it? And as for the Americans, they simply encourage it!"

"A million people died during the famine."

"I know, I know. It was a dreadful time, and we did very little to help. Ireland is part of the United Kingdom and we allowed it to happen. Can you imagine if something that terrible had happened in Surrey?"

"It wouldn't."

"Exactly. It wouldn't. We wouldn't allow it, and yet we allowed it to happen in Ireland."

"This is why the Irish are angry," I said.

"So you are defending them?"

"I don't agree with the bombing campaign, but I understand their anger and their desire for independence from a country that has let them down."

"We could talk about the Irish question all day." Eliza paused from her boiled beef to sip her tea.

"One of the women in your society," I said, "Mrs Lennox, I think her name is. The woman with the feathered hat. She told me she knew Lizzie Dixie."

"Did she?"

"Do you know how she knew her?"

"No idea, I'm afraid."

I sighed. "Perhaps she is married to a politician?"

"What makes you say that?"

"There seems to be a Westminster connection to Lizzie's death," I whispered.

Eliza paused with her cup halfway to her mouth. "Really?"

"But please keep that fact to yourself. In the meantime, I would be grateful if you could find out what Mrs Lennox's husband does."

"I don't think he's a politician, but I will find out."

"Thank you, Ellie."

"I've heard that most people suspect Mr Taylor."

"I don't think it was him. I visited Annie Taylor in hospital a few days ago and she speaks highly of him, despite acknowledging that he can be bad-tempered. If he was capable of murdering his wife, I think she would have picked up on something."

"So who then?"

"I don't know. There are various other possibilities, but I cannot talk about them in a public place."

I glanced around us and saw that the only person within earshot was an elderly lady eating a slice of cake with a fork. Talking about Lizzie's case saddened me. I missed being involved in the investigation, and had also found myself missing James.

"Keep on at Mr Sherman, won't you?" said Eliza, laying down her knife and fork. "I know you have other work to do, but this really is very important. Every piece of coverage we can get in the press makes a difference. It is another step forward in making our case for women's rights. It is quite a national movement now. I am surprised that Mr Sherman cannot see how newsworthy this is."

"He is a man in a man's world. Women's rights are not very important to him."

"And you are a woman in a man's world. You have the opportunity to make something happen."

I took a sip of tea and felt guilty that I hadn't done more to help Eliza. The society wasn't just a hare-brained idea of hers. I knew that people could not continue to ignore the issues of women's rights. I had been so distracted by Lizzie's case and my day-to-day work that I hadn't given proper thought to how I could help my sister. It was people such as Eliza and their relentless campaigning that made a difference.

"I will get something published in the *Morning Express*, I promise. I will harangue Mr Sherman until he gives in."

"Thank you."

Eliza and I said our goodbyes and she left by the door that led into the station while I walked through the door that took me out onto the street. We had agreed to meet next at the new Natural History Museum, where Father's work would soon be on display. I felt excited about seeing it.

A brisk, cold wind blew up Euston Road. I tied my scarf tighter and walked alongside the curve of the Midland Grand Hotel. Built a decade previously, the exquisite hotel was an elaborate, five-storey, red-brick building with hundreds of arched windows. Its tall chimneys and gothic pinnacles soared up into the fog, where they seemed to inhabit another world, like a fairy tale castle. I tried to peer in through its windows as I thought about the next article I had to write about the railway bombings. Then a familiar figure passed me: I recognised at once the broad-shouldered form of Inspector Cullen. His thick grey moustache was prominent between his black top hat and black ulster overcoat. But he didn't see me. I stopped and stared as he disappeared into the main entrance of the hotel.

I continued walking and prepared to cross Euston Road, but as I waited for a gap in the traffic I couldn't stop thinking about Inspector Cullen.

Perhaps he was following up some new information on Lizzie's case. If he was, then he was unlikely to tell me about it.

I had the distinct impression that he was planning to keep me at arm's length. If I wanted to find out what he was up to, I would need to see for myself, and I was certain that there would be little harm in venturing into the hotel to see whether he was still in the entrance hall. If he saw me, I could pretend to him that my visit was purely coincidental.

Which it almost was.

I turned and quickly followed the detective through the elaborate stone arch and up the steps to a revolving door. Once through the door, I found myself in the entrance hall, with gilded arches supported by pink stone columns. People bustled around me and a porter pushed a trolley with suitcases on it.

There was no sign of the inspector.

I walked on into a curved corridor with an intricately tiled floor and red and gold patterned wainscoting. I could hear the chink of cutlery and china from further down the corridor and wondered whether Inspector Cullen was meeting someone here for lunch. I followed the noise and passed the impressive main staircase, which was flanked by stone columns.

I found the restaurant beyond a glass door and peered inside. It was busy with diners and well-lit, with a row of windows along one side and a large chandelier in the centre of the room. Green and gold flocked wallpaper covered the walls and large oil paintings hung from the picture rail in heavy gilt frames.

Waiters busied about among the tables and I could see that a number of wealthy people sat there wearing gold jewellery and fashionable clothes. Some of the ladies had elaborate hairstyles and stylish little hats decorated with ruffles, bows, feathers and flowers.

There was a man walking away from me, escorted by a waiter, and I could tell by his gait that it was Inspector Cullen, newly relieved of his overcoat and top hat. He approached a table that was occupied by two other men.

One had a balding head and thick grey whiskers and the other was younger with a blond moustache. Just the sight of them made me think of lobster sauce.

Sir Edmund Erskine and Hugh Dowdeswell.

What were they planning to discuss? They would surely discuss Lizzie. Was the inspector questioning them, or were they meeting to plan a cover-up?

I watched them at their table and wished I could get close enough to overhear.

A scuffed footstep on the floor tiles behind me caught my attention. I turned around just in time to see a young man walking away from me. I got the impression that he didn't want to be seen.

I hadn't caught sight of his face, but I thought I had caught a glimpse of a pale moustache. His suit was dark and he wore a tweed cap. I recalled a snatch of conversation with James on the rainy Mile End Road.

Slight build, tweed cap and dark clothing.

It was the description of the man who had been seen climbing over the fence of Highgate Cemetery on the night that Lizzie died. The man who had followed us in Kensal Green Cemetery.

The man who was walking away from me now fitted that same description.

CHAPTER 36

"Excuse me!" I called out to the young man.

If he stopped and wondered what I wanted, I could pretend that I had mistaken him for someone else. But he didn't stop. Instead, his pace quickened and this roused my suspicions further.

I followed him.

The man disappeared among a group of people gathered at the foot of the main staircase. I made my way to the curved corridor, assuming that he would leave via the main entrance. But just as I passed the staircase, a movement caught my eye and I glanced up to see the feet of someone progressing quickly up the stairs.

He had wanted me to think he had left the hotel, but he hadn't been quick enough.

I swiftly turned and bumped into a woman, to whom I apologised before making my way up the first part of the staircase, which divided into two elegantly curved staircases beneath an arched window. One led to the left and the other to the right. I was sure the man had taken the staircase to the right, so I lifted my skirts and ran up the flight of stairs as quickly as I could. Once I reached the top, I realised the two staircases converged onto another landing and then divided again to curve round to the next floor.

Where had the man gone?

Three stone archways behind me led to three different corridors on this floor and the walls were decorated with red and gold fleur-de-lis. I heard a noise above me and decided to ascend another flight of stairs. This time I took the staircase on the left. As I climbed, I looked over to the other staircase just in time to see the dark, slender figure reach the top of the stairs.

"Wait!" I called over to the man. "I need to talk to you! Did you send me the letters?"

I reached the next storey, puffing with exertion. I wanted to take deeper breaths but my corset was too tight.

The man was running up to the next storey, I was sure of it.

Why was he running away? What was he trying to hide?

I ran up the next flight of stairs and felt my heavy skirts and petticoats weighing me down. For the first time, I wished I was wearing the practical divided skirt and shoes, as modelled by Mrs Henderson.

Up above me, the ceiling rose into elegant painted vaults, like the interior of a grand church.

I caught sight of the man at the top of the staircase running through one of the stone archways.

I couldn't let him get away. Not now.

With all the strength I could muster, I launched myself up the last flight of stairs as quickly as possible. My handbag thudded against my legs and my face was hot and damp with perspiration. I could feel my spectacles slipping off my nose.

I ran through the same archway as the man had, and saw

him running along a carpeted corridor lit with small lamps. I continued my pursuit and almost bumped into a maid emerging from a room with a chamber pot. She appeared alarmed to see me bowling towards her.

"Is something the matter, ma'am?"

"We need to stop that man," I said breathlessly as I ran past her.

"Is he a thief?" she called after me.

"I don't know!" I called back. "But he is something!"

As I ran on, I realised how foolish my words must have sounded.

He turned right at the end of the corridor and I puffed after him. There was a door at the end of it, which he ran through. I followed.

Where could he possibly be going?

As we turned into another corridor, the man glanced to his right and stopped dead, as if he had suddenly noticed something. Then he moved to his right and disappeared, as if he had stepped through an invisible door.

I heard a metallic, wrenching sound and then a slam. As I got to the place where I had last seen him, I saw that he had got into a lift and, with a shaky, rumbling sound, it was heading downwards.

I had heard about lifts and ascending rooms, but had never encountered one before now. It was an iron cage set in the centre of a stairwell with a great, thick cable attached to its roof. As it rumbled downwards, I could just about see the man inside. I ran down the staircase and called out for the lift to stop, but I wasn't sure if the contraption was capable of stopping on demand. With the loud whirring and clanking noise the lift made, it was unlikely that its occupant would hear me.

I tried to keep up with the lift, but it was moving faster than me. I was at risk of stumbling and falling down the stairs. The lift shuddered to a jolting halt just below me. With a sense of relief, I leapt down the last few steps and turned the corner to the lift entrance, but to my annoyance I heard the machinery whirr into motion again and the lift began to ascend.

"Stop!" I called out, but I knew there was little use in crying out.

I ran back up the stairs again. My legs ached and I felt light-headed from my shallow breathing. I watched with despair as the lift rose above me.

I heard the lift stop again and scrambled up the last few stairs to reach it, but I knew I would not get there in time.

I reached the top stair and stumbled, twisting my ankle as I tried to reach the lift.

"Are you all right?" asked a concerned lady with a small dog under her arm as I flung myself around the corner towards the lift door.

"Yes," I replied, gasping for air. I turned to look inside the lift, but it was empty. The concertina lattice door was pulled open and there was a mirror inside the lift which offered only a reflection of my red, perspiring face. I spun round to look about me, but there was no sign of the man.

"The man," I said to the woman with the dog. "Did you see where he went?"

"What man?" she asked.

It made no sense for him to have vanished in such a way.

I admitted defeat and made my way back down the stairs, mopping my face with my handkerchief.

I found myself at the end of a corridor on the ground floor. I strode along it, my heels clicking against the tiled floor. I passed a number of doorways, hoping to find my way to the restaurant, where I could tell Inspector Cullen about the man who had run away from me. It was likely that the man was still in the building and there was a good chance that he could be found.

I eventually found myself back where the chase had started, by the restaurant. I opened the glass door and stepped inside to be greeted by the hum and chatter of diners and the smell of roasted meat. A waiter in a fitted black jacket, bow tie and white waist apron approached me and I asked him to take me to Inspector Cullen, pointing to the table he was sitting at with Sir Edmund and Hugh Dowdeswell. As we approached them, the men paused from their conversation and frowned at me.

"Miss Green." Cullen stood up immediately and Sir Edmund and Hugh Dowdeswell followed suit.

"What the deuce are you doing here?" asked Cullen. "Whatever has happened? You look as though you have just run across London."

"There is a man here whom we need to apprehend. It is the same man who was seen climbing over the fence of High-gate Cemetery the night Lizzie died. Dark suit, tweed cap. I have just been chasing him, but he got away, I think he could still be in the hotel if we are quick enough. Come, Inspector, let's find him so you can make the arrest."

"Hold your horses," replied Cullen. "I have no idea what you are talking about. Which man?"

"You will find his details in *the case file*. He was seen on the night Lizzie died. Climbing over the fence."

"Yes, yes, you said that. But I still don't understand what you are doing here."

"It's Beth, isn't it?" said Sir Edmund.

"Miss Penny Green," Cullen corrected him. "A scribbler on the *Morning Express*."

"A news reporter?" said Sir Edmund. "Well that makes everything as clear as mud. I knew there was something not quite right about you the other evening. Trying to work undercover again, are you? Just what exactly are you trying to do, woman? Can't a man dine in peace?"

"We need to arrest this man! Please, Inspector, will you come with me?"

"Arrest him on what grounds? For bearing a resemblance to a man seen climbing over a fence in Highgate a month ago? Do you realise how many men there must be in London with dark suits and tweed caps?"

"It's not just his clothing that has aroused my suspicion; it is the way he was behaving."

"Give the man a break," said Sir Edmund. "I think I would be quick to run myself if you began chasing me."

"He is acting suspiciously."

"And so are you," fumed Sir Edward. "Now please excuse me, my mussels are getting cold."

He sat down in his place again and tucked a serviette into his collar. Hugh Dowdeswell also sat down, staring at me in a manner which made my blood run cold.

I appealed to Cullen. "Please, Inspector, he looks just like the man who was seen on the night of Lizzie's murder. And when we attended her funeral in Kensal Green Cemetery we saw a man matching his description there and he ran away."

I could feel my conviction waning as Inspector Cullen fixed me with his narrow, steely eyes.

Perhaps I had been mistaken. Perhaps I was losing my mind.

"Where did you last see this man?"

"He got out of the lift on the second floor."

"So the lift operator must have seen him?"

"I don't remember seeing a lift operator."

"I would sit down yourself, Basil. I am grieved to say that your lemon sole won't keep its heat," said Sir Edmund. "The woman is clearly deluded. She's trouble. You need to speak to Sherman at the *Morning Express* about her."

"I already have," sighed Inspector Cullen.

A search of the Midland Grand Hotel yielded nothing. Maids, bell boys and porters were asked to search each floor and staircase, while the lift operator had been discovered talking to a maid in the laundry room instead of being on duty. He knew nothing of the man in the lift. Inspector Cullen was bad-tempered with me for ruining his lunch and wasting his time.

⚜

I took a train from King's Cross to Ludgate Hill Station and walked along foggy Fleet Street, feeling embarrassed and somewhat ashamed about the whole episode.

But I also felt angry. I was certain that Cullen could not understand the relevance of the man who had run away from me. If he had read James' case notes he would have realised that the man seen climbing over the fence of Highgate Cemetery around the time of Lizzie's death was a crucial witness.

What had the man been doing at the hotel, and why had he run away?

These were important questions; questions which couldn't be answered.

Perhaps the man had wanted to see someone in the restaurant: perhaps Sir Edmund, Hugh Dowdeswell or Inspector Cullen. Perhaps he had a keen interest in the case, which might explain why he had been hanging about in Kensal Green Cemetery.

Perhaps the young man had been hired by Sir Edmund or Hugh Dowdeswell to shoot Lizzie.

Wild theories occupied my mind and I couldn't begin to make sense of which were the most feasible, if any at all.

I felt the need to speak to James. He was the only person I could think of who might help me understand what was happening. As soon as I arrived at the *Morning Express* offices, I went to the telegraph room and sent a telegram to Scotland Yard asking him to meet me the following evening.

CHAPTER 37

My thoughts were so consumed with the chase around the hotel the previous day that I didn't listen properly to the newspaper boy as he cried out the morning headlines.

"Mr Joseph Taylor arrested for murder!"

I had already passed him before I realised the meaning of his words.

"What did you say?" I stopped and asked.

The boy had a grubby face and wore a faded necktie and a patched-up jacket fastened with string. He thrust a copy of *The Star* at me.

"Mr Joseph Taylor arrested for murder!"

"Lizzie Dixie's murder?" I asked.

He nodded at the paper in his out-thrust hand, so I gave him a ha'penny and took it.

I stopped to read:

Mr Joseph Taylor, the famous showman, has been arrested on suspicion of being involved in the murder of his wife, Lizzie Dixie (Mrs

Taylor). Mr Taylor was apprehended on Thursday at his home in Mile End, London...

I didn't stop to read any more.

This was a mistake.

Or a cover-up.

I rolled the newspaper under my arm and marched to the *Morning Express* offices to find out what Edgar knew about this latest development.

"I said it was him all along, didn't I?" Edgar had his feet on his desk and a pipe in his mouth.

"But it can't have been him! I visited Mr Taylor with Inspector Blakely and he told us that he was performing in the show that night."

"He may have been. But Lizzie was murdered at midnight, remember? The show had finished long before then."

I thought of how fondly Annie had spoken of her stepfather when I had visited her in the hospital. I didn't like Taylor, but I struggled to believe that he could be a murderer.

"He pulled the wool over the schoolboy inspector's eyes, that's for sure. Blakely should never have discounted him from the investigation."

"He didn't discount him, he was still gathering evidence. He was working steadfastly before Cullen removed him from the case."

"Working on it too slowly."

"So what information does Cullen have on Taylor?"

"A new witness has been found who says he saw Taylor near Highgate Cemetery on the night Lizzie died."

"That's all he has?"

"I'd say it was a good start, wouldn't you?"

"How does he know the witness is reliable? Someone could be making it up."

"Why would he do that?"

"He could have been asked to pretend that he saw Taylor in Highgate that night."

"A cover-up?"

"Yes, Lizzie had connections with Westminster. With powerful men."

"Lizzie was known for her *connections*." Edgar wiggled his eyebrows and grinned.

"Someone with power may have wanted her silenced and, to divert attention from what he did, he could have paid someone to say he witnessed Taylor close to the scene. That is probably all he had to do. And a close friendship with the detectives investigating the case also helps."

"You are implying that a politician murdered Lizzie, paid someone to frame Taylor and is currying favour with Scotland Yard to avoid any repercussions?"

"Yes."

Edgar laughed. "You should write fiction, Miss Green."

I felt my teeth clench. "This is not a laughing matter, Edgar."

"No, you're right. It is not." He removed his feet from the desk and sat up straight in his chair. "And your theory might have been a possibility if Taylor hadn't admitted to it."

"Admitted to what?"

"To being in Highgate the night that Lizzie died. That blows your cover-up idea out of the water, doesn't it?"

"Taylor says he was in Highgate when Lizzie died?" I felt as though I had been knocked sideways by Edgar's words.

"Yes! So the witness isn't even needed now. Taylor fully admits that he was there."

"But he doesn't admit to her murder?"

"No, but it is only a matter of time, isn't it? They'll get it out of him. He will be taken to Bow Street Magistrates' Court this morning. Cullen should have been on this case from the start, shouldn't he? Then we needn't have wasted so much time."

I couldn't muster the energy to argue with Edgar any further. I walked over to my desk and sat down.

Then a thought occurred to me.

"What about Annie?" I called over to Edgar. "Even if Taylor shot his wife, he would never do that to her daughter! And besides, he couldn't have done it. He was in the same performance as her at the time!"

Edgar shrugged. "Someone different. Inspector Lloyd is working on that case." He pulled the pencil out from behind his ear and began to work. "Busy day today. Heard about the murder in Wandsworth?" I shook my head. "The body of a man has been found under the floorboards in a house in Red Lion Street, next to the brewery. The husband and wife who live there are missing. I will need to get down there shortly."

I sat at my desk with my fists clenched, thinking about Taylor, the anonymous letters and the young man I had chased around the hotel.

It seemed that Lizzie's murder case was solved and Cullen would take all the credit. He had made the case seem so simple, but I believed there was far more to it. My problem was finding the evidence.

CHAPTER 38

J ames was waiting for me beneath a gas lamp outside the Museum Tavern that evening. The sight of him cheered me, as if I were meeting an old friend.

"I can't tell you how pleased I am to see you!" I said breathlessly as I hurried up to him. "So much has happened!"

"Taylor?" he said with a wry smile.

"Yes, and there's more."

"Goodness, let's sit somewhere warm then."

He pushed open the tavern's swing door for me and we stepped into the warmth and pipe smoke, just as we had on the evening we first met.

We sat with our drinks at a table close to the fireplace. James wore a grey suit and removed his jacket to reveal rolled-up shirt sleeves. There was something less boyish about him now. Perhaps he had always had the faint lines beside his eyes, but there was more definition around his cheekbones, as if he had lost some of the boyish plumpness in his cheeks.

He noticed me eyeing him as he folded his jacket and placed it on the bench next to him. I quickly occupied myself with my sherry, embarrassed that he had seen me looking.

"Has Cullen told you much?" I asked.

"Not a great deal." He took a gulp of his stout. "Taylor is rather obviously the big surprise. And I hear Colehill has returned."

"He visited me and was angry at me for losing the diaries."

"Is that so? How unreasonable. I hope you weren't too frightened by him." James looked concerned.

"Not really. He seemed understanding once I explained what had happened. I think he was more bothered about his wife discovering that he had been visiting Lizzie."

"It sounds as though he could be in a peck of troubles there."

"And had you guessed that he is Annie's father?"

"I hadn't, but to hear you say so does not surprise me now that we know he was Lizzie's visitor at her home. The relationship between them must have endured for a number of years."

"He says he will comply with the police."

"Very wise. He has quite a bit of tidying up to do now. I understand that Taylor has admitted to being in Highgate the night that Lizzie died. I was unable to extract that information from him, wasn't I?"

"You would have discovered it soon enough if you hadn't been taken off the case."

"I like to think I would have done. But who knows? Perhaps I wouldn't. Inspector Cullen is a good detective."

"And so are you."

"I have a lot to learn yet." He took another large gulp of his drink and I noticed only half of it remained when he placed his glass down on the table. I hoped he wasn't feeling inadequate because he hadn't uncovered the evidence against Taylor himself.

"You laid the groundwork for Cullen. He showed me the case file you left him. He didn't manage this all by himself."

"Perhaps not, and thank you for trying to make me feel better. The question is, do you think Taylor did it?"

"No, I do not." I told him about my visit to Annie and how she had spoken charitably of her stepfather.

"He could still be a murderer, even if Annie likes him," said James.

"But how do we explain Annie's shooting? I have always been convinced that the same person who shot Lizzie also shot Annie. Taylor would never have done such a thing."

"So if he didn't, then who did?"

"Perhaps Sir Edmund or Hugh Dowdeswell hired someone."

I told James about the young man I had chased around the Midland Grand Hotel and he listened intently. "It has to be the same man, doesn't it?" I said. "The one who was seen climbing into Highgate Cemetery and the one who was watching us in Kensal Green Cemetery."

"The description is certainly the same."

"I think this man could have been hired to kill Lizzie and Annie. Cullen doesn't seem to think this man is important, unless he already knows what happened and is helping Sir Edmund and Hugh cover something up."

"I cannot imagine Cullen being involved in a cover-up."

"But he is friends with Sir Edmund!"

"I will ask Inspector Lloyd if he has a description of the man who shot Annie yet. If it turns out to be similar to the man you chased, you might be on to something."

"If Westminster is behind this, it makes sense that Annie would be targeted because she might have known about Lizzie's work and clients. Perhaps they found out that Annie was meeting with her mother regularly. Perhaps the two women knew something they shouldn't have."

A story began to build in my head of what or who could be at work in all this.

Lizzie had been the paid companion of rich and powerful men. Perhaps her supposed drowning on the Princess Alice had been a reassurance to them that their secrets had died with her. To discover that she was still alive and meeting with her daughter could have been a grave cause for concern.

"I think the same person has to be behind Lizzie's murder and the attack on Annie. A revolver was used in both cases. Taylor couldn't have done it."

"Even if you are right, Taylor needs to provide an innocent explanation as to what he was doing in Highgate."

"He must have somehow discovered that Lizzie was still alive. I wonder if he found out that Sebastian was visiting her."

"Hopefully we will know more once Cullen has interviewed him further. However, if he did murder Lizzie he will be extremely cagey on many subjects as he won't want to incriminate himself."

"It could be the end for Astley's Amphitheatre! And poor Annie. She wouldn't have been expecting this at all. How awful for her. I must visit her again and find out how she is."

"You need to be careful."

"Now you have reminded me, I received another letter."

I took the letter out of my bag and handed it to James. He read the envelope and then the letter inside it.

"What do you think?" I asked.

"It is difficult to know whether this threat should be taken seriously or not. I wish I could identify the handwriting on the envelope from the first letter you received. Do you still have it?"

I nodded.

"It could be from Taylor, Colehill, Sir Edmund, Hugh Dowdeswell or someone else connected with them. Don't take it personally. They all have reputations to protect and they are rightly suspicious of hacks; even nice hacks like you."

I smiled at the vague compliment. "I don't know whether I should be worried."

"I could pass it to Cullen and ask him to look into it."

"No, that shouldn't be necessary. I can't see him making it a priority. He doesn't have a great deal of time for me."

James handed the letter back to me. "I'll see if I can get hold of handwriting samples from each of the men. Sir Edmund and Hugh Dowdeswell should be quite straightforward as politicians write many letters."

"You are busy enough as it is, James. Don't worry yourself about this."

"I should like to work on it; I like a challenge."

"Cullen seems determined to pin this on Taylor. Do we know if he has considered Sebastian at all?"

"I think he should, but Taylor's admission seems to rule anyone else out."

"Even if Sebastian shot Lizzie, he wouldn't harm Annie, would he?"

"I know it sounds improbable to you, but these things do happen. Fathers sometimes lose their minds and murder their families. It is difficult to understand why some men do such things, but it is not unheard of."

"Perhaps he grew frightened about people finding out about the affair."

"That is a possibility."

"And among all this, there is the young man at the hotel. He has to be involved, but I cannot work out how. If only we were able to find out who he is and speak to him."

James sipped his drink thoughtfully. "It's a thorny situation, isn't it? And with Cullen in charge we have our hands tied. I'm not even supposed to be working on this."

"I'm sorry, I shouldn't have asked you to meet me here. You have other work to concern yourself with now."

"Don't apologise, Penny. Having worked on the case, I remain extremely interested in its every turn."

"Have you found much time for your grandfather's garden recently?"

"A little; however, there isn't much to do now. There are a few leeks still in the ground, but I think chess playing season is upon us."

"Don't forget you were going to teach me how to play."

"I haven't forgotten." He grinned and finished off his stout.

"Would you like another drink?" I asked.

"I would be delighted to, but I must go." He checked his pocket watch. "The future Mrs Blakely is paying me a visit this evening and I am already late." He stood up and put on his jacket.

I felt a little stunned by his words.

"The future Mrs Blakely?" I asked, my throat tightening. "I haven't heard you mention her before."

"Have I not? Well, she won't be pleased if I am late."

I picked up my sherry glass but noticed that it was already empty. I told myself there was no reason why there shouldn't be a future Mrs Blakely. James was the right age for marriage and perhaps I should have been more surprised that he wasn't married already. But even as I told myself this, I felt disappointed at discovering her existence.

I stared at the woodgrain in the polished table and wondered what the future Mrs Blakely looked like. She probably had a pretty nose and a well-turned ankle.

"It's dark and cold out there," said James. "Would you like me to hail you a cab? I probably have enough time."

I tried to ignore the despondency that had descended over me and made an effort to speak cheerfully. "Thank you, James, there is no need. I have decided to stay and drink another sherry."

CHAPTER 39

"It is surely one of the most beautiful buildings in London." I stared up at the facade of the British Museum's new Natural History department. I had passed through South Kensington many times and seen this building under construction but had never stood so close to the finished article before.

"It is a wonder, isn't it?" said Eliza. "I feel proud that Father's collection will be on display here."

"So do I."

The sun glinted on the grey granite and cream stone brickwork. We walked up the steps to the main entrance, which had an archway elaborate enough to rival that of Westminster Abbey. Two Romanesque-style towers rose up either side of the main entrance. Glancing further along the building, I could see hundreds of stone-arched windows decorated with sculptures of plants and animals.

Eliza dragged her bicycle up the steps to the entrance and it made such a clattering sound that I worried a wheel or lever was about to fall off. A doorman kindly offered to look after it to save her the trouble of taking it into the museum itself.

The main hall was just as breathtaking as the exterior, with terracotta brickwork and rows of stone arches leading to a grand staircase at the far end. There were glass windows in the ceiling, supported high above our heads by broad iron arches.

"This way," said Eliza, leading me towards the staircase.

Father's collection was in a small, newly opened gallery on the first floor. There was space here to show more of his work and there were some colourful watercolours of bromeliads alongside his beloved orchids. A small piece of card labelled 'Frederick Brinsley Green' gave an overview of Father's works. I felt a lump in my throat when I read the last sentence:

F. B. Green and his guide vanished in the Amazonian jungle in 1875.

"Doesn't his work look wonderful here?" I said brightly, trying to force a smile. I looked at Eliza and saw tears in her eyes. I embraced her and we remained that way for some time.

"Terrible news about Joseph Taylor," said Eliza as we walked back down the main staircase. "I hear the shows at Astley's Amphitheatre are postponed."

"They are."

"And all that dreadful business of his daughter being shot."

I didn't correct Eliza. Most people assumed that Annie was Taylor's daughter.

"And now he has been arrested for murdering his wife! She must have been hiding from him; she must have falsified her death to escape him. But he tracked her down and killed her, and then tried to kill their daughter!"

"Nothing is proven until he has had his trial."

"Of course not, but it looks rather likely, doesn't it?"

"I am not so sure."

"Who else could have done it?"

"Lizzie knew a lot of people."

"A lot of men, you mean? There were always such rumours, weren't there? Do you think it could be someone she had an affair with?"

"It is not unlikely. It must be someone who knew she was still alive. I wish I could find out who. I feel I owe it to Lizzie. She funded the expedition to find Father which discovered more of his drawings."

"It would have been preferable for him to come back in person."

"Of course it would. And if there were ever another expedition to find Father then at least the hut where his drawings were found would be a good place to begin looking again. The hut would never have been discovered without Lizzie's help. That is why I want justice for her so badly."

"Perhaps when Taylor's trial is underway you will feel satisfied that justice is being served."

"I may, although I cannot deny the nagging sensation I have that he is not the murderer."

The afternoon sky had clouded over, casting a grey gloom through the windows of the reading room. The electric lights flickered on and off, much to the consternation of my fellow readers, and my eyelids felt heavy as I leafed through *The Short History of Ireland*.

The two men named as suspects in the underground railway explosions, McCafferty and O'Riordan, had been cleared in connection with the bombings. There was little more to report on, other than some experimental explosions which were being carried out in Woolwich to ascertain how much explosive material the bombers had used.

"Penny?"

James had walked up to my desk without me noticing.

"What are you doing here?" I whispered. "Did you enjoy your evening?"

"Enjoy it?" He looked at me quizzically.

"With the future Mrs Blakely?"

"Oh that. Yes, thank you. Take a look at this." He spoke as quietly as possible and placed a letter addressed to Inspector Cullen on my desk.

"What is it?"

"A letter from Sir Edmund to Cullen. Do you recognise the handwriting?"

"No."

"Good. Then the anonymous letters you have received are not from Sir Edmund."

"Is that all you came here to tell me?"

James appeared affronted by my blunt reply and picked up the letter again.

"Thankfully, it isn't," he said, tucking the letter into his inside pocket. "I came here to tell you that Cullen has asked me to write a report to the magistrates outlining the evidence against Taylor. I have been given three days to complete it."

"But you're not even convinced that Taylor is the murderer."

"No, I'm not."

"This whole affair is a mess!" I threw down my pen in

annoyance, causing the ink to splatter across my page. "The wrong man has been arrested and now you have to convince the magistrates that he should stand trial when you don't even believe he murdered Lizzie!"

"Madam, you are disturbing my work," said a man with bushy red whiskers who was seated next to me.

"I do apologise."

"We can't talk here any longer," whispered James. "But let me reassure you that I am actually bringing you good news. Inspector Cullen has put me in charge of the case again while he works on the Wandsworth murder. May I be permitted to visit you this evening? There are further developments."

"Of course." I felt my heart skip. "That is wonderful news, James."

I felt myself smiling as he departed.

CHAPTER 40

I hurriedly tidied my room that evening in anticipation of James' visit. I dusted the shelves, swept the floor and gathered the papers on my writing desk into a neat pile. The paraffin lamp emitted a rather gloomy light, so I lit some candles and placed them around the room to make it look as cheery as possible. Then I positioned my chair so that it was angled at a comfortable distance from the end of my bed. I could sit on the bed and James could sit on the chair.

I took my place on the bed and waited. As Tiger walked across my lap, I wondered what James would make of my lowly lodgings.

Was I destined to live in this room for the rest of my days?

My thoughts were interrupted by a rap at the door and I opened it to find Mrs Garnett standing there with James. He greeted me with a broad smile.

"It is the detective again," she said. "Has someone else been shot?"

"Not that I know of," I replied. "Do come in, James."

"You will keep your door open while he visits, won't you?" asked Mrs Garnett, one eyebrow raised in suspicion. "He may be a detective, but I don't usually permit gentleman callers at this hour. He must leave by eight o'clock."

"Absolutely," I replied.

"Please don't worry yourself, Mrs Garnett," said James. "I am here on police business and this will not take long."

As he stepped into the room, Mrs Garnett sucked her lip disapprovingly and left.

"Can I offer you a drink of something?" I asked. "Coffee? Cocoa? Sherry?"

"Sherry would be wonderful, thank you."

I gestured to the seat by my writing desk. James took off his hat and placed it on my desk, hanging his coat over the back of the chair. I reached under my bed for the bottle of sherry and saw Tiger hiding under there, her eyes flashing at me.

With a horrible lurch in my stomach, I realised I had no glasses with which to drink the sherry. I walked over to my stove and took down the two tin cups from their hooks on the wall. I poured out the sherry and handed James' drink to him apologetically. He thanked me and made no mention of the tin cup.

I sat on the bed and took a gulp of sherry, feeling awkward that James was in my room. I was pleased to see him, but welcoming him here felt as though I was allowing him access to a private part of my life. My lodgings told him more about who I was, and I wasn't sure I felt comfortable about that. Most of all, I was worried what he would think of me.

"I cannot tell you how pleased I am that you're back on the case, James."

"I am also very happy about it." He leant forward with an elbow on each knee and his cup of sherry cradled in his hands. "But I have to work quickly now. I was too slow before and time is not on my side. Cullen wants me to have the report written for the magistrates, but before I do that I need to rule out the other possible suspects."

"Who do you think they are?"

"I think there are two other people who might have harmed Lizzie. The first is someone at Westminster. It may not be Sir Edmund or Hugh Dowdeswell, but they are the best starting point we have. The other is Sebastian. I propose to rule Sebastian out first, as that will be a little simpler than the Westminster connection."

"And how do you propose to do that?"

"By finding an alibi for him. The most obvious person is his wife."

"That makes sense."

"Once I have done that, I will need to tackle Sir Edmund and Hugh Dowdeswell."

"Oh dear." I had a sinking feeling in my chest. "I fear this will not be quick. While you are investigating the politicians, Cullen will be pressuring you for the report on Taylor."

"I know, it will not be easy. But I have promising news from Inspector Lloyd. So far, the description he has of the man who fired the shots at Annie in the amphitheatre is that he wore a tweed cap and had a pale moustache."

I felt a buzz of excitement. "So it could be the same man that was seen at Highgate the night that Lizzie died? And the one I saw at the cemetery and in the hotel?"

"The description is similar, so we can be hopeful that there is a connection. I feel rather frustrated that we have been unable to find that man so far. He has been crucial to our investigation ever since the beginning. I will issue another request for information via the press. Your colleague, Edgar, can write a useful paragraph again for me, I am sure."

"If only I had caught up with him at the hotel!"

"You did your best. Don't worry, I have a feeling that he is never too far away. I think he is watching our every move. Hello! What a pretty cat."

I felt Tiger rub against my skirts. I leant down and stroked her. "She must like you," I said. "She doesn't usually come out from under the bed when visitors are here."

James drained his cup and placed it on my desk.

"More sherry?" I asked.

"Thank you. Firstly, let me tell you a most interesting thing I discovered this morning."

James reached into the pocket of his jacket and brought out an envelope. "I spoke with Taylor first thing. He was frank about being in Highgate the night that Lizzie died, but he says he didn't go into the cemetery because the gates were locked. He may have been a fit man in his youth, but he would struggle to clamber over the fence as the young man managed to."

"So what was he doing there?"

"He was sent something."

James pulled a square of red silk from the envelope. "Someone posted this to his home." He held the square of silk in one hand and unfolded it with the other. I leaned forward to take a closer look.

Inside the piece of silk was a gold locket, and it struck me that it was quite an expensive one because the small bird it displayed was moulded in gold, with jewels on its wings and tail. It was sitting on a branch, which was also carefully crafted in gold, and next to it was a delicate little nest with three small pearls for eggs.

"Someone posted this to Taylor?"

James nodded and moved his hand towards me. "Open it."

Carefully, I picked up the locket and fitted the nail of my thumb into the clasp at its side. The little case opened and inside were two small, oval-shaped photographs. The picture on the left was of Lizzie, with her dark hair brushed over one shoulder and flowers pinned above her right ear. It was Lizzie as I remembered her, so it was likely to have been taken before the sinking of the *Princess Alice*.

On the right-hand side of the locket was a photograph of Sebastian, looking about ten years younger than he was now. He wore a high collar and was scowling slightly at the camera.

"Where did this come from? Did it once belong to Lizzie?"

"Either to her or Sebastian, I imagine."

"So one of them sent this to Taylor? What was the writing on the envelope like? I might be able to recognise Lizzie's writing."

James handed me the envelope and I was aware that he was watching my face, as if he were trying to read my reaction.

The handwriting was in black ink and crudely executed, as if a child wrote it.

I leapt up from my bed and dashed over to my writing desk, where I had stashed the two anonymous letters in a little drawer. I pulled them out and compared them with the envelope which had contained the locket.

"They're all written in the same ink!" I exclaimed. "And the handwriting has been disguised on two of them, but whoever sent them forgot to disguise it on the first envelope. The same person sent all three!" I waved them excitedly. "The postmark is also the same!"

"There is something else in the envelope which contained the locket," said James.

I looked inside and found a small piece of folded paper. I opened it and saw the same childish writing again.

"Highgate Cemetery, midnight tomorrow," I read.

I staggered backwards and slumped down onto my bed. "This was posted the day before Lizzie was murdered," I said. "Do you think it was sent by the man who murdered her?"

"It is possible. I would say with certainty that it came from someone who knew about the plan to murder Lizzie. This person wished to frame Taylor. He wanted Taylor to be near the cemetery at the time Lizzie died."

"Why didn't Taylor tell us about this before now?"

"Because he believes he would have been arrested for her murder. Now that he has been arrested, he feels he has nothing to lose by showing it to us. He claims it is proof that he didn't murder Lizzie; that he was invited there and simply went to find out why someone had sent it to him."

"Did he say what he thought about seeing Sebastian and Lizzie's photographs together in the locket?"

"He says it wasn't a surprise, and that he knew their relationship had never really ended. It was the cause of many arguments, but he admits that he kept mistresses throughout their marriage. Perhaps that's what drove Lizzie back to Sebastian. By the time Lizzie was supposedly drowned on the *Princess Alice*, her marriage to Taylor had long since deteriorated."

"Annie told me that Lizzie wished to leave him."

James nodded. "I've followed up on the rest of Taylor's story and I think he is telling the truth. Having been unable to make his way inside the cemetery, he left and stayed at the Dalrymple Hotel nearby. I spoke to the owner of that hotel earlier today, who confirmed Taylor's story. The following morning, Taylor returned home and I visited him shortly after that to tell him of Lizzie's death."

"I cannot believe Cullen failed to uncover any of this."

"He would have done, I am sure."

"Did Taylor hear the gunshots?"

"He says that he did not. He says that he would already have been at the hotel by that time."

"Did Sebastian send him the locket?"

"I don't know. But we do know that it was someone who knew about Lizzie and Sebastian's relationship and, most crucially, they knew that something was to happen that night at Highgate Cemetery."

"It is eight o'clock!" Mrs Garnett called up the stairway.

"I am sorry you didn't have time to have another sherry," I said to James as I gave him back the locket, letter and envelope. "Here, take the other letters too. They are part of your investigation now."

I shuddered as I pondered why the same person had written to, and threatened me, in this way.

He stood up and put on his coat. "You have met Mrs Colehill before?"

I nodded.

"Would you like to visit her with me tomorrow morning? She may be less alarmed by my line of questioning if you are with me. We need to find out whether she can provide an alibi for Sebastian on the night Lizzie died."

"Poor Mary, she will be upset about Sebastian's affair with Lizzie."

"She must be. At least if we can rule him out of any involvement in the murder, she and her husband can be left in peace to reconcile their differences."

"I am not sure that I am looking forward to it, but I will accompany you when you speak to Mary."

"Until then."

James put on his hat and bid me goodnight.

CHAPTER 41

Thick fog cloaked Cadogan Square the following morning, and the bare-branched trees loomed like spectres. I couldn't see the Colehills' home until I was almost upon it. James was waiting for me by the steps.

"The locket," I whispered. "You're not going to mention it to Mary Colehill, are you? I am certain that it will upset her terribly."

"No, I won't mention it. All I wish to ask is whether she can account for Sebastian's movements on the night that Lizzie died."

The maid told us that Mrs Colehill was at home and showed us into the drawing room. I warmed myself by the lively fire while James inspected the family photographs arranged on top of the harpsichord.

Mary Colehill entered the room wearing an attractive, brown-coloured ticking day dress. Her waist was tightly laced and a brown and cream ribbon was tied in her hair.

She smiled at me, but I saw a look of concern in her large blue eyes as she glanced at James.

"Good morning, Mrs Colehill, I am sorry to trouble you. My name is Inspector James Blakely and I believe you already know Miss Green?"

Mary nodded and smiled again.

"Miss Green has been working with me in relation to the sad case of Lizzie Dixie, and she is accompanying me this morning as her familiarity to you will hopefully put you at ease."

"Of course, Inspector, I understand. Miss Green has been a guest at our home before and I know her sister well. Do please take a seat and I will ask the maid to bring you some refreshments."

"There is no need to go to the trouble, Mrs Colehill. Our visit this morning will be a brief one."

"Very well then." Mary took a seat on the settee and smoothed her skirts while James and I both sat on chairs facing her.

"Mrs Colehill, you are aware, I am sure, of the terrible murder of Lizzie Dixie."

"Yes." The smile left her face. "A police inspector visited Sebastian recently to discuss it with him. And I hear that her daughter was also shot! Is she expected to make a recovery?"

"Thankfully, Annie has recovered well and will be returning home from hospital tomorrow."

"That is good news!" I said.

"Indeed it is," said Mary.

"Mrs Colehill," continued James, "you may have heard that an arrest has been made in connection with this awful murder, and I am at the stage where I am ruling out the involvement of anyone else who might have known Lizzie. I would therefore like to ask you just one question, Mrs Colehill, if you are happy for me to do so?"

"Of course."

"It concerns your husband, Mr Colehill."

Mary nodded.

"And in asking this question, I am by no means suggesting that your husband had any involvement with Lizzie Dixie's death. Is that clear to you, Mrs Colehill?"

She nodded again and pursed her lips together anxiously as James took a notebook and pencil out of his pocket.

"I wonder if you could tell me where your husband was on the night of the twentieth of October?"

"I gave this some thought when the last police inspector visited, and Sebastian and I have established that he was here, just as he is most evenings. He was at the theatre first, of course, but after the performance he came home, as he does every night. Would you like me to fetch my diary to show you?"

"There is no need, Mrs Colehill, thank you. What time does Mr Colehill usually arrive home after an evening's performance?"

"About eleven o'clock."

"And has he stayed out any later than that recently?"

"No, although he occasionally stays overnight somewhere."

"So you are satisfied that the night of the twentieth of October was the same as any other? Your husband returned home about eleven o'clock and did not go out again after that time?"

"That is correct. Would you like to confirm it with the butler? He always locks up the house once Sebastian is home."

"Thank you, Mrs Colehill, but your word is enough. You have been extremely helpful."

James closed his notebook and placed it back in his pocket along with the pencil.

"That is all you need from me?"

"That is all, Mrs Colehill. Thank you."

We all got up from our seats.

"Sebastian could not have had anything to do with this sorry business," said Mary. "I understand that you have enquiries to make, but he wouldn't squash a fly, I can assure you. If he ever discovered that he had been considered a suspect, the news would destroy him..."

"Please be assured that he is not a suspect, Mrs Colehill."

"Thank you." She smiled, but then her face fell and she pulled a handkerchief from her sleeve to wipe a tear from her cheek. "Please excuse me being rather upset. You will be aware that I have learnt of an indiscretion of my husband's. It has caused me enormous sadness."

"We understand, Mrs Colehill, and we will not trouble you any further," James replied. "My very best regards to you and your family."

"Sebastian has his alibi confirmed," said James as we walked down the steps of the Colehills' home. "Now let's see what he has to say about the locket."

"Would you like me to accompany you?"

"Have you no deadline for today?"

"It's not due until tomorrow."

"Good, then let's go directly to Drury Lane."

CHAPTER 42

Once again, I found myself waiting in a red velvet seat in the auditorium. The gas lamps flickered dim and low, and the air felt close.

"I remember seeing Lizzie on this very stage in *Lady Audley's Secret*," I said in an attempt to hide my nerves. "She played Alicia and that was the night Gladstone came here."

A thud came from the back of the auditorium, as if something had fallen. Startled, I turned around in my seat but was unable to see much in the gloom.

"Did you hear that?" I whispered to James, although I wasn't sure why I was whispering.

"Yes, I did," he said in a low voice. "This theatre is rumoured to be haunted, isn't it?"

"I think all theatres are supposed to be haunted. But where do you think that noise came from?" I looked around again, and felt a prickling sensation at the back of my neck.

"A ghost?"

"Don't say that!"

"You don't believe in ghosts, do you?"

"Of course I don't!" But the sensation at the back of my neck remained.

The door at the side of the stage opened and Sebastian strode out, just as he had during my previous visit. He made his way up the steps by the side of the seating and stopped when he reached the row in front of us.

"Good morning, Inspector Blakely."

"Good morning, Mr Colehill."

James stood and offered his hand. Sebastian leant forward and shook it, then took a seat in the row in front of us.

"Miss Green," he said with little warmth as he sat down.

"Hello Sebastian."

"What can I do for you, Inspector?" Sebastian crossed his long legs and sat sidelong in his seat, so that James had to address his profile.

James removed something from his inside pocket. "Can I ask if you recognise this, Mr Colehill?" He leant over the seat in front of him and handed Sebastian the locket.

I held my breath.

Sebastian's brow furrowed as he took the locket from James. "I haven't seen this in a long while." He held it up by its chain and inspected it. "Are the pictures still inside it?"

"You do recognise it?"

"Yes. How did you come by it?"

"Firstly, can you tell me who it belongs to, Mr Colehill?"

"It was Lizzie's."

"And when did you last see it?"

"I don't remember. A long time ago."

"Can you be more exact, Mr Colehill? Was it before or after she was presumed drowned on the *Princess Alice?*"

"Tell me where you found it first." There was a sharp tone to Sebastian's voice.

"It was posted to Mr Taylor the day before Lizzie was murdered."

Sebastian's eyes opened wide in surprise, but I couldn't tell whether his reaction was genuine or false.

"And who posted it?"

"That is what I am trying to ascertain, Mr Colehill. Now you see why it is so important that you tell me when you last saw this locket."

"It wasn't me who posted it, that's for sure!"

"I am not suggesting that it was, Mr Colehill. If the locket was in Lizzie's possession, perhaps she posted it?"

"Why would she do that?"

"I have no idea."

"It is a long time since I last saw this locket."

"After the sinking of the *Princess Alice*?"

"I don't remember. I'm certain that I gave it to her a long time before then. And then I remember that we had an argument about something. It was nothing important, just a misunderstanding. And that was when she returned it to me."

"So the locket was in your possession?"

"For a while, yes, but I must have put it somewhere. And perhaps I gave it back to Lizzie again, I don't remember."

James held out his hand for the locket.

"Do you want it back?"

"For the time being. It is being kept as evidence at the moment. The locket was accompanied by a short note."

"What did it say?"

"It instructed Taylor to visit Highgate Cemetery at midnight the following evening."

"Really?"

"Which was the day and time when Lizzie was shot."

Sebastian's face paled and he turned away. "So it was planned."

"What was?"

Sebastian turned back to face him. "Lizzie's murder was planned."

"We have known that for some time, Mr Colehill."

James was still holding out his hand, and Sebastian gently lowered the locket into his palm.

"Who would do this?" said Sebastian, slowly shaking his head.

"That is what I am trying to discover, Mr Colehill," said James, putting the locket back in his pocket.

"But I thought it was Taylor. I suppose it still is, isn't it? Someone sent him the locket and the note, so he went to the cemetery, saw Lizzie there and shot her."

"It is possible, although Taylor says he didn't go into the cemetery that night because the gates were locked. A young man was seen climbing over the fence of the cemetery shortly before Lizzie was shot. Did Lizzie know someone who might fit that description? Perhaps he visited her at her home in Highgate or she mentioned him to you?"

"No, never. She didn't see anyone. I allowed her to meet Annie once a month, but that was all. She was supposed to be dead and that was why she kept herself hidden away. Perhaps Taylor paid him to do it."

"Who?"

"The man you mention. Perhaps Taylor paid him to shoot Lizzie."

"We cannot rule that out, and we will continue to speak to Taylor about that night."

"Good, good."

Sebastian turned his attention to me. "How much of this conversation will appear in the newspaper, Miss Green?"

"None of it," I replied. "As you know, Taylor has been arrested and it would be untoward to publish anything further at this time."

"Taylor has been arrested and you would think he hadn't by the way you are chasing me over this. I had nothing to do with it! If those blasted diaries hadn't been lost, you would have known the truth by now. Would you like to hear exactly what happened?"

CHAPTER 43

"Once I have explained this, I expect you to remove me from your enquiries, do you hear?" said Sebastian. "You have full assurance of my honesty now. Please don't ignore what I say and maintain some foolish notion that I killed the woman I loved!"

James and I remained silent. Sebastian removed his handkerchief from his pocket and dabbed at the back of his neck.

"Lizzie hid because she was desperate. She had spent a lifetime working to get to where she was, and once she got there she realised it wasn't what she wanted at all. Her husband treated her deplorably, her career was fading and younger actresses were being offered the best parts. Most frustratingly for her, she had realised that she would never have what she really wanted."

"Which was what?"

"Me, of course!" Sebastian laughed. "I met her first when she was nineteen years old, and a fetching young thing she was too. She was my secret for a while. Perhaps we should have married, but you knew what sort of girl she was. She had already found herself in trouble with Mr Burrell. I did the

Burrell family a favour by taking her under my wing. And just as I was there for her in the beginning, so I was there for her at the end. When it all became too much, I took her under my wing a second time. I placed her in that house and she became my secret once again."

"But after the sinking of the *Princess Alice*... how did you know that she was still alive?" I asked.

"It was mayhem down there at Woolwich, an absolute tragedy. I had been due to meet her off the boat at Swan Pier by London Bridge, but when I got wind of the sinking I had my carriage take me down to North Woolwich Pier. Have you ever watched six hundred souls drown? It is not a pretty sight. Of course, I feared the worse as I fought my way through the crowds to the water's edge. I helped drag people out of the river and saw some of them die right in front of me. The screams. The panic. And the speed of it all! The boat was already fully under the water by the time I got there. Lizzie had managed to get into one of the *Bywell Castle*'s lifeboats. I found her wandering among the crowd, shivering and bewildered. I don't think she fully realised what had happened. I knew she had been on the boat with one of the men who paid her for companionship, but he was already dead by then. He had helped her onto the rescue boat. You knew she was a whore, didn't you?"

I winced at his use of the word and said nothing.

"Yes, she was a whore all right." Sebastian became more animated as he relaxed into the flow of his words. "Taylor turned a blind eye because her clients paid a lot of money. I told her she would have to stop all that once she was mine — that there was to be no one else — and I think she was happy to leave that life behind. I have always felt it was providence that I should have found her in that crowd. It was one of those moments when I knew that she wanted to come to me. And she could finally have me, so long as she did what I said.

She didn't want to be in the limelight any more, but she was too well-known to do anything else. Even if she had retired, she would never have left it. The only way to leave was to die. I explained that to her. I told her she could still see Annie if she made her swear to secrecy, and it worked. They even pulled someone out of the water who they believed to be her! It was such luck!"

He laughed again.

"It worked perfectly for five years. I told her what her funeral was like and she was amused to hear me describe Taylor's tears. She cared nothing for him, of course. I was the only man she ever loved, and I was the only one who could control her. She needed it, of course. She couldn't exactly control herself, could she?"

I felt a bitter taste in my mouth. I didn't like the way he spoke about Lizzie. She had loved him and he had clearly enjoyed the power he had over her.

"I saw her the day she died. She wasn't in her best mood. And now I shall continue to be honest with you, just so you understand that every word I tell you is the truth. Lizzie was not an easy woman to get along with. We argued often and we argued on that day. *Ah ha!* I hear you cry. *What a perfect motive for murder!* But no, I could never sink to such depths, tempting though it was at times. I loved her deeply. She drove me half mad most of the time, but when I found out she was really gone..."

Sebastian trailed off. He turned his head away and looked at the scarlet curtains, which had been pulled across the stage.

"It was as if my world had fallen apart," he said quietly. "I was plunged into a grief I could never admit to or show. I had to return to my wife and family each day, pretending that nothing had happened!"

He turned to face us again. "Can you imagine what that

was like? And when I found out she had been killed, I realised that someone else, someone other than Annie, had known that she was still alive. I have wracked my brains over and over, but I cannot decipher who that person could be!"

There was a long pause before James spoke.

"Are you certain that Lizzie had nothing to do with anyone else while she was in hiding?" he asked.

"Absolutely certain."

"There were two politicians at her funeral whom she had known well in the past. Could she have seen them at all?"

Sebastian shook his head.

"Could they have somehow found out she was still alive?"

"Perhaps there is a chance they might have, I can't rule it out. But I can't understand how they would have done so. And even if they did, why would anyone kill her? And for my daughter to be attacked too... Frankly, it's an outrage that no one has been arrested for the attack on Annie!"

Strange sobs emanated from Sebastian's throat, and I was reminded of the evening that he had cried in his conservatory. He made me feel uncomfortable.

But while it is entirely possible that I was easily fooled, I believed every word he had just told us.

CHAPTER 44

We walked past the Gaiety Theatre and down to The Strand, from which point James could take an omnibus to Westminster and I could walk to the *Morning Express* offices. The fog had a brown tinge to it and flakes of soot floated through the air, landing on the lenses of my spectacles.

"What do you make of Sebastian's story?" I asked.

"I think Mr Colehill spoke with a reasonable portion of honesty. There could be many events which he left out of his account, of course."

"He couldn't have killed Lizzie, could he? His wife has provided an alibi and he has been honest with us about his relationship with Lizzie. And he would never harm Annie. I can't say I am fond of the man, but I regret having suspected him."

"Without doubt, he has been up to some fishy business, but that doesn't mean he is the murderer. We have no evidence against him, so my focus must now shift to Westminster and to Sir Edmund and Hugh Dowdeswell. That will no doubt be a hard nut to crack."

"I think someone at Westminster hired the young man in the tweed cap."

"I will ask for the politicians' help in finding him."

"Do you think they will help? Cullen may have offered to shield them from the rest of the investigation."

"There is only one way to find out, and that is to talk to them."

We paused by the tavern at the corner of the street.

"Good luck, James."

"Thank you. I will need quite a bit of luck."

"Please let me know what happens and if I can help in any way. I know that time is against you now."

"Yes, it is. I will do my best to get to the bottom of this. Cullen wants the report on Taylor by tomorrow evening."

I sat at the typewriter in the *Morning Express* offices and typed a paragraph about a man named Augustus Smith, who had claimed responsibility for the underground railway explosions but had later been certified by a doctor as suffering from delirium tremens and admitted to the Woolwich Union Infirmary.

I was making good progress with my typewriting and could manage to type a reasonable number of words each minute. Once I had finished, I wound the paper off the roller and read my paragraph. There were only a few mistakes and I felt quite pleased with it.

"That looks marvellous," came a voice from over my shoulder.

"Hello Edgar," I replied, without turning to look at him.

"It looks as though it is already published when it's type-written like that."

"If you ignore the mistakes."

"Are there mistakes?" He leant over my shoulder to squint at the paper and I held my breath to avoid the stale mixture of beer and tobacco.

"Oh yes, I see them now. Quite a few mistakes, in fact."

I rolled the paper up so he could look no longer at it.

"What can I do for you, Edgar?"

"You can typewrite my articles, if you like."

"No thank you."

"I was only joking! There is no need to give me a stare like Medusa. Has the schoolboy inspector written his report for the magistrates yet?"

"He is working on it at this very moment."

I thought about James and wondered whether Sir Edmund and Hugh Dowdeswell would speak to him. I struggled to see how he would be able to link Lizzie's murder to anyone at Westminster in the short time he had left.

"Cullen's already made an arrest in the Wandsworth murder case. There is no stopping him, is there?"

"It seems not."

"Miss Green!" Mr Sherman marched into the news room, leaving the door to slam shut behind him. "There is room for a column on the West London Women's Society in Saturday's edition."

"An entire column? That's wonderful news. Thank you, Mr Sherman!"

"It seems that the wife of our fine proprietor, Mr Conway, recently attended the annual meeting of the National Society for Women's Suffrage and happens to have a good friend in the American Women's Suffrage Association. She appears to have convinced Mr Conway that women's rights are an increasingly important topic of news."

"Mrs Conway sounds like a well-informed lady."

"The deadline is tomorrow."

Eliza arrived at my lodgings shortly after breakfast the following morning. I had sent her a telegram informing her of the good news about the article and she was to help me write it. Before long the floor of my room was strewn with pages of notes from the West London Women's Society's meetings and discussions.

"How many words did you say a column should be?" asked Eliza.

"A thousand."

"That is a lot of words! So we could cover suffrage, rational dress and employment."

"That sounds sensible."

"Good, I'm so glad you agree. This is such wonderful news, Penelope!" Eliza clapped her hands together with glee. "This could be the start of something wonderful, don't you think?"

"I do. We don't have a lot of time, though. Shall we begin with suffrage?"

"Of course. I shall gather up the notes."

Eliza stepped over to a pile of papers near the door, picked it up and brought it over to me.

"Suffrage is something we have discussed at a number of our meetings, and we have all taken turns to write notes. I have collated them together here." She leafed through the papers. "The difficulty is deciding where to start."

I sighed, realising that the article would not be written quickly. I could feel the deadline looming and was desperate to find out how James was getting on with his Westminster investigations.

Would he stumble across some new evidence, or would he be forced to make Taylor stand trial?

"I found out who Mrs Lennox's husband is."

"What was that?" I asked, distracted by a piece of paper which had caught my eye.

"Mrs Lennox who was at the society meeting. Do you remember? You asked me to find out who her husband was. He's a physician. What are you looking at?"

"Who wrote this, Ellie?" I asked, pointing to a sheet of sloping handwriting in black ink. There was something familiar about it.

"I don't know," replied Eliza. "One of us in the society."

She leafed through the pages, covering up the one I had been interested in. I grabbed it before it became lost in the pile of paper.

"What are you doing?"

"I need to find out who wrote this; I recognise the handwriting."

I couldn't think where I had seen it before.

"Give it here," said Eliza, taking the piece of paper and examining it. "This was the meeting we held on the fifth of October. Let me see... I think it was Mary Colehill."

I felt sure that my heart had stopped beating for a moment.

"Mary Colehill? You are certain of that?"

Now I remembered where I had seen the handwriting. It matched the writing on the envelope of the first anonymous letter I had received.

If Mary had written that letter, she had also written the second letter and sent the locket to Taylor.

"I need that piece of paper," I said.

"What is the matter, Penelope? You have strange blotches on your cheeks."

"I need to check it against something."

Perhaps I was mistaken, but I would find out for sure once I had checked the handwriting against the letters James had in his possession.

Eliza slowly handed me back the piece of paper, staring at me with a concerned look on her face. I took it from her and got up to fetch my handbag and coat. "Don't worry, I will bring this back to you. I just need to take it to Scotland Yard."

"Scotland Yard, Penelope? *Now? What on earth?*"

"I will return as quickly as possible. While I am gone, perhaps you can make a start on the article and show me what you have written when I get back. I'm so sorry, Ellie, but something quite unexpected has turned up."

"So I gather," replied my sister as I dashed from the room.

CHAPTER 45

The train journey from Moorgate to Westminster Bridge station seemed to take an eternity. I sat in second-class, reading and rereading the page of notes Mary Colehill had written.

Could I be sure that it was the same handwriting as the address on the envelope of the first letter I had received? Or was I simply clutching at straws?

James had to finish his report on Taylor by the end of the day. If I had new evidence, we needed to work as quickly as possible.

Sebastian hadn't been truthful with us the previous day. He must have made his wife write the letters so that no one could link them to him. He had told her to threaten me. Mary was far too mild-mannered to write the letters of her own accord.

A few sentences from her notes on suffrage remained in my head:

Women should no longer be considered nonentities. It is time to strike off the shackles and allow their voices to be heard. It is time to fight against the injustice which has been endured for so long.

As I turned these words over in my mind, it occurred to me that they might not apply only to women's suffrage.

Had there been something else in her mind when she wrote them? Could she have been referring to the injustice she felt as a result of Sebastian's love affair with Lizzie?

Had Mary found out about them sooner than we realised?

I leaned back in my seat, closed my eyes and tried to calm my thoughts. I needed to determine whether my mind was working properly and not running away with itself like a horse broken free from its carriage.

Had Mary killed Lizzie?

I pictured Mary in her pretty day dress with her sweet smile and decided it was impossible.

But it wasn't impossible that she had found out about Sebastian and Lizzie. Their love affair had continued for many years and there must have been cause for Mary to grow suspicious.

Mary might have found out about the affair and wanted to exact her revenge.

Everything seemed to fit into place all of a sudden. If Mary had discovered Sebastian and Lizzie's affair, she would have felt angry and betrayed. She might also have felt a strong sense of resentment towards their daughter, Annie.

All of a sudden, I had established a possible motive for the attacks on Lizzie and Annie.

But was I right?

The train remained halted for some time at Charing Cross

Station, the engine belching out so much smoke and steam that the platform was barely visible after a short while. I felt my stomach cramp with impatience and I pondered whether it would be quicker to get out of the train and run to Westminster. I knew I had little chance of picking up a decent speed in my skirts and boots, so I was relieved when I heard the guard blow his whistle for the train to depart.

As soon as I alighted at Westminster Bridge Station, I ran as quickly as I could up Whitehall towards Scotland Yard. It was raining, but I couldn't run with my umbrella open, so I screwed up my face against the raindrops and accepted that I would have to get wet.

A few scruffy boys ran alongside me, laughing.

"What's the 'urry, lady?" they called out.

"I have just solved a murder!" I shouted back at them.

They wrinkled their foreheads in puzzlement.

I was so out of breath that I could barely speak by the time I reached the Yard, and I was horrified to discover that James was not there. After making some enquiries and eventually speaking to the inspector's long-nosed colleague, I was told that he was at the Palace of Westminster.

I cursed under my breath as I had run past the palace on my way to the Yard. I left by the way I had come and ran back down Whitehall towards the Houses of Parliament and the unmistakeable clock tower that housed Big Ben. The clock told me that it was almost ten o'clock, and I wondered what progress James was making with Sir Edmund.

Presumably none, if Mary was indeed our suspect.

The ornate, sand-coloured Houses of Parliament with their many mullioned windows were grimy with soot. I passed the ancient Westminster Hall to St Stephen's Entrance, where a footman asked me what my business was.

It took me a while to convince him that I urgently needed to speak with Inspector Blakely, and eventually it was decided that the inspector be brought out to me rather than allow a hysterical, rain-soaked woman into the hallowed palace. Even showing the footman my card did nothing to help my cause.

I put my umbrella up and waited by a statue of a unicorn clutching a shield.

Eventually, James appeared in the doorway.

"Penny! You have heard?" He stepped out and joined me under my umbrella.

"About what?"

"Cullen allowed Taylor to walk free yesterday evening."

"Taylor is no longer a suspect?"

"Apparently not. Cullen has decided that he was framed, which I have to say was also my conclusion. It means we have to focus our efforts on the Westminster connection. I can't say it has gone well this morning, however."

"It's all beginning to make sense now. I don't think anyone in Westminster had anything to do with Lizzie's murder."

"Why do you say that?"

"Look at this."

I gave him the handle of my umbrella to hold while I scrabbled around in my handbag. I found the crumpled page of Mary's notes and thrust it at him.

"Mary wrote this. Mary Colehill!"

I took the umbrella from James and his eyebrows knitted tightly together as he examined the page.

"Don't worry about what it says," I said. "Look at the handwriting. It's the same as the writing on the envelope."

"Which envelope?"

I felt a snap of impatience in my chest, but I did my best to remain calm as I explained to James about the neatly written address on the envelope of the first anonymous letter that had been sent to me.

As I spoke, James' brow smoothed out and his blue eyes widened. He glanced back at the page of writing and a smile began to spread across his face.

"Penny, I think you are right! Keep this safe in your bag. I don't want it to get wet and have the ink spoiled." He handed the piece of paper back to me. "The other letters are in the case file on my desk. Let me fetch my coat from Sir Edmund's office so we can compare the handwriting at once."

۞

The damp had seeped through to my skin from my rain-soaked jacket by the time we arrived at James' office. I noticed that he sat just a few desks away from Cullen, but thankfully the more senior inspector was nowhere to be seen.

I gave James the page of Mary's handwriting and he placed it on the desk, smoothing it out with his hand. A few spots of rain had already smudged the ink.

Then he opened the case file and leafed through it until he found a large envelope. Inside it were three smaller envelopes: one that had contained the locket and the other two the anonymous letters which had been sent to me.

"The ink is the same colour," said James. "There are no guarantees that they were all written by the same person, but it certainly helps us."

He placed the neatly written envelope next to the page of notes and we looked from one to the other repeatedly. The envelope was written slightly more neatly. Mary's handwriting was looser on the page of notes, which was to be expected when writing so many words at speed.

"You are not mistaken, Penny. I can say without much doubt that the person who wrote this page of notes is the very same person who wrote the address on this envelope."

"Mary sent these letters; I can scarcely believe it. To think how friendly she was towards me when she was actually sending me threatening letters. Why would she do such a thing?"

"Only one person can tell us, and that is Mary herself."

"Do you think she is the murderer?"

"I don't know."

"She could have hired the young man to kill Lizzie. She would never have done it herself."

"Perhaps not. It is most urgent that I discuss this with her. Are you certain that she is the author of these notes?"

"That is what Eliza told me."

"I need to get hold of proven examples of Mary's hand-writing before I can use this as evidence. Your sister's word is crucial, but we still don't have any actual proof that Mary wrote these. Once I can get a sample of her handwriting, which she testifies is hers, I will have that and the three letters analysed by a graphologist. Before I do that, however, we can ask her whether she is the author of the notes and the letters and see what she says."

"Shall we go and see Mary now?"

"Absolutely. A cab would get us there in ten minutes or so."

James took off his overcoat and jacket, leaving him standing there in his shirt and waistcoat.

"What are you doing?"

I watched him open a drawer in his desk and take out a leather shoulder holster.

"You need a *gun*?"

"With a bit of luck, I won't." He put the holster on and took a revolver out of its case on his desk. "But it is best to be prepared."

CHAPTER 46

James asked the cab driver to wait in Cadogan Square as we called at the Colehills' house. The maid answered and told us that neither Mary nor Sebastian was at home.

"May I ask for their whereabouts?" asked James. "I need to speak to Mrs Colehill about some urgent police business."

"Mr Colehill is at Drury Lane, sir, and Mrs Colehill is at a society meetin'."

"The West London Women's Society?" I asked.

"Yes ma'am, that's the one."

I gave James a questioning look. We both knew that Eliza wasn't at the meeting, and would have been had the society been scheduled to meet.

Could Mary have lied to the maid about her whereabouts?

I remained silent, not wishing to arouse the maid's suspicion.

"Thank you for your time," said James. "We will go and visit Mr Colehill at Drury Lane."

"Why are we going to see Sebastian?" I whispered to

James as we descended the steps and the maid closed the door behind us.

"We're not. I didn't want the maid telling anyone where we're going."

"Where are we going?"

"The King Henry pub on Mile End Road, please, driver!" he called out. "As quick as you can!"

We leapt into the cab and the horse trotted on.

"Taylor's house?" I asked.

"Do you remember me telling Mary yesterday that Annie was returning home from hospital?"

A sickening sense of dread stirred in my stomach. "You think Mary has gone after her?"

"I don't know, but I'm worried that Annie isn't safe."

"Hopefully Taylor is with her now that he's been released."

"Hopefully, but I want to be sure that she has someone there to protect her. Until we have found Mary, I will request that someone from H Division is at the Taylor home to guard her."

The cab made its way around Belgrave Square, with its impressive stuccoed townhouses and its trees dripping with rain.

James checked his pocket watch and tutted. "It is going to take us some time to reach Mile End. I can only hope Mary doesn't reach it before us."

"Do you really think she could be the murderer? I can't imagine her doing such a terrible thing. She is so mild-mannered."

"She is either mild-mannered or a talented actress. I fear that she is the latter, and that she has been one step ahead of us the entire time."

"You think she framed Taylor?"

"Yes, she sent him the locket, didn't she? And she

instructed him to be in Highgate Cemetery at the time of the murder. Presumably, she was hoping someone would see him there and suspect that he was behind Lizzie's murder."

"She achieved that."

"She did. Rather clumsily, perhaps, but she had us fooled for a while."

"And what of the young man witnessed at the scene of both shootings? The man who was at the cemetery and the hotel?"

"I feel certain that she will lead us to him."

❦

We exited the cab outside The King Henry pub and ran up the steps to Mr Taylor's house.

James knocked at the door while the rain drummed on the glass porch over our heads. The maid answered and I was relieved to hear that both Annie and Mr Taylor were at home.

"This is good news," said James as we passed the large stuffed bear in the hallway. "Once I am satisfied that Annie and Mr Taylor are well, I will ask H Division to mind them."

"I wonder where Mary is," I whispered.

"Not you again!" Mr Taylor barked at James as we were shown into the drawing room. "You've only just let me go! Can't you leave a man in peace?"

He stood on the hearthrug smoking a cigar, while Annie rested on the red velour settee. She returned my smile.

"Please be assured that you are no longer a suspect, Mr Taylor," said James. "We are here because we are concerned for Annie's safety."

Annie frowned.

"Don't worry. You're safe now the inspector's here,

Annie," I explained. "We are concerned because the person who shot you has yet to be caught."

"He's hardly going to shoot her in my home, is he?" said Taylor. "What nonsense."

"We are close to catching the culprit," said James. "I will ask my colleagues in Stepney to look after you until the individual is caught."

"It could be weeks, even months, until you catch the man," said Mr Taylor. "I don't want bobbies hanging around here until the Yard finally gets its act together. We want to be left in peace now, do you hear? My priority is to ensure that Annie recovers well enough to be able to perform again. That is all that matters, isn't it, Annie?"

But Annie didn't reply. Instead, her wide eyes were fixed on the doorway behind us.

I spun around to see the maid standing as still as a statue, her face white. A revolver had been pressed up against her temple by a young man in a tweed cap and a dark suit. He had a pale moustache and stared back at me with cold, empty eyes.

As I studied his face, I noticed there was something soft about his features.

He was either extremely youthful or he wasn't a man at all.

It was then that I realised *he* was in fact a woman.

And the woman was Mary Colehill.

CHAPTER 47

Mary's fair hair was tucked up inside the cap and the brim had been pulled down low over her eyes. Her moustache looked convincing enough. *Perhaps she had made it with her own hair*, I thought.

With her square jaw and dark, baggy suit, she was passable as a slim-built young man. I was afraid to make any sudden movements and I sensed that James felt the same way. He stood still and silent next to me, presumably thinking up a plan to manage the situation.

"Mary?" I ventured.

She glared back at me and pressed the gun harder still against the maid's head. The poor maid's eyes and mouth were open wide in terror.

"Come here, Annie," said Mary.

"No!" said Mr Taylor from behind me.

Mary gave him a cold glance, and from the corner of my eye I noticed Annie stand up and walk towards Mary. I also noticed James slowly moving his hand beneath his jacket, to where I knew his revolver sat in its holster.

My heart pounded in my ears.

The maid cried out as Mary suddenly pushed her away and grabbed hold of Annie. She moved the gun so that it was pressed up against Annie's head and the maid cowered by the tiger skin rug.

I was wary that anything I said might make matters worse, but I felt I had to try and calm the situation. "Mary, please don't do this. Annie hasn't done anything to hurt you. Please leave her alone. Can't you see that she has already suffered enough?"

"What do you know about suffering, Penny?" asked Mary.

Annie's face remained calm and expressionless. I was impressed by her bravery. I decided it was best to keep Mary talking as a way of distracting her while James hopefully found his gun.

"I don't know a lot about suffering, Mary, but I know what you must have been through. I cannot imagine what it must have been like to find out about Sebastian and Lizzie. You didn't deserve that; you have a lovely family What Lizzie and Sebastian did was wrong."

"She was *your* friend."

"She may have been, but I still believe she was wrong. In fact, she kept the affair so well-hidden that I didn't know about it while she was alive."

"My husband and children are the most important things in my life," said Mary, her voice cracking slightly. "I do whatever I can to protect what we have. I tried to warn you that this would happen, but you ignored me. How many letters did I need to send to convince you to stay away?"

"I didn't know whether to take the threats seriously or not."

She laughed. "Do you need any more convincing now?"

"Mary, please don't do this. You have too much to lose."

Mary glanced at James, then her arm moved and a sudden shot made Annie scream. I leapt back, startled.

"James!" I cried out. He lay on the floor, on his left side. I knelt down beside him.

"I'm all right," he said through clenched teeth.

He gripped his arm with his hand and I could see a dark patch of blood begin to spread across the sleeve of his jacket.

"She shot you?"

"Yes, in the arm, but I'm all right." He kept moving his eyes to his left shoulder and I saw that he was lying on top of his revolver. He looked up at me, wide-eyed, and I understood from his glance that he wanted me to pick up the gun.

"Move away from him!" said Mary. "On your feet!"

"He needs a doctor."

Mary pointed her gun at me. "Get up!"

I grabbed the revolver and stood up, pointing the barrel at Mary. The gun felt cold and heavy in my shaking hands.

Mary gave me a half smile and pointed her gun back towards Annie's head. "I can kill her with just one shot."

I wondered why she was hesitating. Perhaps she wasn't quite callous enough to shoot someone at such close range.

I glanced over at Taylor and the maid, and it was then that I remembered the shotgun above the case containing the stuffed otter. I was sure that Taylor had already stepped back so that he was closer to it.

With James injured, Taylor had become our only hope. I needed him to get hold of his shotgun and help save Annie. I had never fired a gun before and I had little confidence in my ability to do anything with the weapon I now held.

"Please let Annie go," I said to Mary. "Think of Sebastian. Think of your children."

Mary's eyes grew watery. "Sebastian doesn't know that I found out about his affair with that whore. He thinks I'm his little woman, caring for his children and waiting patiently for him to come home every evening. He has no knowledge of the many times I followed him or how frequently I read his letters from that insufferable woman. She thought she could take him away from me. He wouldn't go, of course; he would never leave me."

"So why do this?" I asked. "Why kill Lizzie?"

"My husband is now one of the most successful theatre proprietors in the country. What would happen to him if people discovered the truth? Lizzie had been a thorn in my side for so long. I knew my family could never live in peace until she was gone. In everyone else's mind she had drowned, so what harm could I do in killing a woman who was believed to be dead and buried?"

"Let Annie go," I said.

"Sebastian's daughter with *that woman*? For as long as she is alive, I am reminded of his betrayal."

"That's enough, Mary!" said Taylor, grabbing his shotgun off the wall as I had hoped he would. He pointed it at Mary. "Do what the woman says and let Annie go. This was not part of the agreement."

"Agreement? What agreement?" I asked.

"Let Annie go," said Taylor. "*Now!*"

He took a step towards Mary and she lowered her gun. Annie moved away from her.

Then Taylor swung his shotgun round and pointed it at me.

"What are you doing?" I asked. I was still pointing my gun at Mary. "Mr Taylor, what was the agreement?"

"The agreement," he replied, "was that we would kill Lizzie. Do you want to know how Mary found out about their affair? I told her. I knew about them before the boat sank, and I found out that Lizzie was still alive when I followed Annie one day. I couldn't understand who she kept meeting in Vauxhall Pleasure Gardens. To think that my own wife pretended to me that she had drowned! Just so she could carry on with that man. There is no greater deceit than that, is there, Miss Green? You must know how it feels. She deceived you too. But I confronted her that night in Highgate Cemetery. Both Mary and I were there. We sent her a message and pretended it was from Sebastian asking to meet him there. And the fool turned up! She would have done anything for him. We told her what we thought of her, didn't we, Mary? She tried to apologise, but her words meant nothing to me by then. I no longer cared."

"But you couldn't bring yourself to shoot her, could you?" said Mary. "That was left to me." Her face was so contorted that I no longer recognised her, especially when she was dressed in men's clothing.

"But the locket," I said. "Why did Mary frame you with the locket?"

"I wanted it to look as though I'd been framed. I knew I would be one of the main suspects from the start, so if I could show that I was being framed the detectives hopefully wouldn't delve any deeper. Which they didn't. It all worked extremely well until Mary took matters into her own hands. It seems that killing Lizzie wasn't enough for her; she wanted Annie dead too. Now, Annie may not be my daughter, but I've been a father to her since she was a young girl. I love her as if she were my own."

Mary raised her gun again and pointed it at Taylor.

"Do you see what I mean, Miss Green?" he said. "This woman likes to take matters into her own hands."

He turned his shotgun on Mary. "Annie, get out of the room!" he shouted.

Mr Taylor and Mary were holding each other at gunpoint and I felt terrified of the outcome.

Who was to shoot first?

I felt relieved that Annie was leaving the room and would not witness any bloodshed. The revolver was still in my shaking hand, but I felt unsure what to do with it. I glanced over at James and he gestured to me to pass him the gun, even though he was still lying on the ground. I knew he was a far better shot than I, but he was injured.

Would he be able to fire the gun accurately?

Whatever decision I made would be risky. I stooped to one side and slid the gun across the floor to him.

"Stop!" Mary cried out.

I looked up and saw the barrel of her gun trained on me.

I tried to cover myself with my arms, but the shots rang out.

CHAPTER 48

"Welcome back!"

Mr Sherman and the entire staff at the *Morning Express* were gathered in the news room. They broke out into hearty applause as I stepped through the door and I felt my face flush hot.

I had never seen Mr Sherman grin before, and even Miss Welton had a smile on her face. Among the staff, I saw Edgar, Frederick and even the compositors and printers from downstairs, as well as some of the messenger boys.

"Let me help you with your coat, Miss Green," said Mr Sherman, stepping forward. I allowed him to help me. It wasn't easy with my arm in a sling, and the injury was still painful when I moved too much.

Mary had managed to fire at me and Mr Taylor before James had shot her in the leg and disarmed her. Mr Taylor had died of his injuries at the Royal London Hospital. His shotgun had later been found to be empty of ammunition. Thankfully, Annie was unharmed and James' wound was not too serious.

Only one of Mary's bullets had hit me. It had travelled through my right forearm, which I had been holding across my chest, and had been halted by the boning of my corset. My ribs had been bruised, but were thankfully undamaged. The injury to my arm had required surgery and I wondered whether I would ever be able to use it properly again.

"The return of Miss Green calls for a celebratory drink!" said Mr Sherman. "This bottle of champagne has been given to us by our fine proprietor, Mr Conway!"

He set about opening it while I walked over to my desk and sat down.

"Are you sure you are ready to return to work?" asked Edgar with a look of concern on his face.

"I think so. I had to; I felt that I was losing my mind sitting about in my lodgings doing nothing. My sister visited me every day and that made it even worse."

Edgar laughed. "It's terrible bad luck, though, isn't it?" he said.

"What is?"

"You could have at least asked her to shoot you in your left arm. You're a writer and now you can't write!"

"But at least I am alive." I smiled. "All is not lost. I am going to try typewriting."

"Really? On Miss Welton's machine?"

"Yes, I can type with my left hand."

"You are very determined. I think that if I were shot in the arm I would sit at home, enjoying plenty of rest and waiting to make a full recovery."

"I can imagine you doing just that."

We both smiled.

"To Miss Green! And her health!" Mr Sherman held his glass high.

"To Miss Green!" my colleagues echoed.

Feeling embarrassed by the attention, I reached out for my glass and took a sip of champagne.

"And the Colehill woman will hang!" someone cried out.

I felt pleased that justice would finally be served for Lizzie and Annie, but I couldn't stop thinking about the Colehill children. Although their mother had committed a dreadful crime, it didn't seem fair that they should lose her.

"I hear that Sebastian Colehill wants to have her death sentence commuted to life imprisonment instead," said Frederick. "He is encouraging his wife to confess and repent, in the hope that it will save her. I should think he's also hoping a lot of the blame will be pinned on Taylor for encouraging her to do such awful things."

"Sebastian may feel partially responsible," I said. "He could never have known that his wife was capable of murder, but he may be questioning the way he treated her. I hope she receives a life sentence rather than the death sentence for the sake of her family."

"I propose another toast," said Mr Sherman. "Let us drink to the satisfactory ending of this entire affair!"

Everyone raised their glasses in celebration. I took a sip of my drink and wondered how poor Annie must be feeling.

Although Lizzie's murderers had been found, there seemed little to celebrate.

CHAPTER 49

The full report on the underground railway bombings had been given to the Home Secretary by Colonel Majendie and Captain Cundill. I sat in the reading room and perused a copy of it.

The report's conclusion was that the bombs at Praed Street and Charing Cross had been malicious acts that could be linked to similar bombings on account of their 'savage disregard for life'. It seemed the Fenians were behind the campaign, although this was yet to be proven.

I slowly tidied my papers into my handbag, a troublesome process with only one functioning arm, and then got up to fetch my coat and hat from the cloakroom. I was due to meet Eliza for lunch.

As I walked towards the door, a man strode in wearing a familiar bowler hat and a dark overcoat.

"James!" I exclaimed. "This is a surprise."

He greeted me with a wide smile and I noticed that his eyes matched the blue of his tie.

"How are you, Penny? How's the arm?"

"Getting better, thank you. And how is your arm?"

"Recovering well."

We grinned at each other with our matching slings.

After the altercation with Mary, James and I had both been admitted to the Royal London Hospital. I hadn't seen as much of him as I would have liked since we had been discharged, but I had heard that he was busy with a new case.

"What brings you here?" I asked.

"I came to say my goodbyes. I have been asked to work on a case up north in Manchester for a while."

He must have noticed my face fall.

"Not for too long," he added, "and I will need to be in London some days during Mary Colehill's trial. Quite a lot of my time will be spent on the London and North Western Railway. Do you think you will attend the trial?"

"I can't say that I plan to sit through it all, but I will attend on some days, out of interest. Edgar will do the reporting on it. I hear Sebastian is already trying to secure a life sentence instead of the death penalty."

"That is understandable. And hopefully she will confess to everything, which would make the life sentence more probable. You look as though you are ready to go somewhere."

"I am due to have lunch with my sister. I'm meeting her outside."

"I shall walk out with you."

We walked down the steps of the British Museum and I found myself wishing that James didn't have to go away to Manchester. I wondered whether we would ever have an opportunity to work on a case together again.

"You are one of the easiest detectives at the Yard to work with," I said. "Until you came along, I had been forced to work with Cullen and a rather odd man with a deformed ear."

"Inspector Royden?"

"Yes, that was him. I wonder what happened to his ear."

"I heard he was savaged by a dog when he was a child."

"Oh dear. That explains the skin as well."

"The scarring?"

"Yes. Oh! Here comes my sister."

We reached the bottom step and watched Eliza stride towards us from the gate in the railings.

"Well, it was a pleasure working with you, Penny."

James turned to me and held out his free hand. I shook it and his hand felt strong and warm around mine.

We regarded each other for a moment, shaking hands for longer than was usual or necessary.

"Enjoy Manchester," I said.

Eliza was almost upon us.

"It will be an experience, that's for sure." James grimaced. "It hasn't gone down well with the future Mrs Blakely, though, as it means the wedding will have to be put back."

"Oh no, for how long?"

"Not too long. How nice to see you again, Mrs Billington-Grieg." James and Eliza were already acquainted, having frequently met at my hospital bedside.

"Hello, Inspector Blakely."

"I don't mean to be rude, but I must go. I have a train to catch."

"Going anywhere nice?"

"Manchester."

"Lovely." Eliza beamed.

"Goodbye, James," I said.

He gave me a small wave and walked away. I watched him leave and wondered why my throat felt so tight and uncomfortable.

"You were rather attached to him, weren't you, Penelope?" said Eliza.

"He is a kind person," I said, blinking back a tear.

"He is a charming gentleman." Eliza took my left arm. "And talking of nice people," she continued, "I must tell you all about the dinner I had last night with Mrs Conway, the wife of your newspaper's proprietor, and a host of other fine people from the National Society for Women's Suffrage. We may not have published the article in the *Morning Express* yet, but you have helped me enormously in making connections."

"That's wonderful news, Ellie!"

We walked out into the street and I glanced fondly at the Museum Tavern across the road.

"No, Penelope, not the pub. We are dining at The Holborn Restaurant, remember?"

I smiled and allowed Eliza to march me off down the street.

THE END

THANK YOU

Thank you for reading *Limelight*, I really hope you enjoyed it!

Would you like to know when I release new books? Here are some ways to stay updated:

- Join my mailing list and receive a free short mystery: *Westminster Bridge* emilyorgan.co.uk/short-mystery
- Like my Facebook page: facebook.com/emilyorganwriter
- View my other books here: emilyorgan.co.uk/books

And if you have a moment, I would be very grateful if you would leave a quick review of *Limelight* online. Honest reviews of my books help other readers discover them too!

HISTORICAL NOTE

❀

Women journalists in the nineteenth century were not as scarce as people may think. In fact they were numerous enough by 1898 for Arnold Bennett to write *Journalism for Women: A Practical Guide* in which he was keen to raise the standard of women's journalism:-

"The women-journalists as a body have faults... They seem to me to be traceable either to an imperfect development of the sense of order, or to a certain lack of self-control."

Eliza Linton became the first salaried female journalist in Britain when she began writing for *the Morning Chronicle* in 1851. She was a prolific writer and contributor to periodicals for many years including Charles Dickens' magazine *Household Words*. George Eliot – her real name was Mary Anne Evans - is most famous for novels such as *Middlemarch*, however she also became assistant editor of *The Westminster Review* in 1852.

In the United States Margaret Fuller became the *New York*

Tribune's first female editor in 1846. Intrepid journalist Nellie Bly worked in Mexico as a foreign correspondent for the *Pittsburgh Despatch* in the 1880s before writing for *New York World* and feigning insanity to go undercover and investigate reports of brutality at a New York asylum. Later, in 1889-90, she became a household name by setting a world record for travelling around the globe in seventy-two days.

The tragedy of the SS Princess Alice is sadly not fiction. The accident is still Britain's worst ever public transport disaster. The Princess Alice was a pleasure steamer which collided with the coal carrier SS Bywell on the River Thames near Woolwich in September 1878. The loss of life is believed to have been between 600 and 650 with exact numbers of how many survived and died remaining vague. About a dozen victims were never identified.

The Fenians were part of the Irish Republican Brotherhood based in the United States and began an armed uprising against British rule in Ireland in the 1860s. They bombed Clerkenwell Prison in 1867 in a failed attempt to free one of their members. The Fenians began their dynamite campaign in Britain in the 1880s and not only targeted London but also Chester, Liverpool, Glasgow and Salford. Miraculously no one was killed or suffered severe injury when the train at Praed Street Station (now Paddington underground station for the district and circle lines) was blown up on 30th October 1883. More attacks continued in London until 1885 when financial support for the campaign began to wane.

The West London Women's Society is fictional but a representation of the local women's rights groups which were being established in the nineteenth century. By the 1880s both sides of the Atlantic saw organisations such as the

National Society for Women's Suffrage and the American Women's Suffrage Association growing from strength to strength. The Rational Dress Society was formed in 1881 in response to the cumbersome clothing which women wore. With pastimes such as cycling and tennis becoming more popular, women found themselves restricted by corsets and heavy petticoats and skirts. Dress reform was controversial for a long time with Lady Harberton refused entry for lunch at a hotel in Ockham, Surrey in 1899, for wearing baggy knickerbockers.

I have used a combination of fictional and actual locations in *Limelight*. Here are some of the actual ones:

The iconic circular reading room at the British Museum was in use from 1857 until 1997. During that time it was also used a filming location and has been referenced in many works of fiction. When the British Library moved to a new location in 1997, the reading room was restored and subsequently used for exhibition space but it has been closed since 2014 while the British Museum decides on its future. When I visited the museum last year I asked staff what the plans were for its future and whether it was possible to sneak a look inside. They told me they didn't know what the future plans were and no I wasn't allowed inside – and neither were they!

The Museum Tavern, where Penny and James enjoy a drink, is a well-preserved Victorian pub opposite the British Museum. Although a pub was first built here in the eighteenth century much of the current pub (including its name) dates back to 1855. Celebrity drinkers here are said to have included Arthur Conan Doyle and Karl Marx.

Publishing began in Fleet Street in the 1500s and by the

twentieth century the street was the hub of the British press. However newspapers began moving away in the 1980s to bigger premises. Nowadays just a few publishers remain in Fleet Street but the many pubs and bars once frequented by journalists – including the pub Ye Olde Cheshire Cheese - are still popular with city workers.

Highgate Cemetery was laid out in the 1830s at a time when London was running low on space to bury its dead. The cemetery is famous for its funerary architecture and the tombs of well-known people such as Karl Marx, George Eliot and Douglas Adams. Neglected after the Second World War, much of it is now overgrown and it's a fascinating, atmospheric place with a host of ghost stories attached to it. Such is the interest in the cemetery that guided tours are run each day. Kensal Green Cemetery also opened in the 1830s and is an impressive place to visit; as well as being the fictional resting place of Lizzie Dixie it's also the burial place of Isambard Kingdom Brunel, Wilkie Collins and William Makepeace Thackeray.

Joseph Taylor is fictional but Astley's Amphitheatre was real and located south of Westminster Bridge. It opened in the 1770s and was built by Philip Astley who is considered to be the father of the modern circus. The amphitheatre has featured in a lot of fiction and was rebuilt a number of times before finally being demolished in the 1890s. Part of today's St Thomas's Hospital now stands over it.

Sebastian Colehill's Theatre Royal in Drury Lane is showing the musical *Charlie and the Chocolate Factory* as I write this. The first theatre was built on the site in the 1660s and the current building is the fourth one and opened in 1812. The ghosts of Charles Macklin and Joey Grimaldi – which worry

Penny during her visits – are said to haunt the theatre. The Victorians loved their ghost stories as you know!

Penny Green lives in Milton Street in Cripplegate which was one of the areas worst hit by bombing during the Blitz in the Second World War and few original streets remain. Milton Street was known as Grub Street in the eighteenth century and famous as a home to impoverished writers at the time. The street had a long association with writers and was home to Anthony Trollope among many others. A small stretch of Milton Street remains but the 1960s Barbican development has been built over the bombed remains.

My research for *Limelight* has come from sources too numerous to list in detail, but the following books have been very useful: *A Brief History of Life in Victorian Britain* by Michael Patterson, *London in the Nineteenth Century* by Jerry White, *London in 1880* by Herbert Fry, *London a Travel Guide through Time* by Dr Matthew Green, *Women of the Press in Nineteenth-Century Britain* by Barbara Onslow, *A Very British Murder* by Lucy Worsley, *The Suspicions of Mr Whicher* by Kate Summerscale, *Journalism for Women: A Practical Guide* by Arnold Bennett and *Seventy Years a Showman* by Lord George Sanger.

THE ROOKERY

A Penny Green Mystery Book 2

❦

London 1884. When a thief robs Penny Green, she finds herself caught up in a horrifying murder.

Someone is terrorizing the residents of St Giles Rookery and Scotland Yard sends Inspector James Blakely to investigate.

Penny and James must overcome their complicated relationship to work together, but each new murder threatens to derail their work for good.

Find out more at: emilyorgan.co.uk/the-rookery

GET A FREE SHORT MYSTERY

꧁꧂

Want more of Penny Green? Sign up to my mailing list and I'll send you my short mystery *Westminster Bridge* - a free thirty minute read!

News reporter Penny Green is committed to her job. But should she impose on a grieving widow?

The brutal murder of a doctor has shocked 1880s London and Fleet Street is clamouring for news. Penny has orders from her editor to get the story all the papers want.

She must decide what comes first. Compassion or duty?

The murder case is not as simple as it seems. And whichever decision Penny makes, it's unlikely to be the right one.

Visit my website for more details:
emilyorgan.co.uk/short-mystery

THE RUNAWAY GIRL SERIES

Also by Emily Organ. A series of three historical thrillers set in Medieval London.

Book 1: Runaway Girl

A missing girl. The treacherous streets of Medieval London. Only one woman is brave enough to try and bring her home.

Book 2: Forgotten Child

Her husband took a fatal secret to the grave. Two friends are murdered. She has only one chance to stop the killing.

Book 3: Sins of the Father

An enemy returns. And this time he has her fooled. If he gets his own way then a little girl will never be seen again.

Available as separate books or a three book box set. Find out more at emilyorgan.co.uk/books

Made in the USA
San Bernardino,
CA